CARDBOARDIA

THE OTHER SIDE OF THE BOX

PIXEL ■ INK

Text copyright © 2021 by Richard Fairgray and Lucy Campagnolo

Illustrations copyright © 2021 by Richard Fairgray

Pixel+Ink is a division of TGM Development Corp

Printed and bound in May 2021 at Toppan Leefung, DongGuan, China.

Cover design by Richard Fairgray and Tyler Nevins

Interior design by Richard Fairgray

www.pixelandinkbooks.com

Library of Congress Control Number: 2021935122

HC ISBN 978-1-64595-040-0

PB ISBN 978-1-64595-099-8

eBook ISBN 978-1-64595-090-5

First edition

1 3 5 7 9 10 8 6 4 2

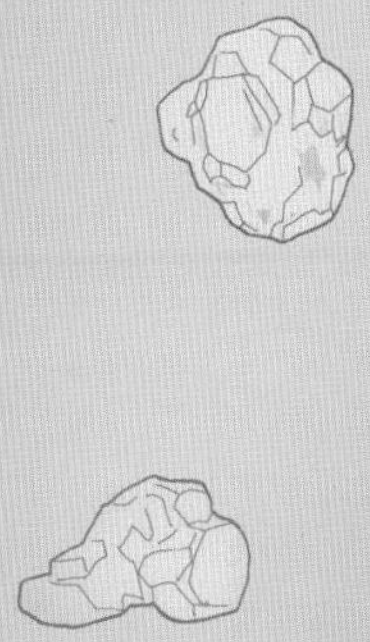

CARDBOARDIA

THE OTHER SIDE OF THE BOX

Written by RICHARD FAIRGRAY
and LUCY CAMPAGNOLO

Illustrated by RICHARD FAIRGRAY

PIXEL ◼ INK

New York

Lucy would like to dedicate this book to her mother, Leone Campagnolo.

Richard would like to dedicate this book to BOTH of Lucy's parents.

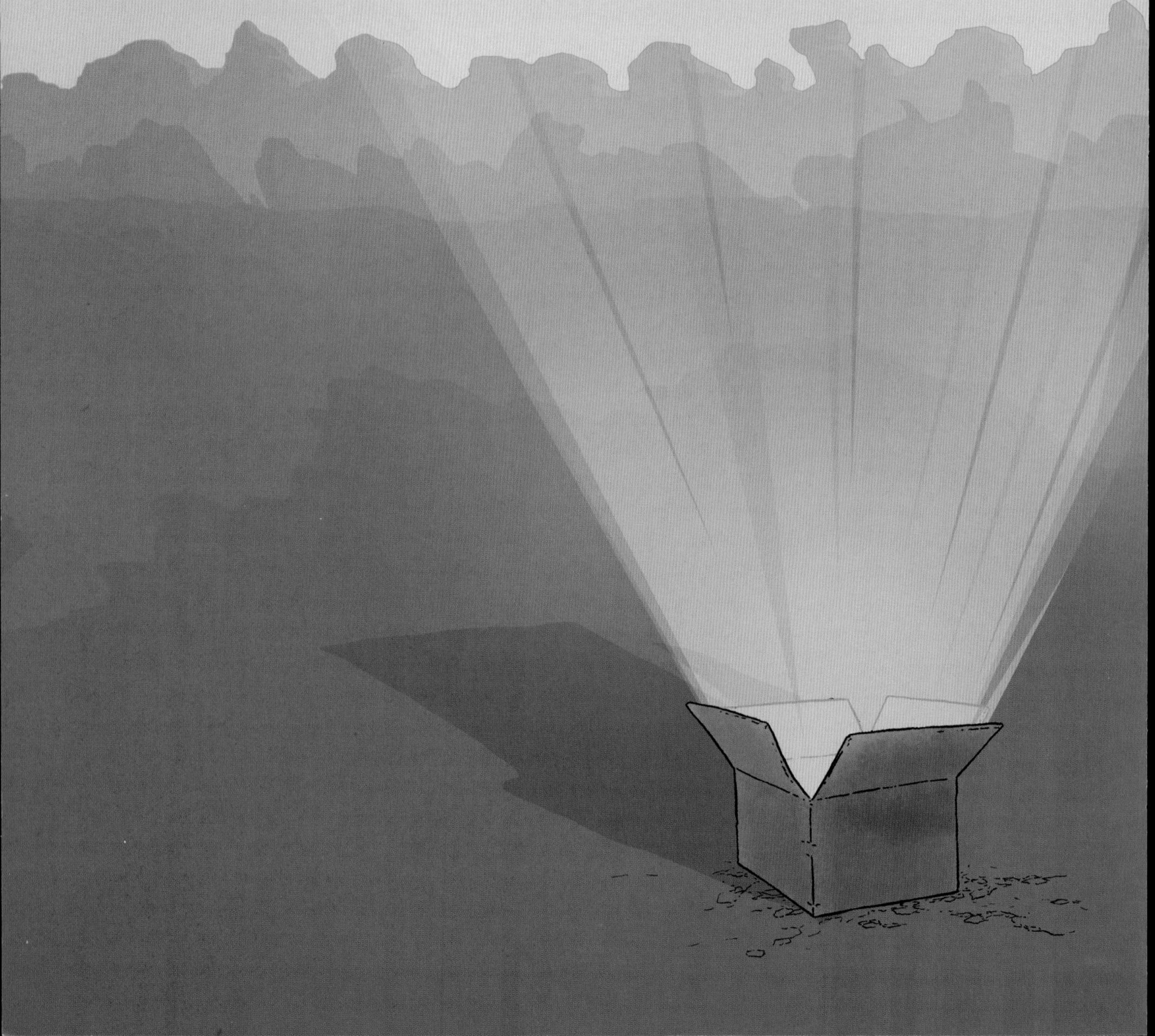

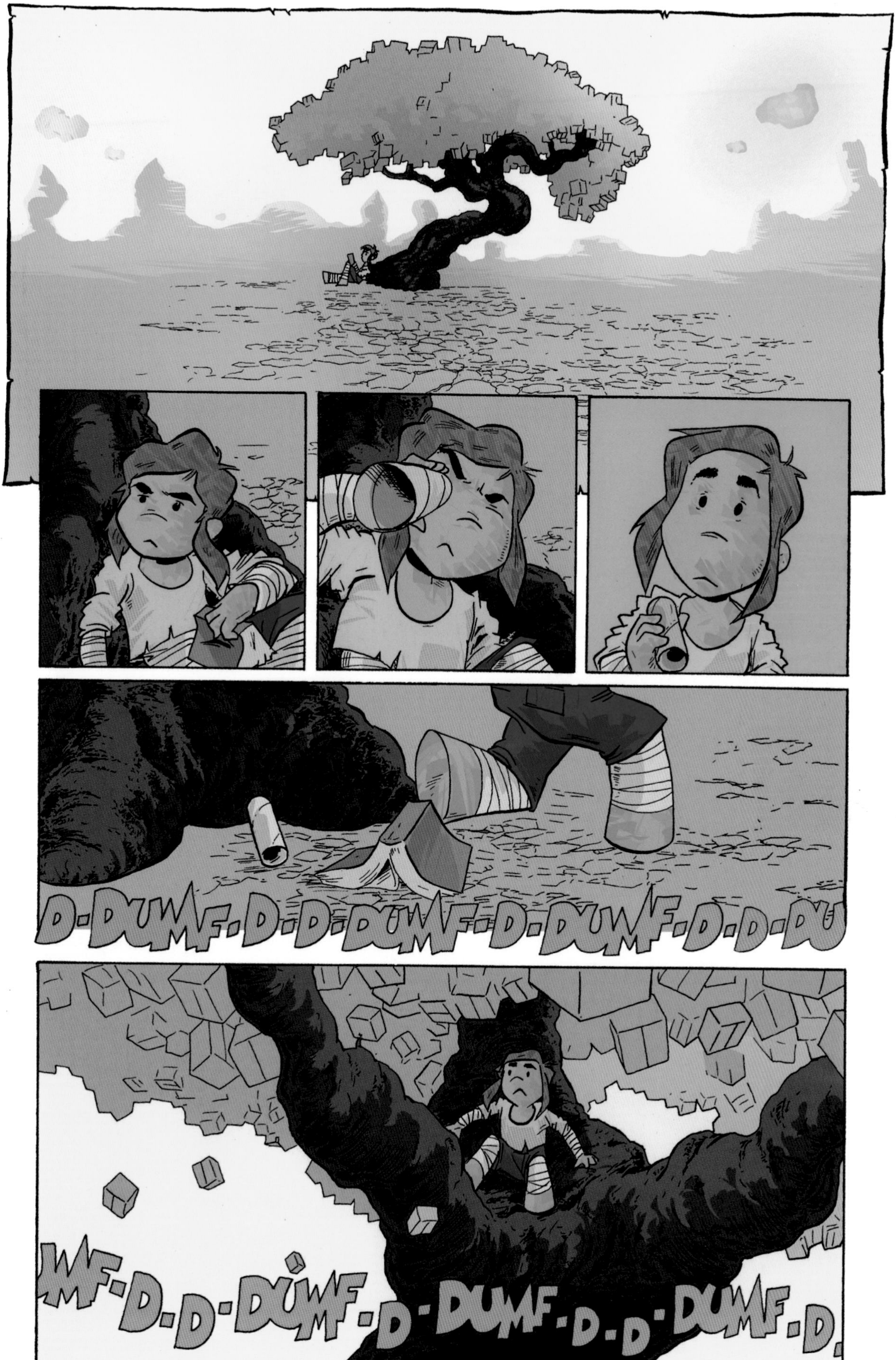
D-DUMF-D-D-DUMF-D-DUMF-D-D-DU
MF-D-D-DUMF-D-DUMF-D-D-DUMF-D

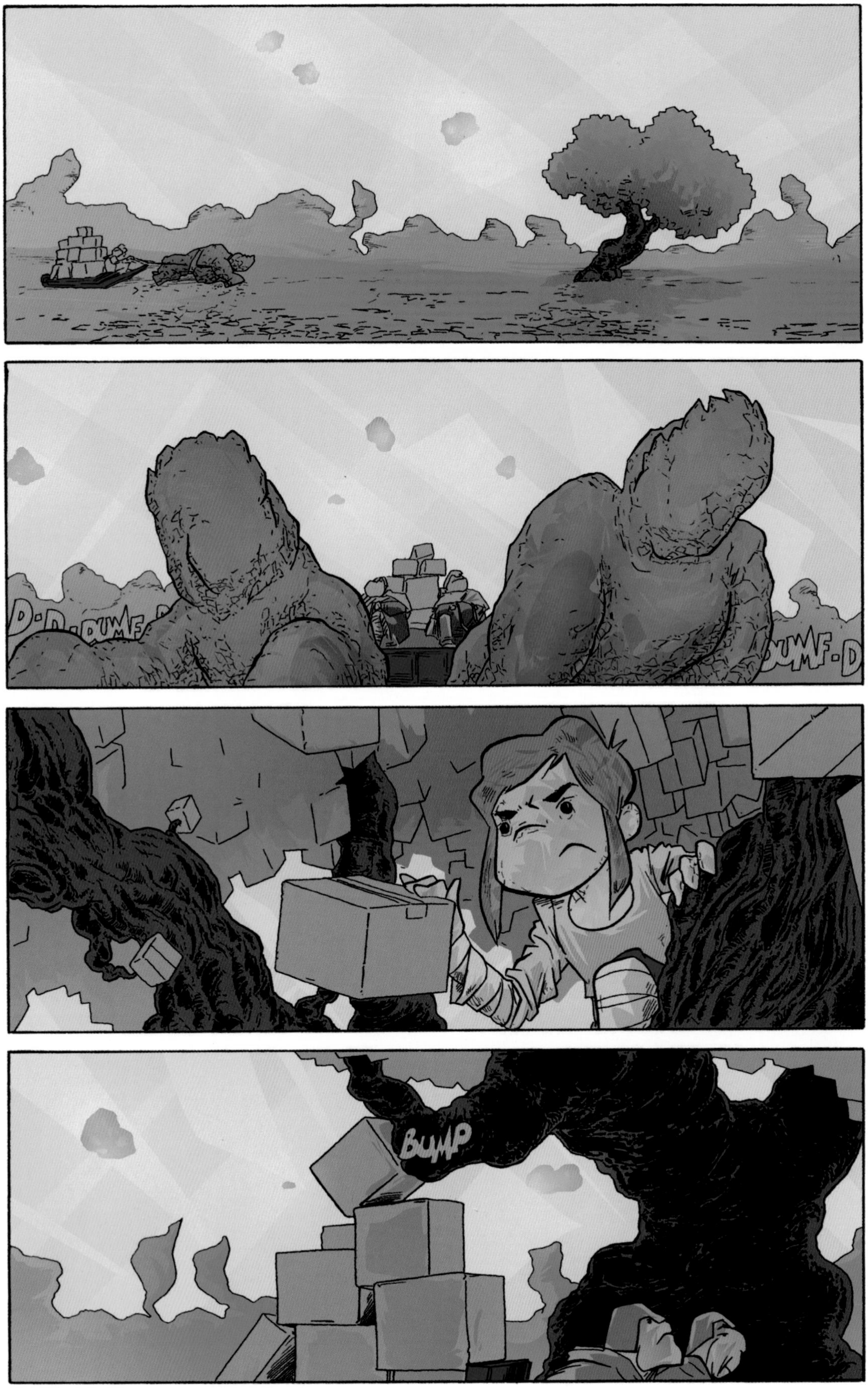
D-D-DUMF
DUMF-D
BUMP

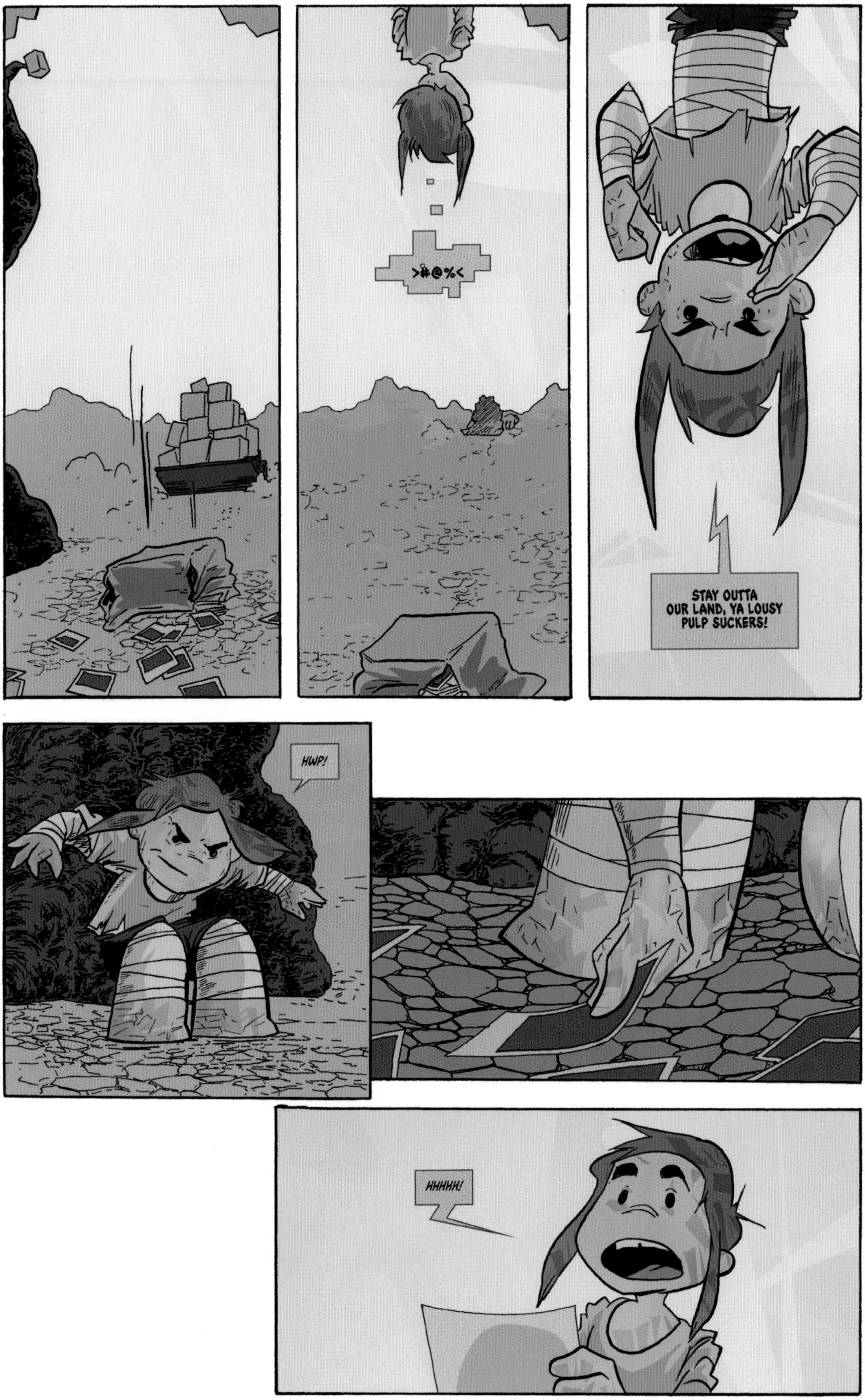
>#@%<
STAY OUTTA OUR LAND, YA LOUSY PULP SUCKERS!
HWP!
HHHHH!

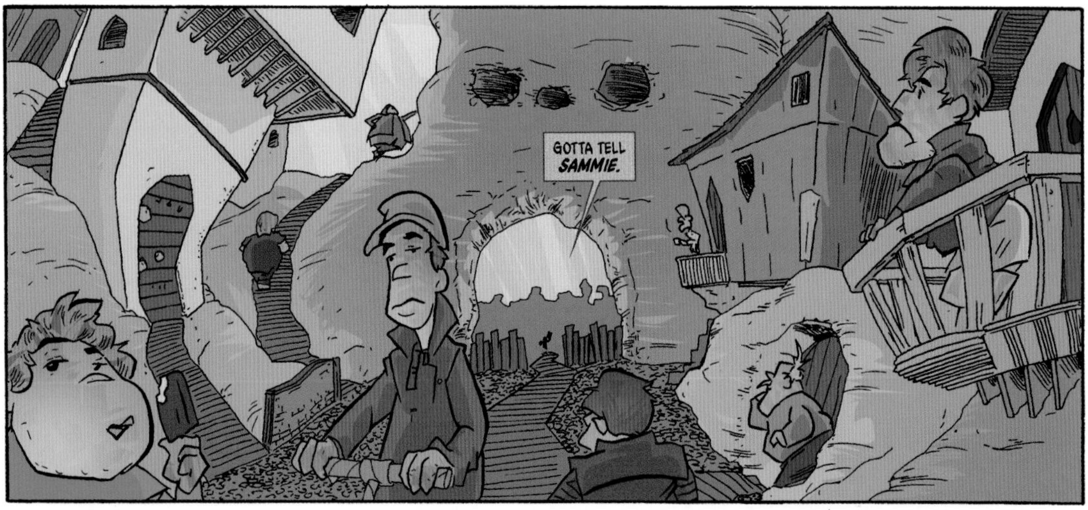
GOTTA TELL SAMMIE.

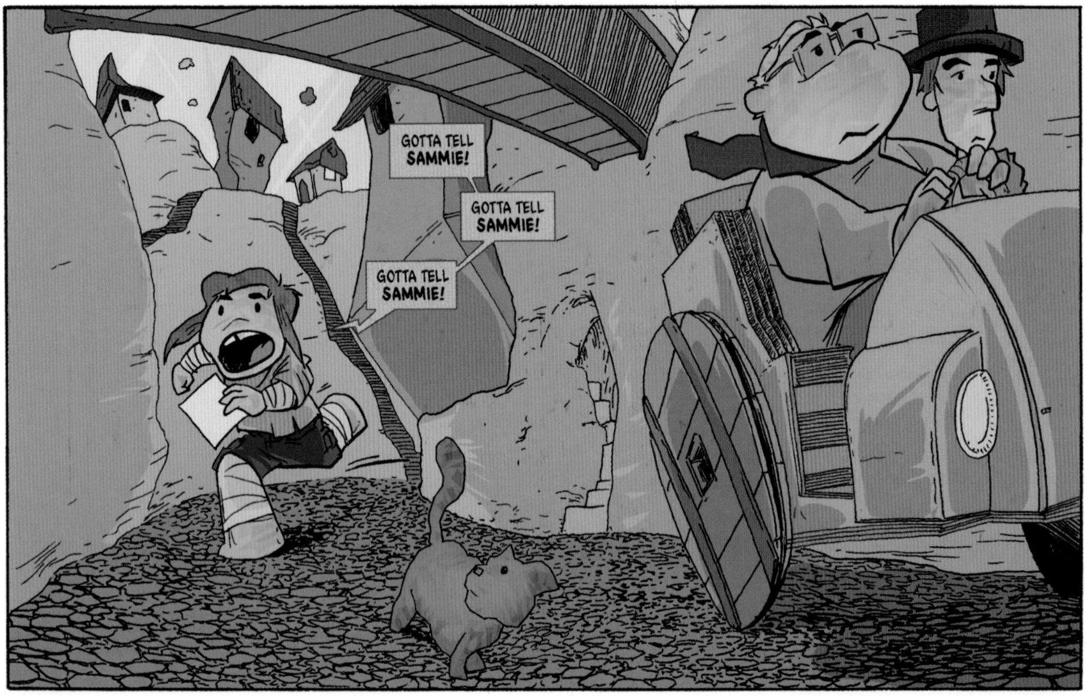
GOTTA TELL SAMMIE!
GOTTA TELL SAMMIE!
GOTTA TELL SAMMIE!

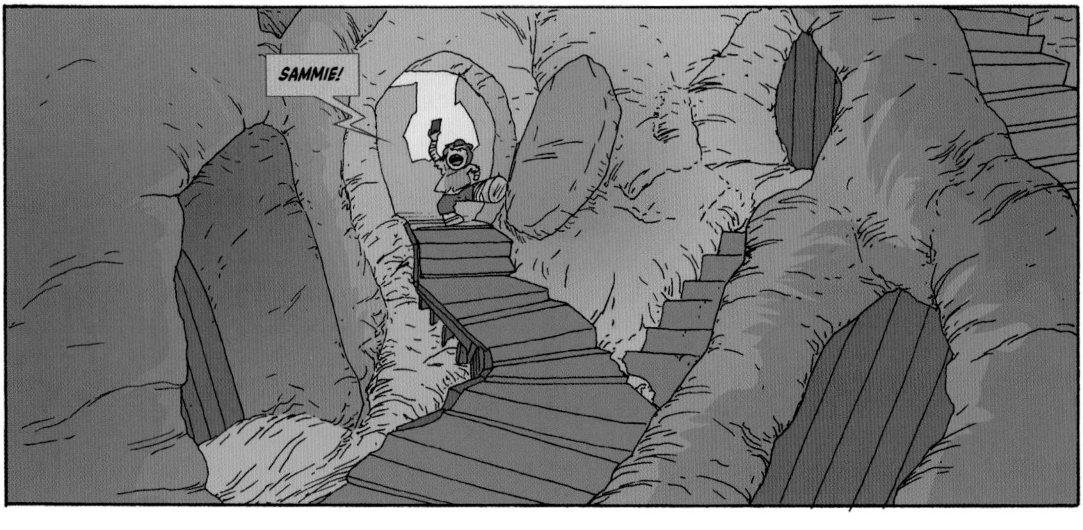
SAMMIE!

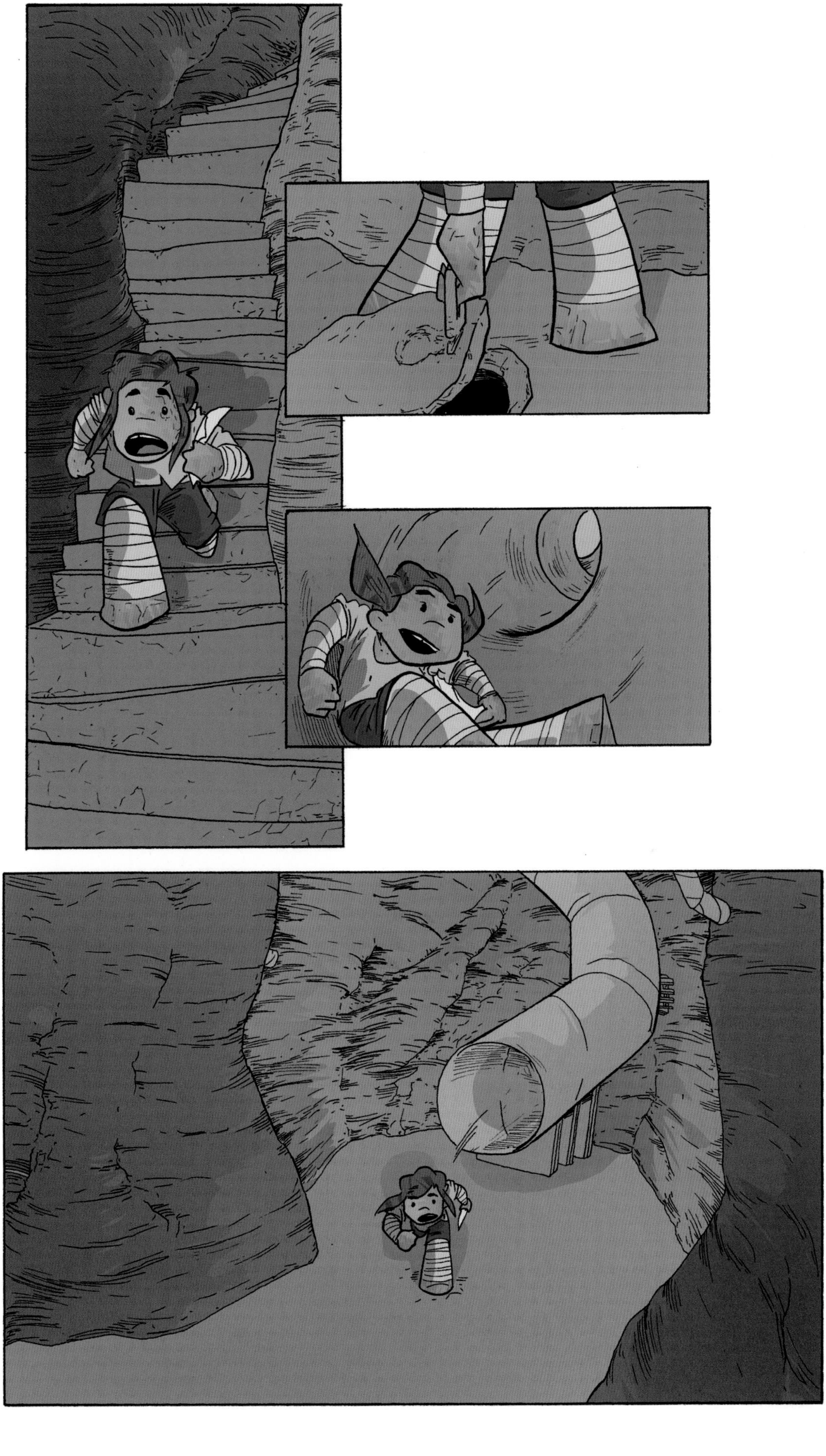

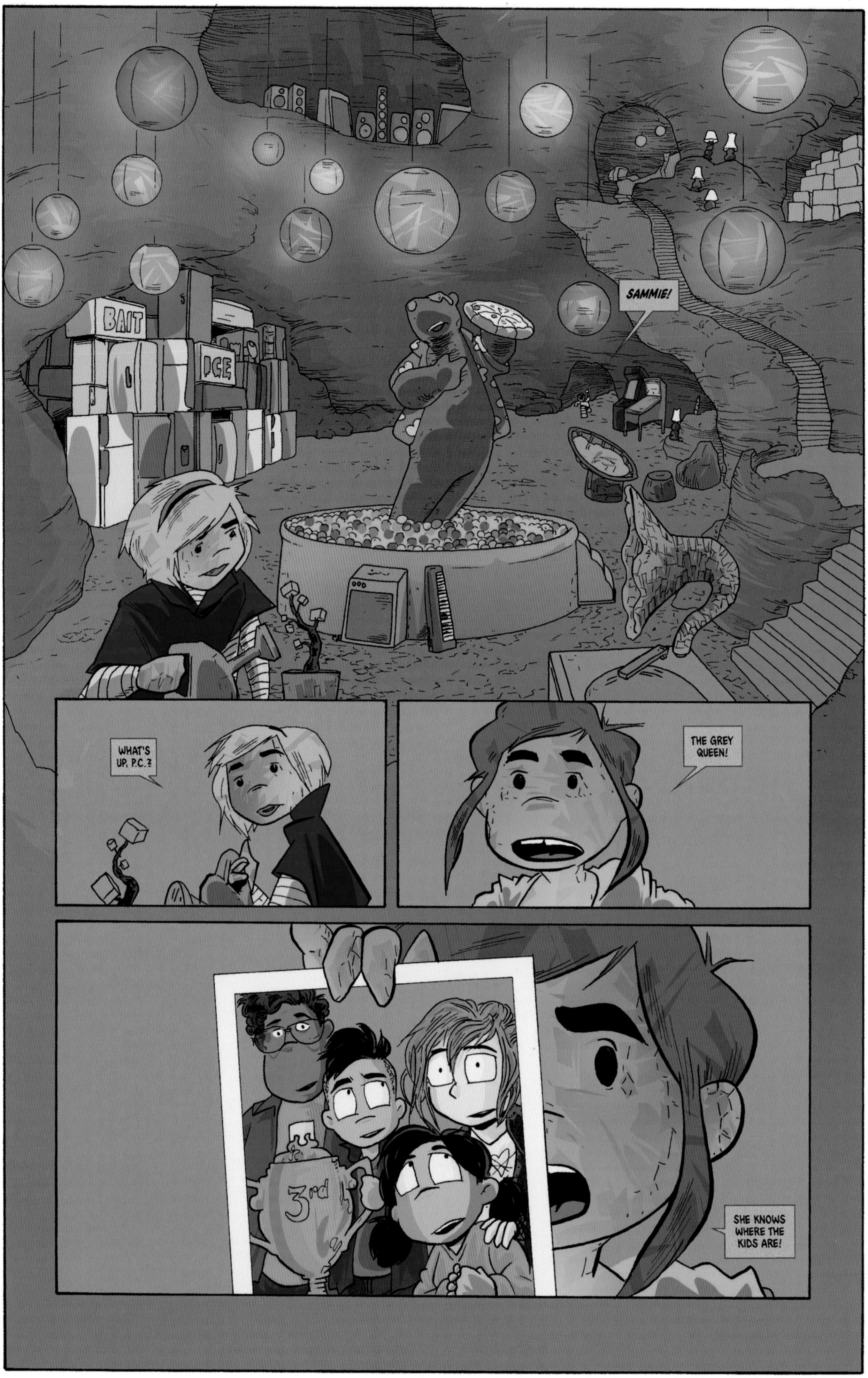
BAIT
ICE
SAMMIE!
WHAT'S UP, P.C.?
THE GREY QUEEN!
3rd
SHE KNOWS WHERE THE KIDS ARE!

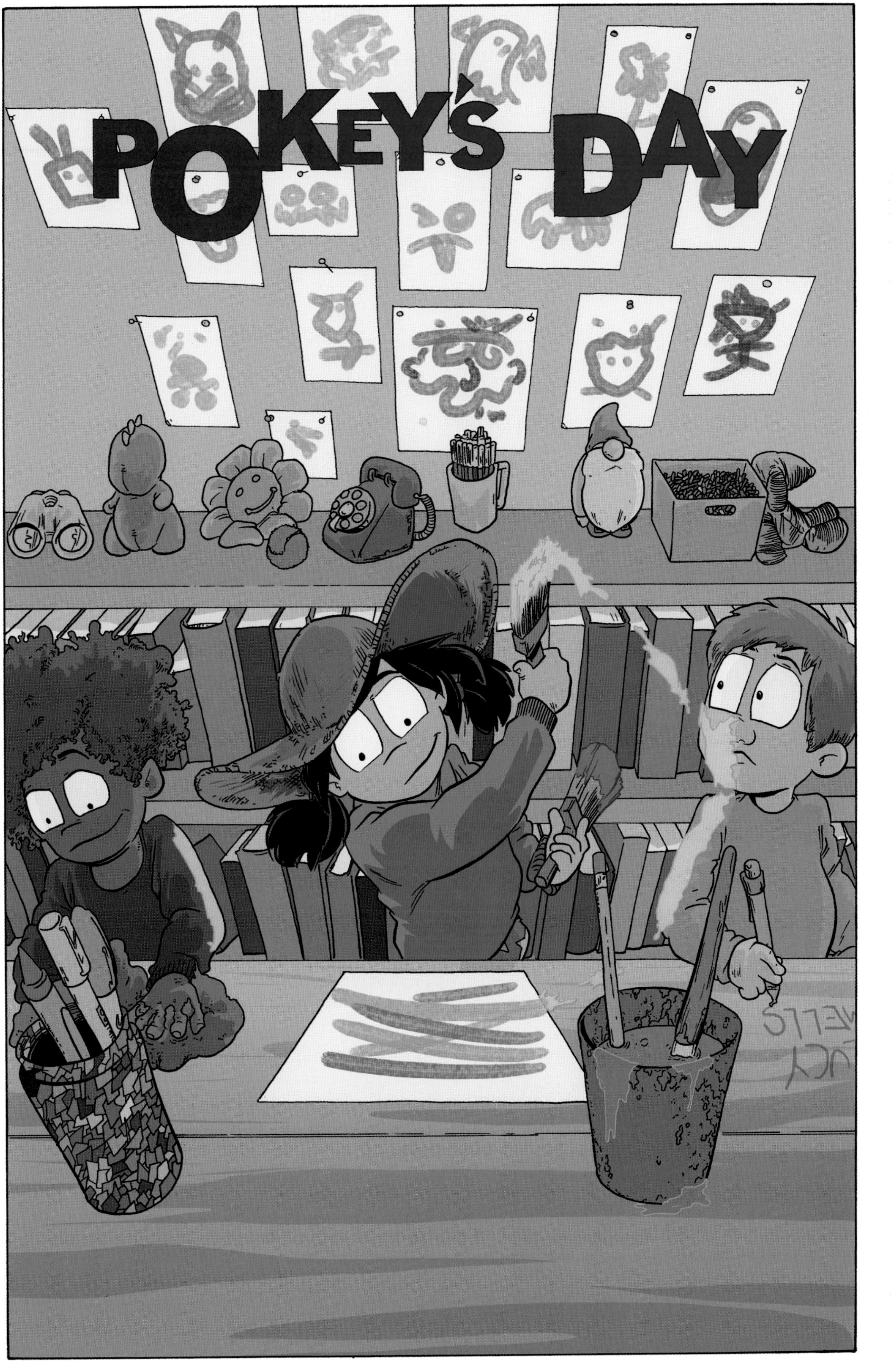
POKEY'S DAY

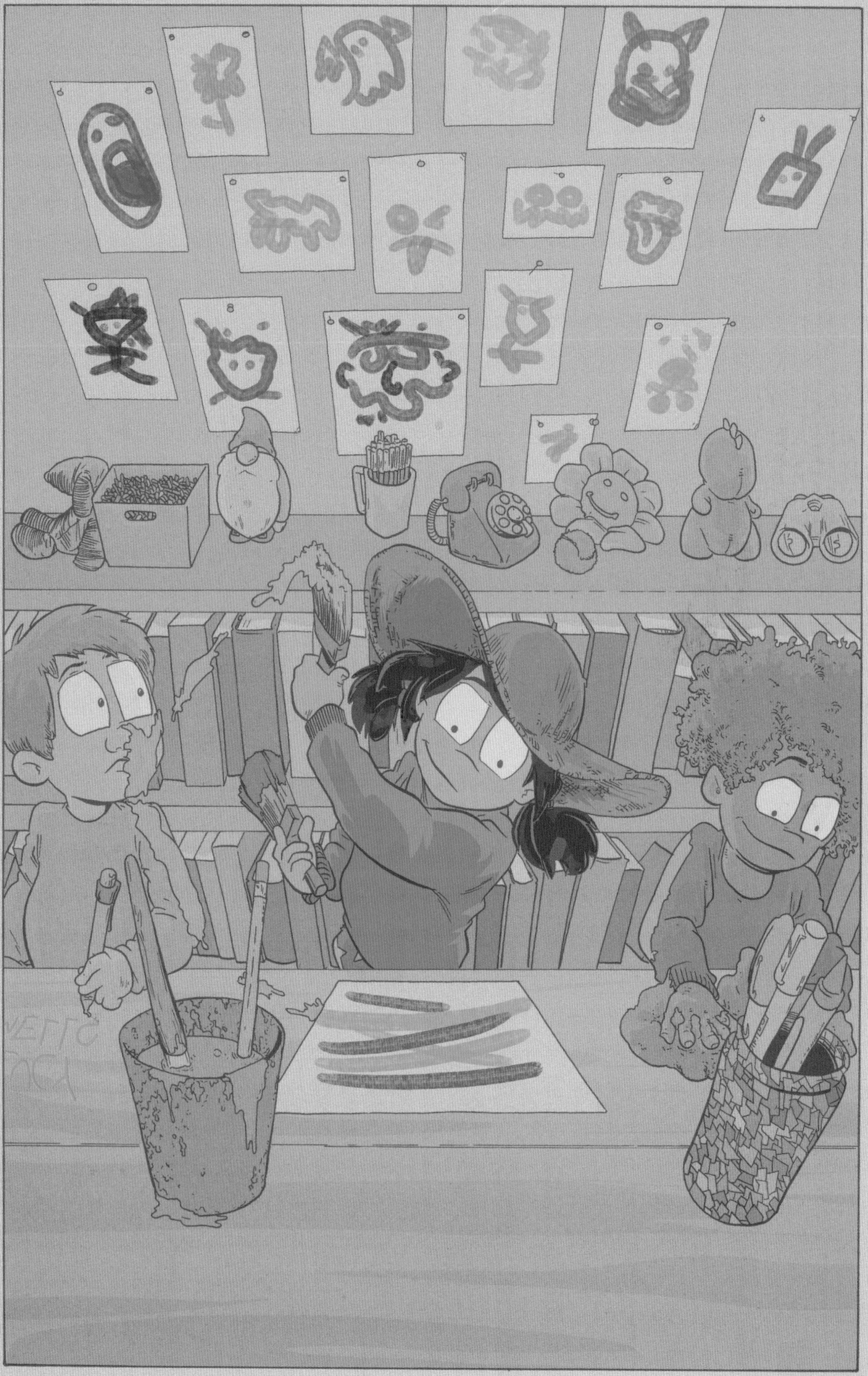

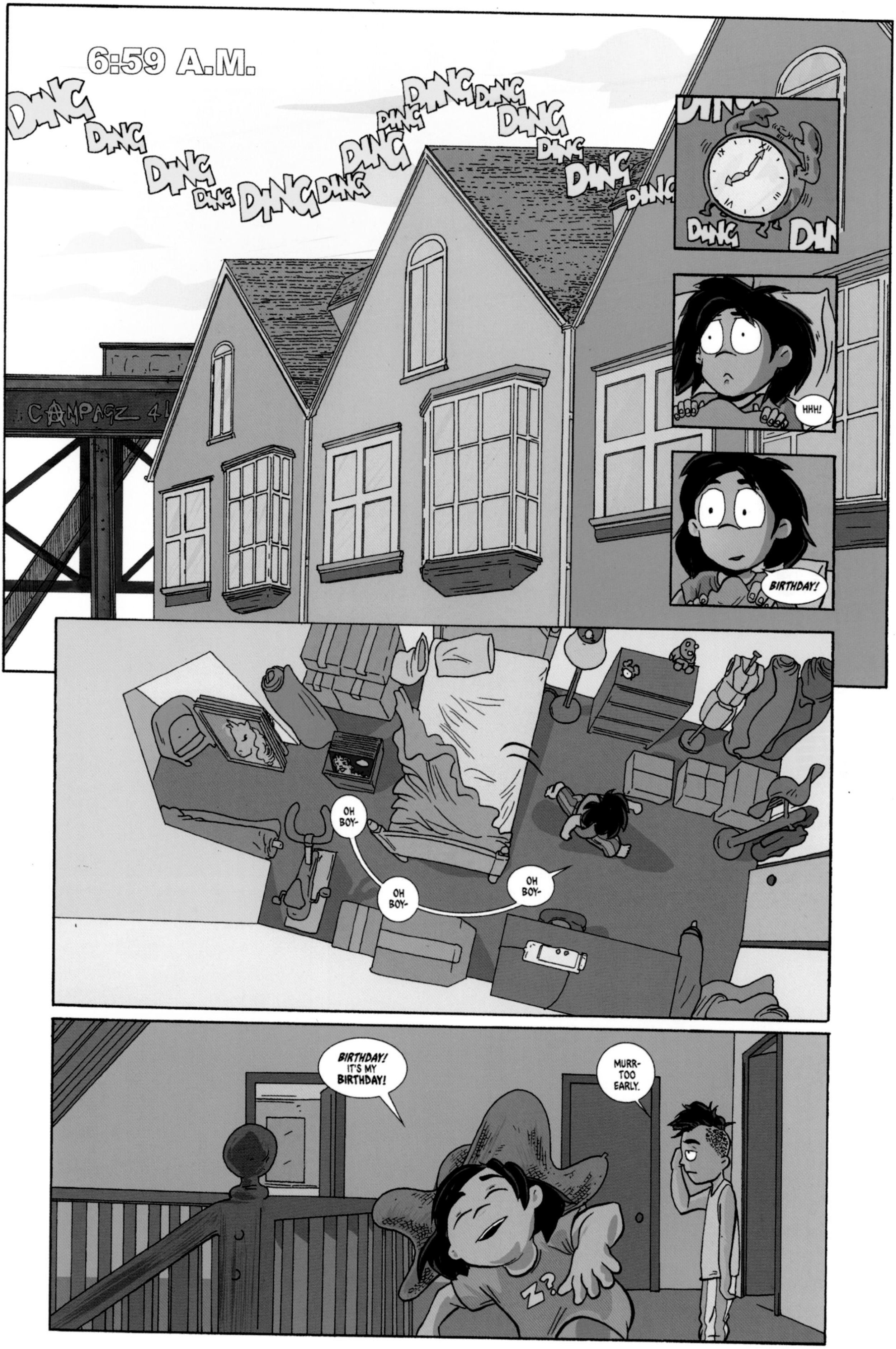
6:59 A.M.
DING DING DING DING DING DING DING DING DING DING DING DING DING DING
DING DING
HHH!
BIRTHDAY!
OH BOY-
OH BOY-
OH BOY-
BIRTHDAY! IT'S MY BIRTHDAY!
MURR- TOO EARLY.

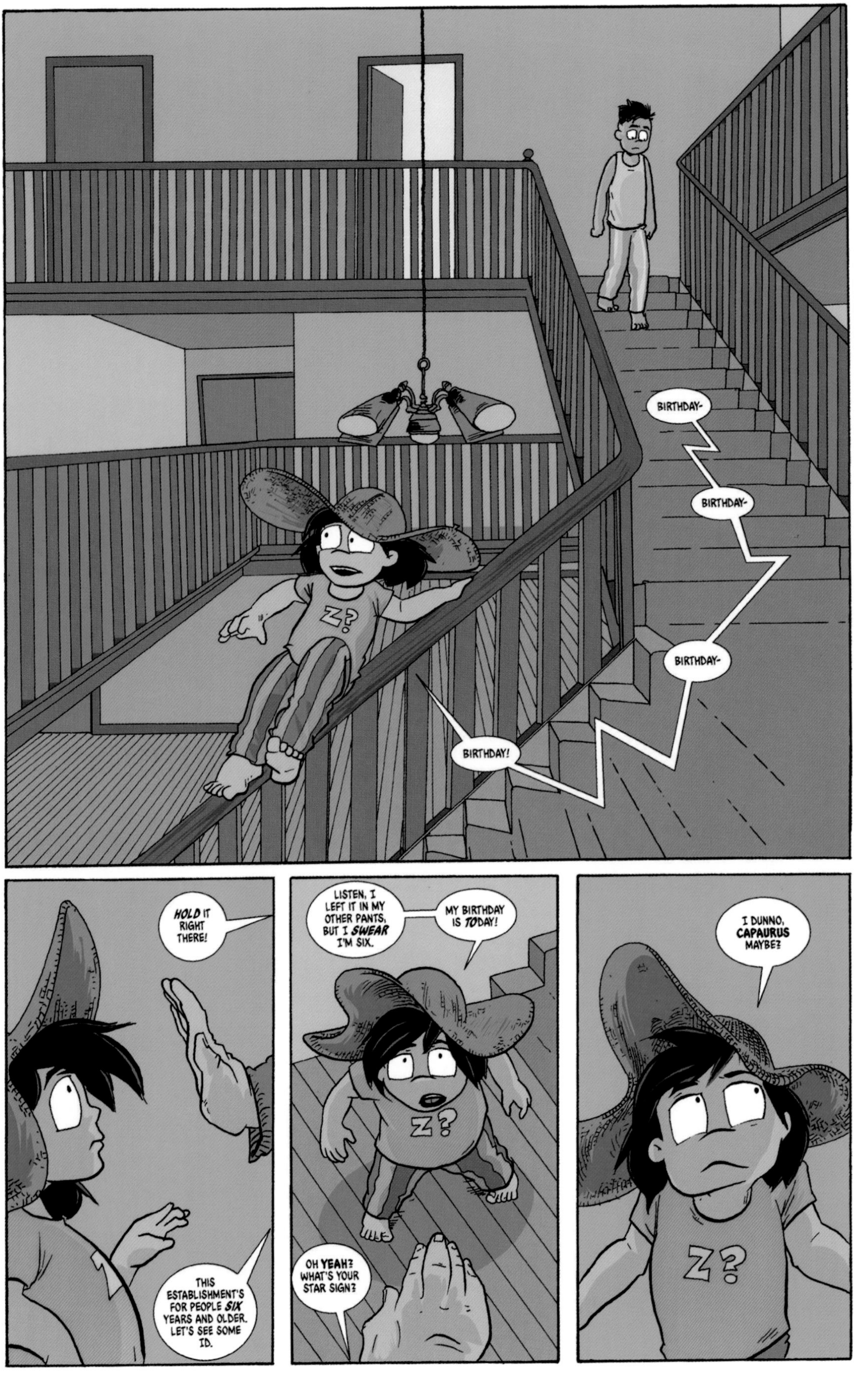
BIRTHDAY-
BIRTHDAY-
BIRTHDAY-
BIRTHDAY!
HOLD IT RIGHT THERE!
THIS ESTABLISHMENT'S FOR PEOPLE SIX YEARS AND OLDER. LET'S SEE SOME ID.
LISTEN, I LEFT IT IN MY OTHER PANTS, BUT I SWEAR I'M SIX.
MY BIRTHDAY IS TODAY!
OH YEAH? WHAT'S YOUR STAR SIGN?
I DUNNO, CAPAURUS MAYBE?

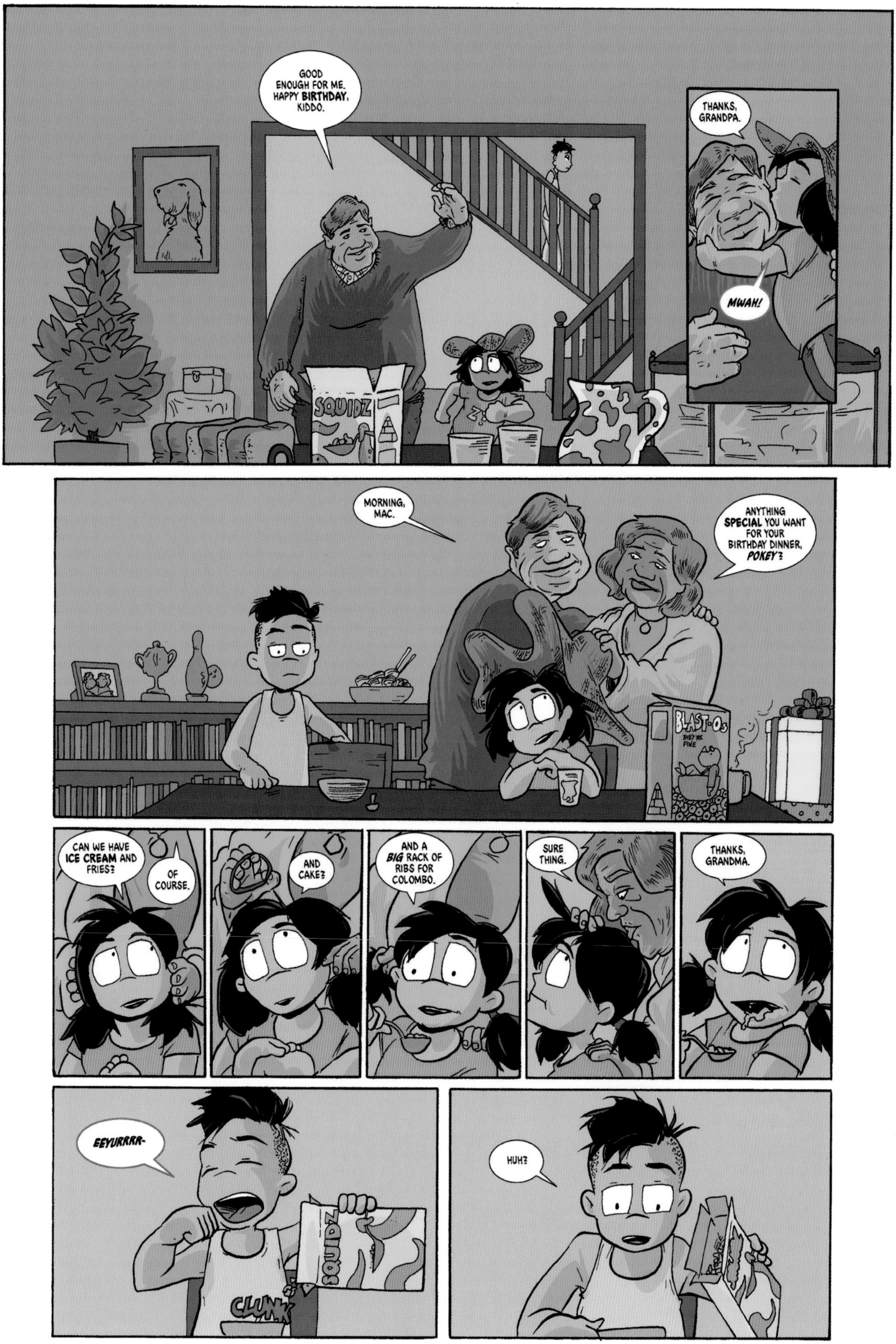
GOOD ENOUGH FOR ME. HAPPY BIRTHDAY, KIDDO.
THANKS, GRANDPA.
MWAH!
SQUIDZ
MORNING, MAC.
ANYTHING SPECIAL YOU WANT FOR YOUR BIRTHDAY DINNER, POKEY?
BLAST-Os
THEY'RE FINE
CAN WE HAVE ICE CREAM AND FRIES?
OF COURSE.
AND CAKE?
AND A BIG RACK OF RIBS FOR COLOMBO.
SURE THING.
THANKS, GRANDMA.
EEYURRRR-
SQUIDZ
CLUNK
HUH?

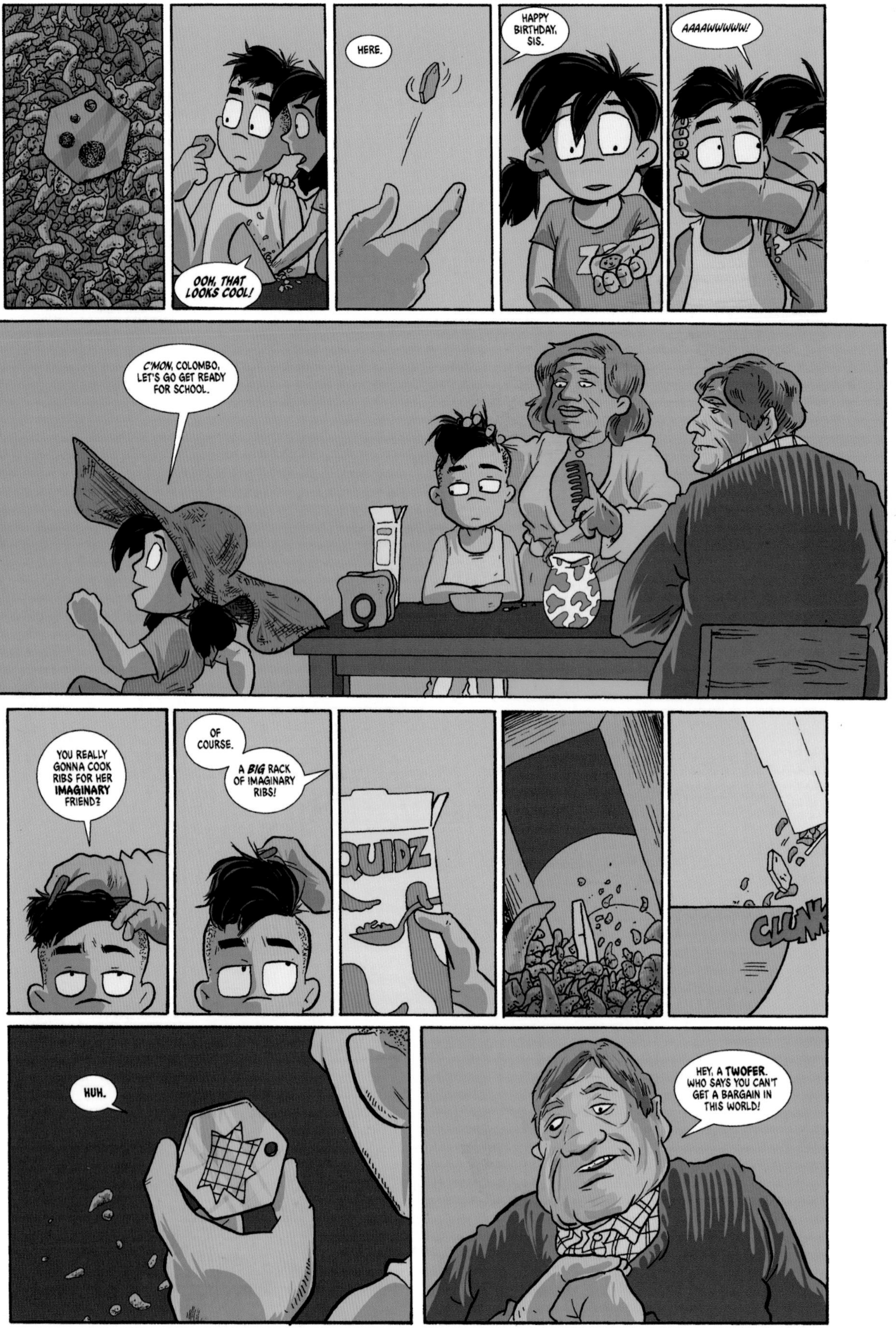
OOH, THAT LOOKS COOL!
HERE.
HAPPY BIRTHDAY, SIS.
AAAAWWWWW!
C'MON, COLOMBO, LET'S GO GET READY FOR SCHOOL.
YOU REALLY GONNA COOK RIBS FOR HER IMAGINARY FRIEND?
OF COURSE.
A BIG RACK OF IMAGINARY RIBS!
QUIDZ
CLUNK
HUH.
HEY, A TWOFER. WHO SAYS YOU CAN'T GET A BARGAIN IN THIS WORLD!

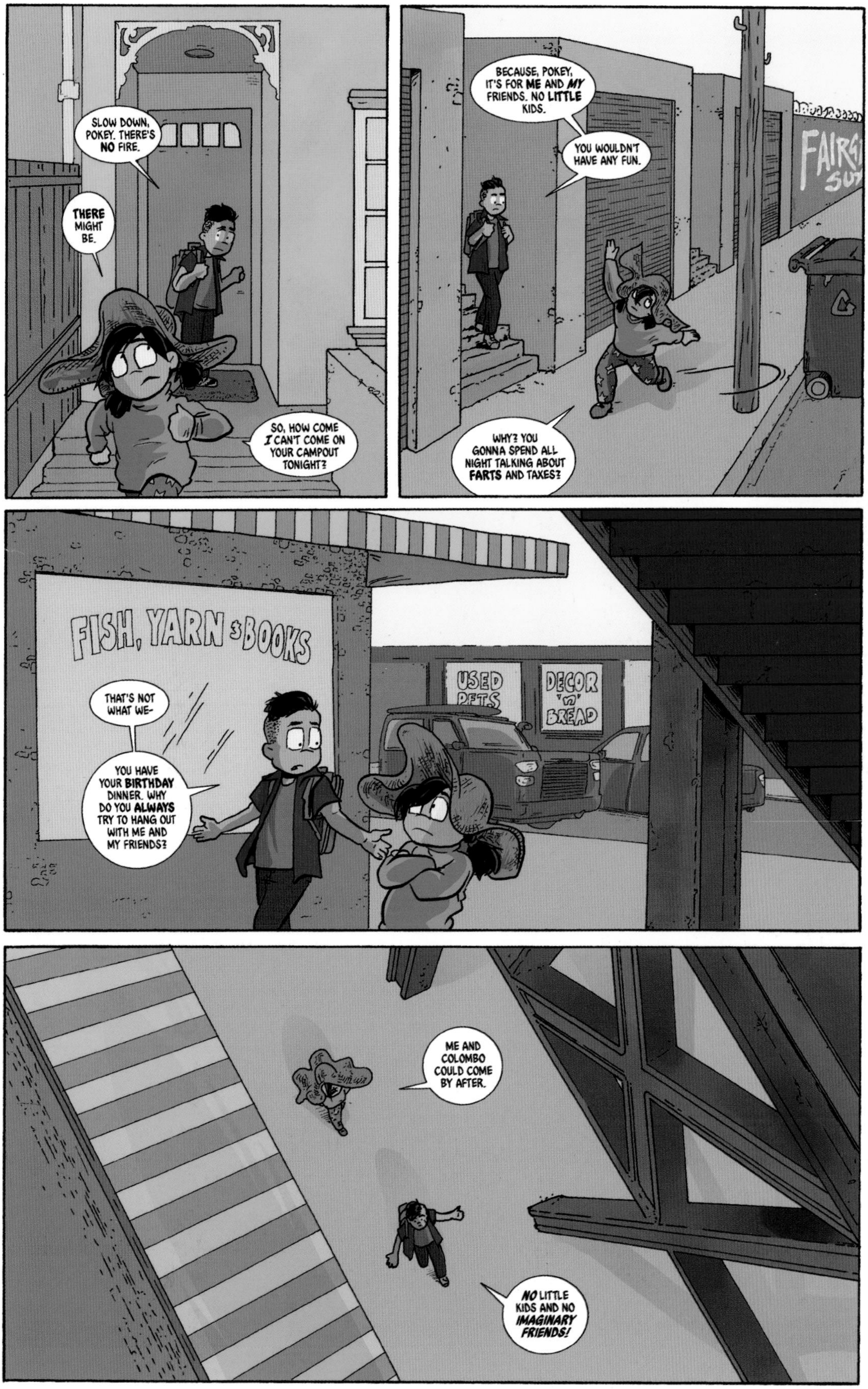

SLOW DOWN, POKEY. THERE'S **NO** FIRE.
THERE MIGHT BE.
SO, HOW COME *I* CAN'T COME ON YOUR CAMPOUT TONIGHT?
BECAUSE, POKEY, IT'S FOR **ME** AND ***MY*** FRIENDS. NO **LITTLE** KIDS.
YOU WOULDN'T HAVE ANY FUN.
WHY? YOU GONNA SPEND ALL NIGHT TALKING ABOUT **FARTS** AND TAXES?
FISH, YARN & BOOKS
USED PETS
DECOR 'N' BREAD
THAT'S NOT WHAT WE-
YOU HAVE YOUR **BIRTHDAY** DINNER. WHY DO YOU **ALWAYS** TRY TO HANG OUT WITH ME AND MY FRIENDS?
ME AND COLOMBO COULD COME BY AFTER.
NO LITTLE KIDS AND NO ***IMAGINARY FRIENDS!***

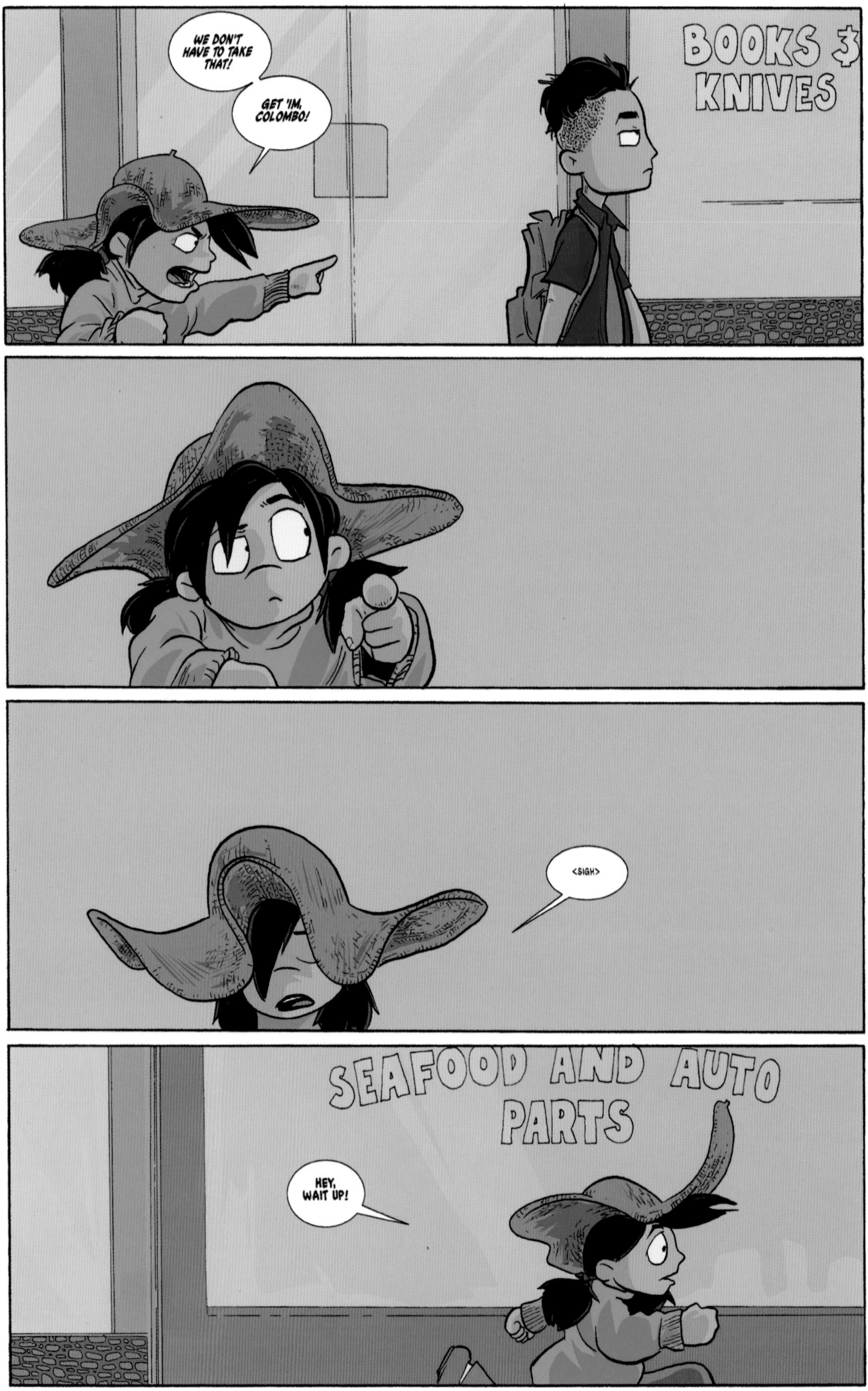
WE DON'T HAVE TO TAKE THAT!
GET 'IM, COLOMBO!
BOOKS & KNIVES
<SIGH>
SEAFOOD AND AUTO PARTS
HEY, WAIT UP!

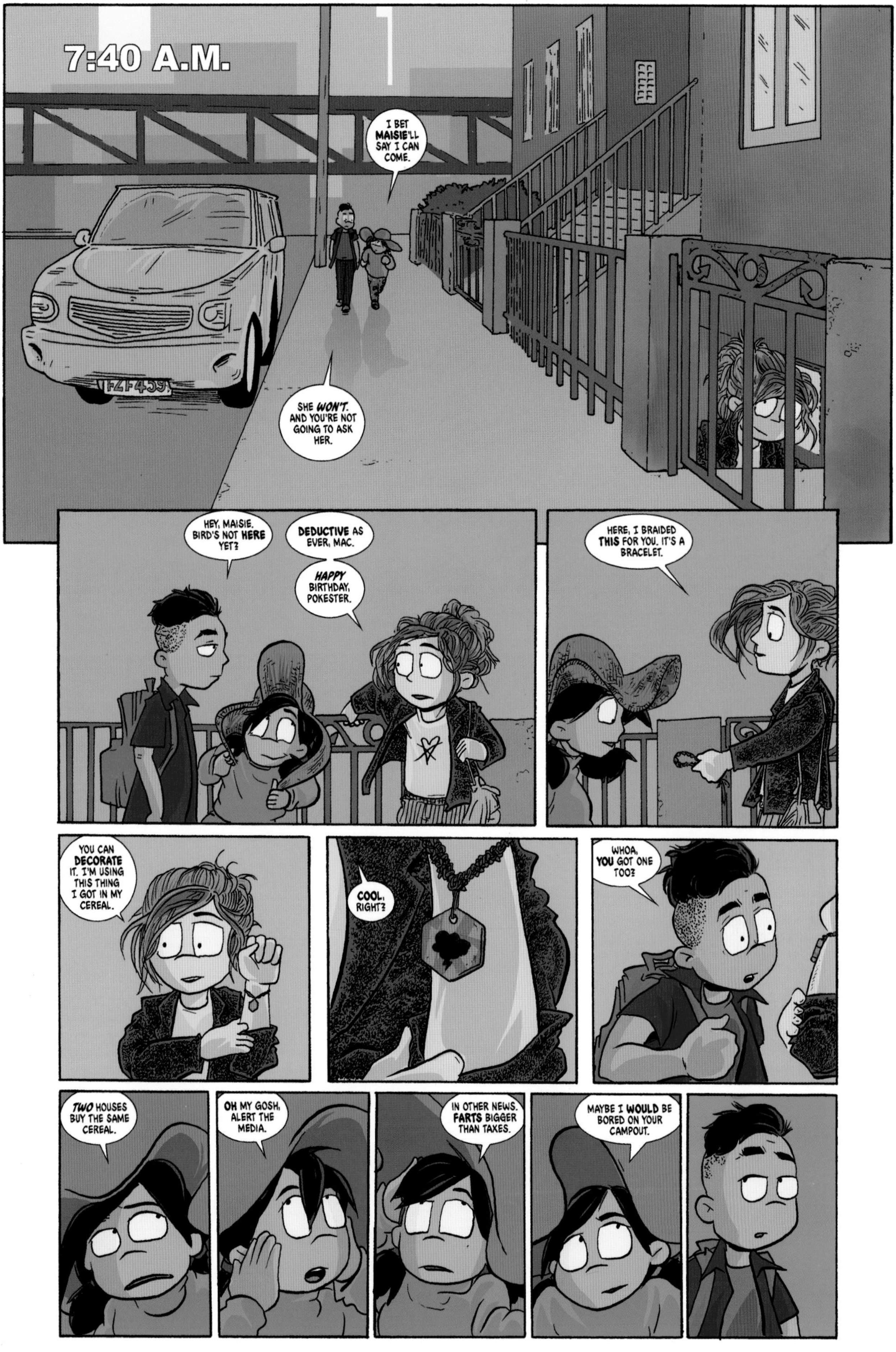
7:40 A.M.
I BET MAISIE'LL SAY I CAN COME.
SHE WON'T. AND YOU'RE NOT GOING TO ASK HER.
HEY, MAISIE. BIRD'S NOT HERE YET?
DEDUCTIVE AS EVER, MAC.
HAPPY BIRTHDAY, POKESTER.
HERE, I BRAIDED THIS FOR YOU. IT'S A BRACELET.
YOU CAN DECORATE IT. I'M USING THIS THING I GOT IN MY CEREAL.
COOL, RIGHT?
WHOA, YOU GOT ONE TOO?
TWO HOUSES BUY THE SAME CEREAL.
OH MY GOSH, ALERT THE MEDIA.
IN OTHER NEWS. FARTS BIGGER THAN TAXES.
MAYBE I WOULD BE BORED ON YOUR CAMPOUT.

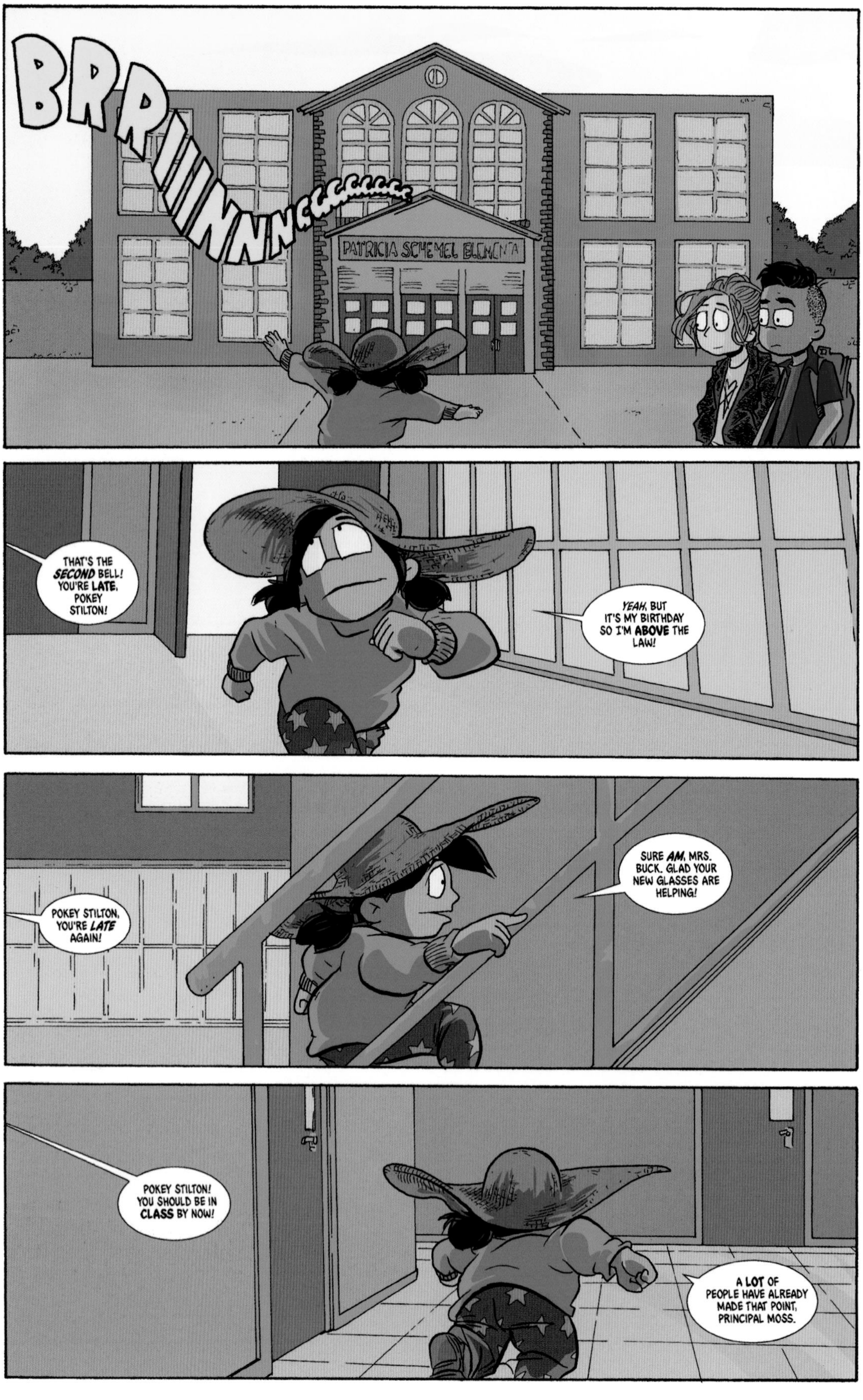
BRRIIIINNNNGGGGGGG
PATRICIA SCHEMEL ELEMENTA
THAT'S THE SECOND BELL! YOU'RE LATE, POKEY STILTON!
YEAH, BUT IT'S MY BIRTHDAY SO I'M ABOVE THE LAW!
POKEY STILTON, YOU'RE LATE AGAIN!
SURE AM, MRS. BUCK. GLAD YOUR NEW GLASSES ARE HELPING!
POKEY STILTON! YOU SHOULD BE IN CLASS BY NOW!
A LOT OF PEOPLE HAVE ALREADY MADE THAT POINT, PRINCIPAL MOSS.

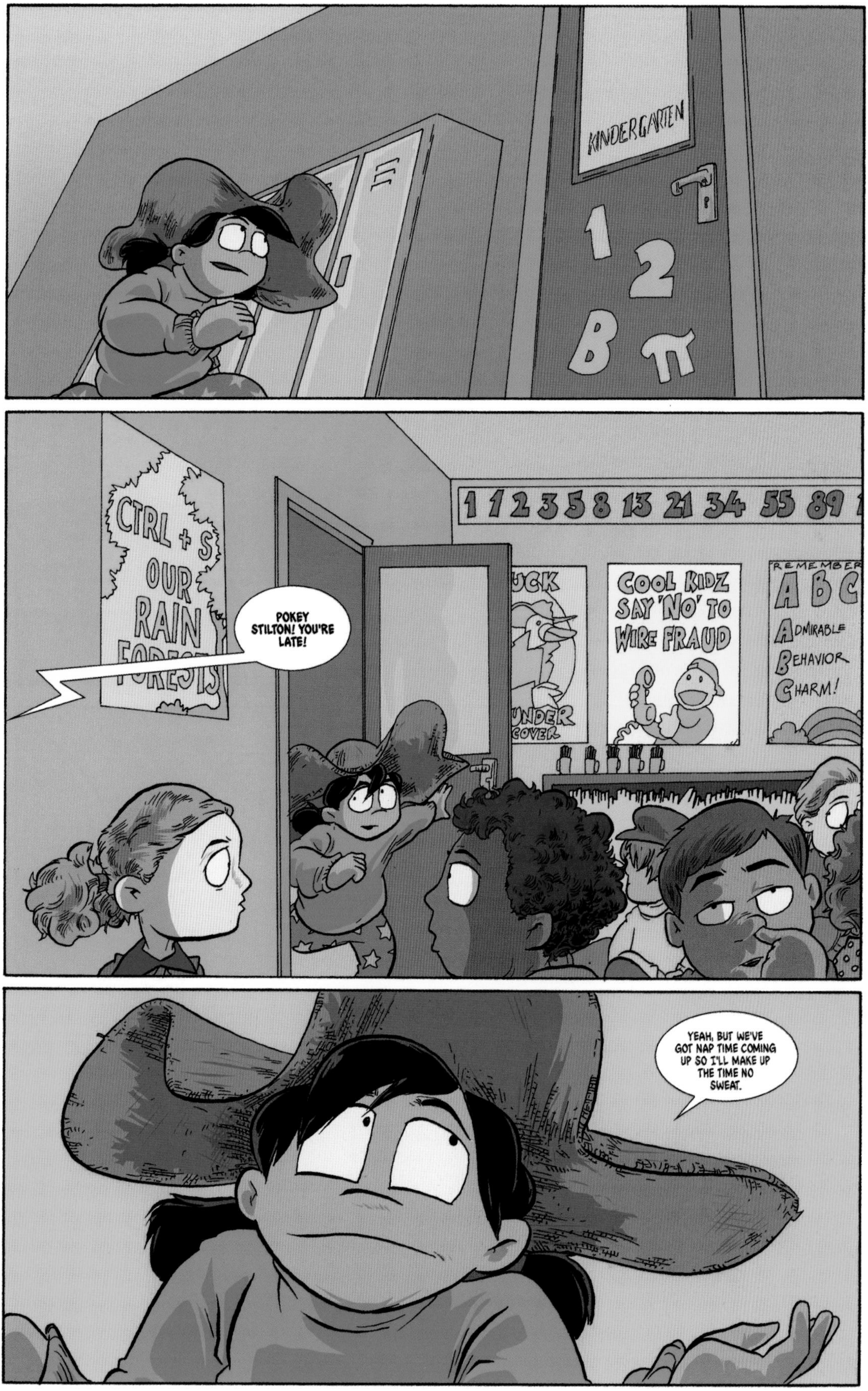
KINDERGARTEN
1 2 B π
CTRL + S OUR RAIN FORESTS
1 1 2 3 5 8 13 21 34 55 89
COOL KIDZ SAY 'NO' TO WIRE FRAUD
REMEMBER A B C ADMIRABLE BEHAVIOR CHARM!
POKEY STILTON! YOU'RE LATE!
YEAH, BUT WE'VE GOT NAP TIME COMING UP SO I'LL MAKE UP THE TIME NO SWEAT.

ARTS AND/OR CRAFTS

NAP TIME

COORDINATION STUDIES

LUNCH

HUWP!

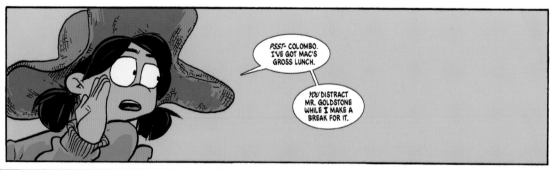

PSST- COLOMBO. I'VE GOT MAC'S GROSS LUNCH.

YOU DISTRACT MR. GOLDSTONE WHILE I MAKE A BREAK FOR IT.

MATH EQUALS FUN

READING IS FINE

TEETH ARE BONES YOU CAN TOUCH

CANN FOO

POKEY STILTON! WHERE DO YOU THINK YOU'RE GOING?

<SIGH> COME ON, COLOMBO.

ALEXANDER BURKE! STOP PUTTING GLUE IN THERE!

FIRE HOSE (SQUIRTS WATER)

MARCHING BANNED

CAFETERIA

BLOOD DRIVE

COLOMBO, EVEN WHEN I CAN'T RELY ON YOU, I CAN RELY ON ALEX BURKE DOING SOMETHING STUPID.

LET'S GO SAVE MY BROTHER'S LUNCH!

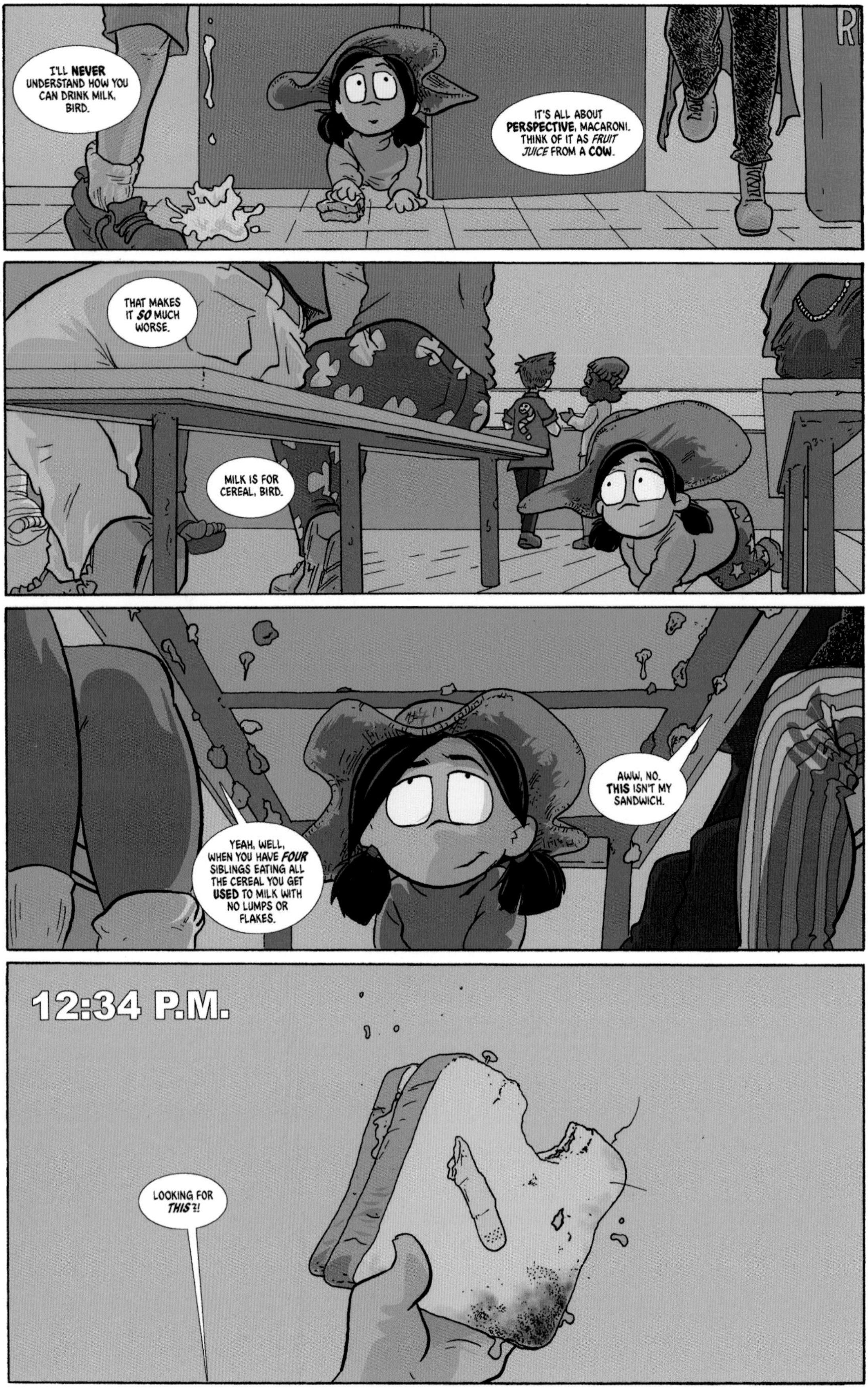
I'LL **NEVER** UNDERSTAND HOW YOU CAN DRINK MILK, BIRD.
IT'S ALL ABOUT **PERSPECTIVE**, MACARONI. THINK OF IT AS *FRUIT JUICE* FROM A **COW**.
THAT MAKES IT ***SO*** MUCH WORSE.
MILK IS FOR CEREAL, BIRD.
YEAH, WELL, WHEN YOU HAVE ***FOUR*** SIBLINGS EATING ALL THE CEREAL YOU GET **USED** TO MILK WITH NO LUMPS OR FLAKES.
AWW, NO. **THIS** ISN'T MY SANDWICH.
12:34 P.M.
LOOKING FOR ***THIS***?!

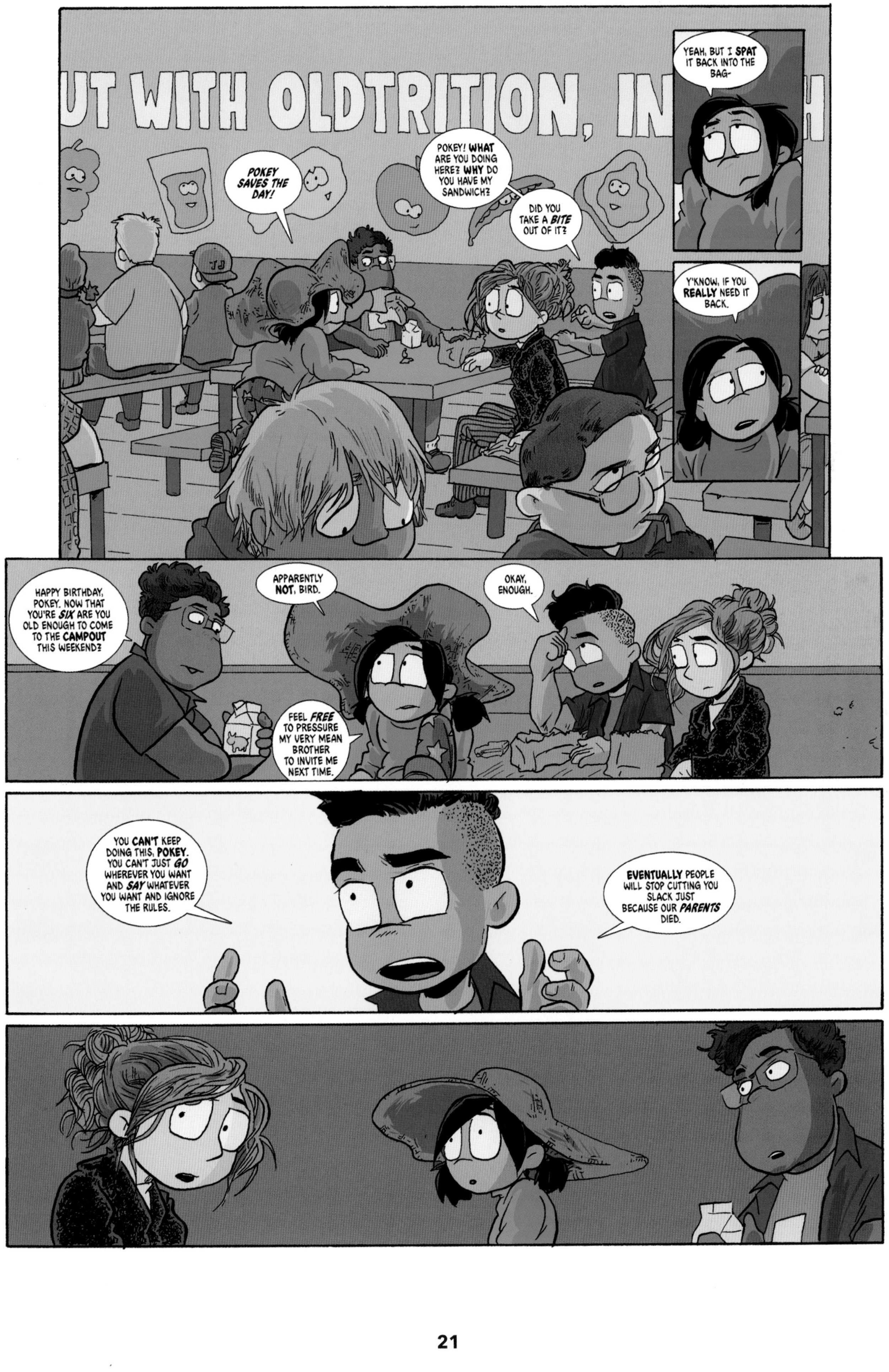
UT WITH OLDTRITION, IN H
POKEY SAVES THE DAY!
POKEY! WHAT ARE YOU DOING HERE? WHY DO YOU HAVE MY SANDWICH?
DID YOU TAKE A BITE OUT OF IT?
YEAH, BUT I SPAT IT BACK INTO THE BAG-
Y'KNOW, IF YOU REALLY NEED IT BACK.
HAPPY BIRTHDAY, POKEY. NOW THAT YOU'RE SIX ARE YOU OLD ENOUGH TO COME TO THE CAMPOUT THIS WEEKEND?
APPARENTLY NOT, BIRD.
FEEL FREE TO PRESSURE MY VERY MEAN BROTHER TO INVITE ME NEXT TIME.
OKAY, ENOUGH.
YOU CAN'T KEEP DOING THIS, POKEY. YOU CAN'T JUST GO WHEREVER YOU WANT AND SAY WHATEVER YOU WANT AND IGNORE THE RULES.
EVENTUALLY PEOPLE WILL STOP CUTTING YOU SLACK JUST BECAUSE OUR PARENTS DIED.

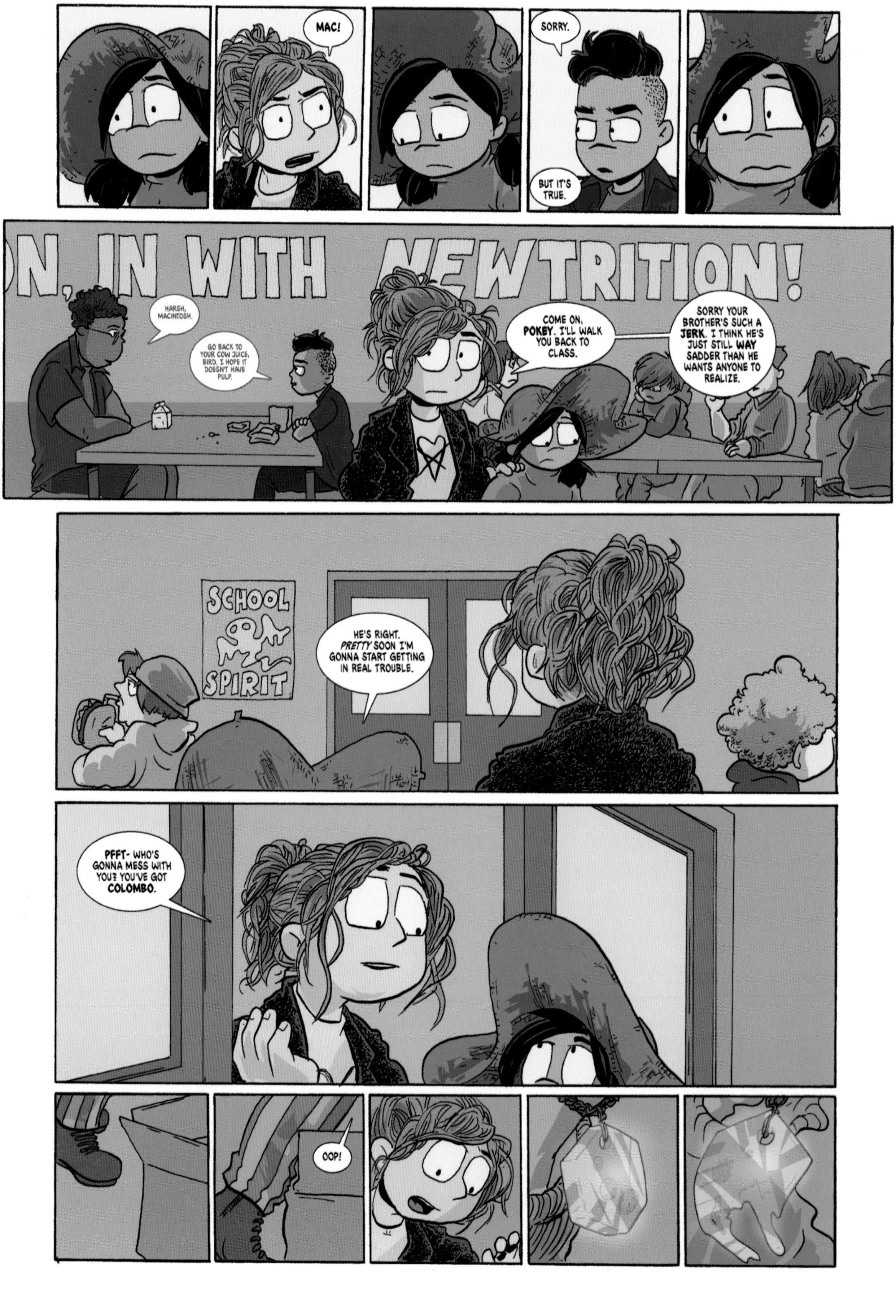

MAC!
SORRY.
BUT IT'S TRUE.
...ON, IN WITH NEWTRITION!
HARSH, MACINTOSH.
GO BACK TO YOUR COW JUICE, BIRD. I HOPE IT DOESN'T HAVE PULP.
COME ON, POKEY. I'LL WALK YOU BACK TO CLASS.
SORRY YOUR BROTHER'S SUCH A JERK. I THINK HE'S JUST STILL WAY SADDER THAN HE WANTS ANYONE TO REALIZE.
SCHOOL SPIRIT
HE'S RIGHT. PRETTY SOON I'M GONNA START GETTING IN REAL TROUBLE.
PFFT- WHO'S GONNA MESS WITH YOU? YOU'VE GOT COLOMBO.
OOP!

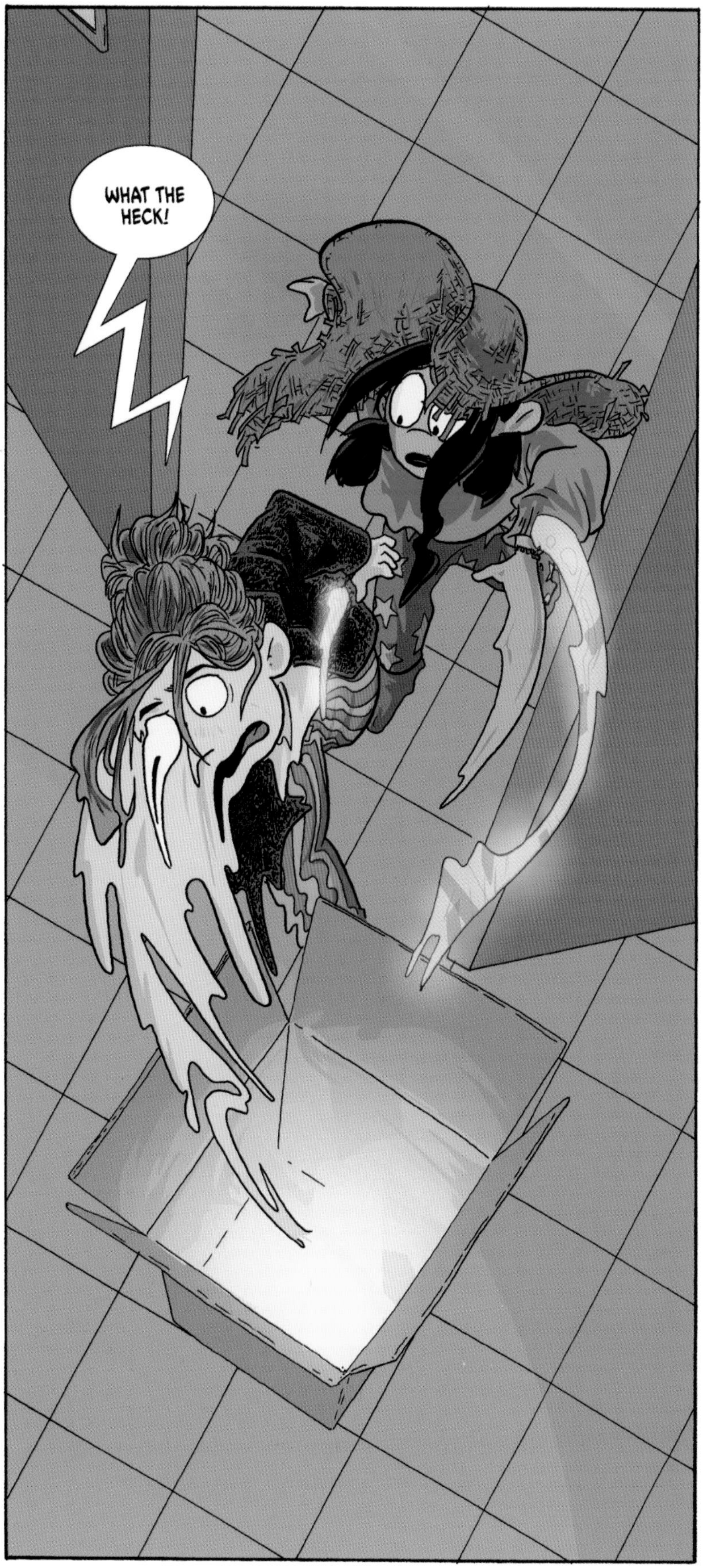
WHAT THE HECK!

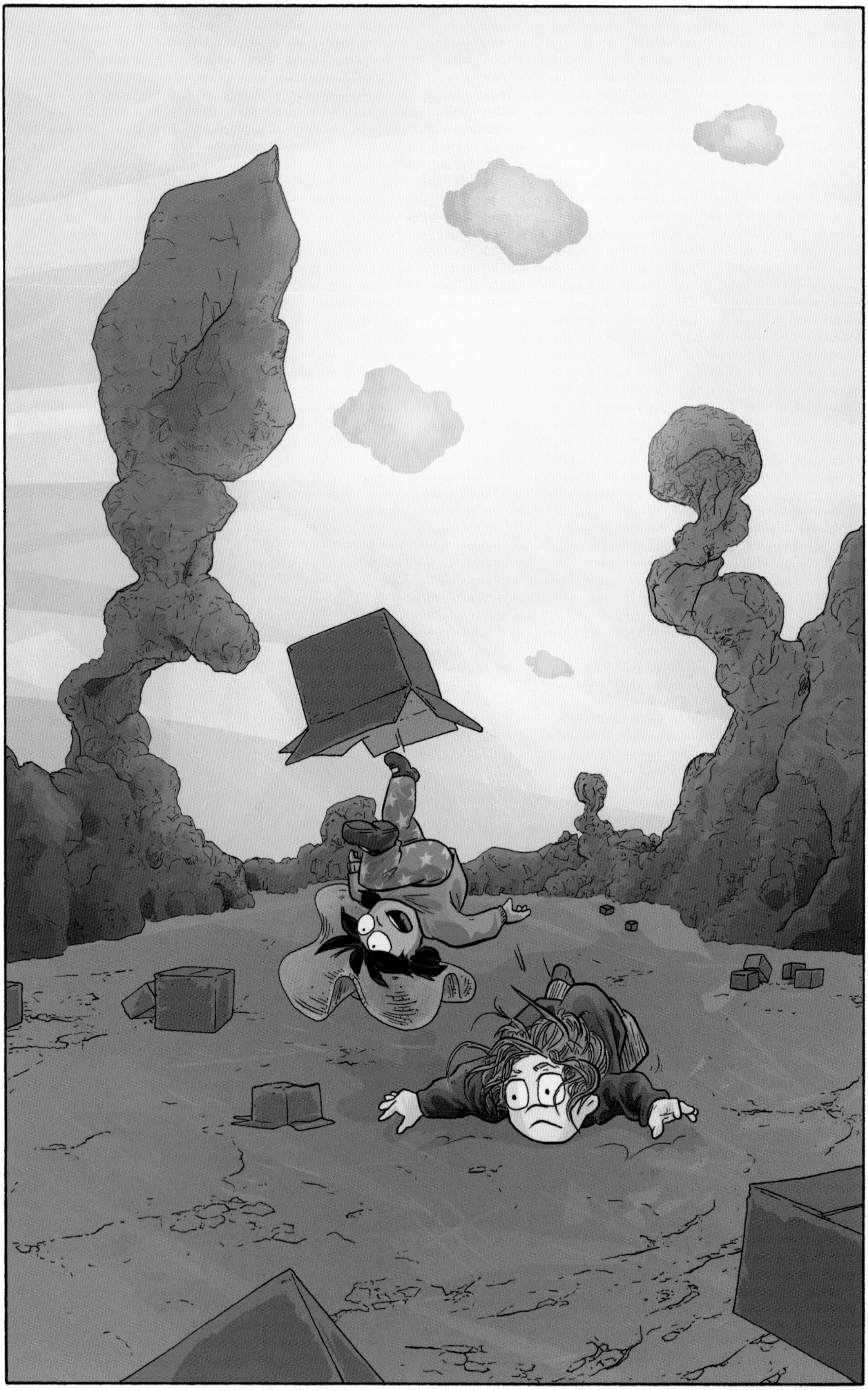

TO BE CONTINUED.

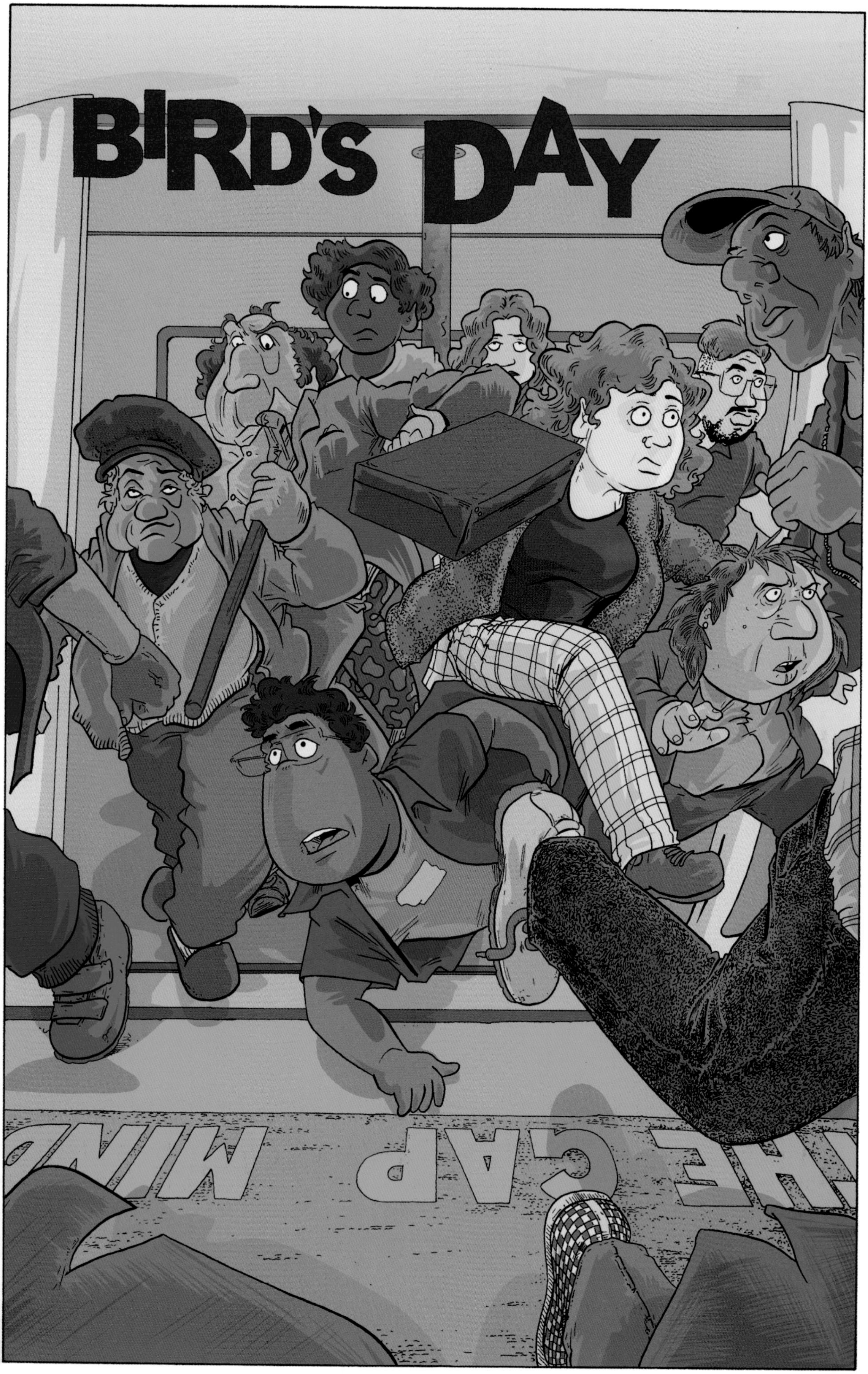
BIRD'S DAY

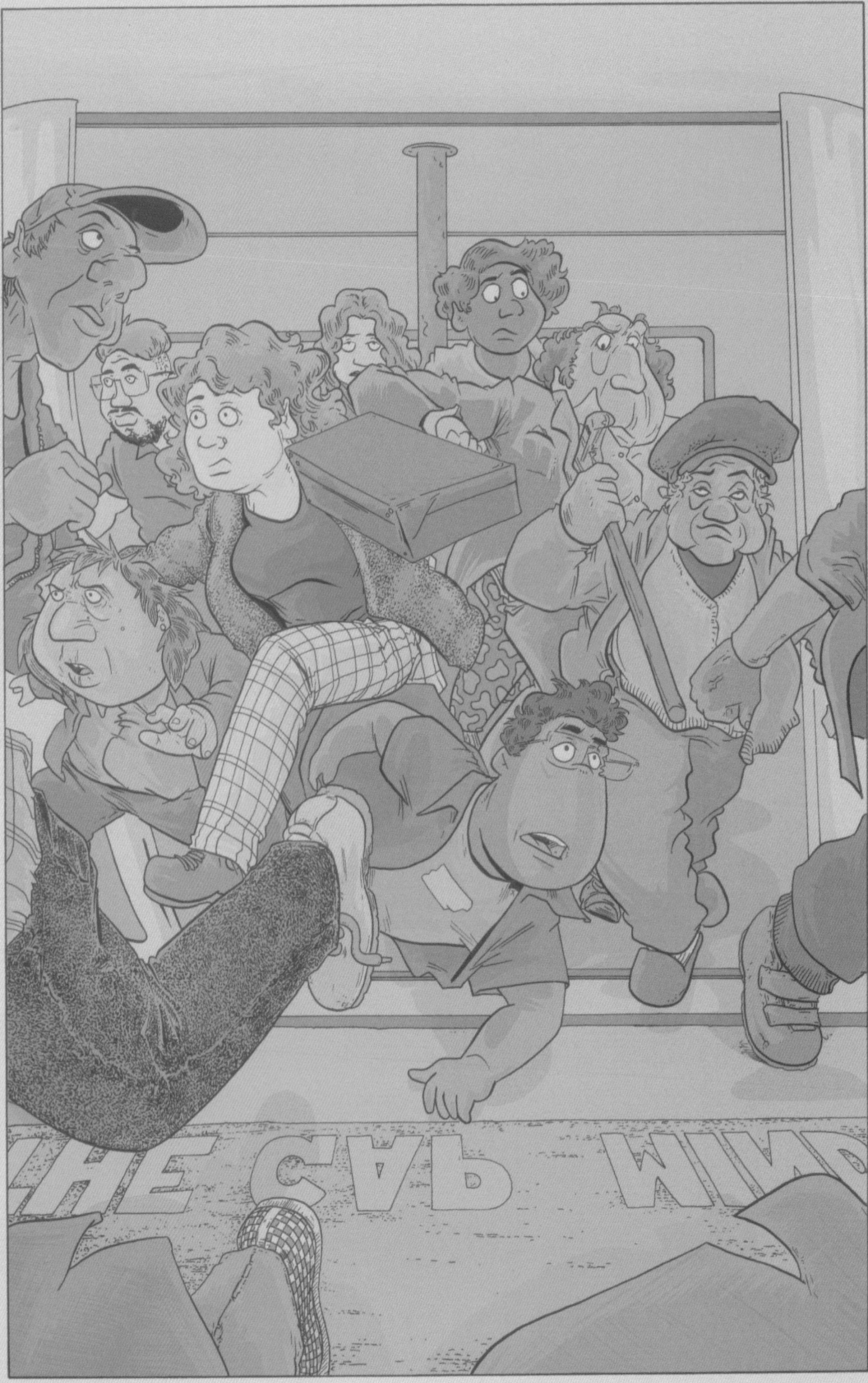

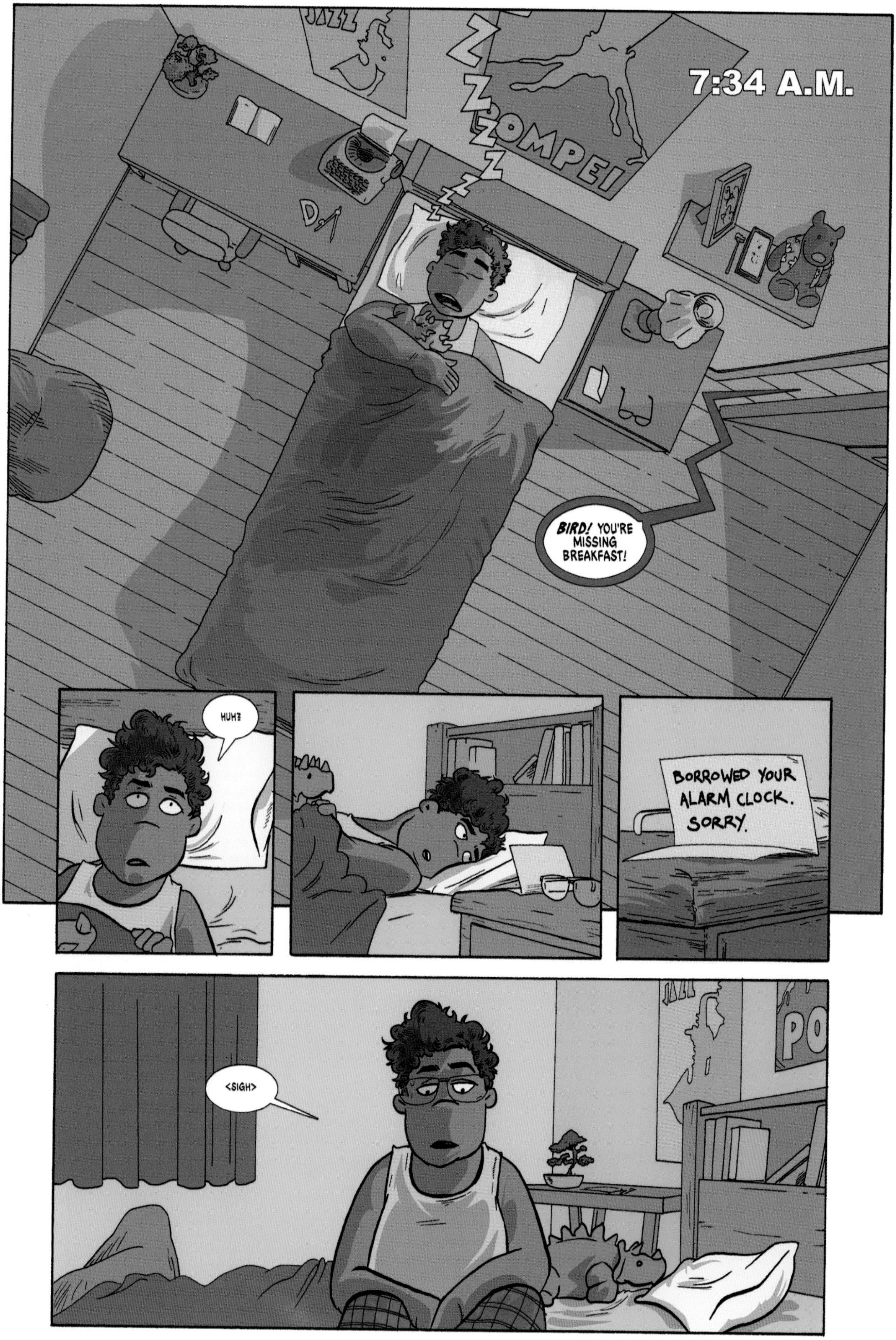
JAZZ
Z
Z
POMPEI
7:34 A.M.
BIRD! YOU'RE MISSING BREAKFAST!
HUH?
BORROWED YOUR ALARM CLOCK. SORRY.
<SIGH>

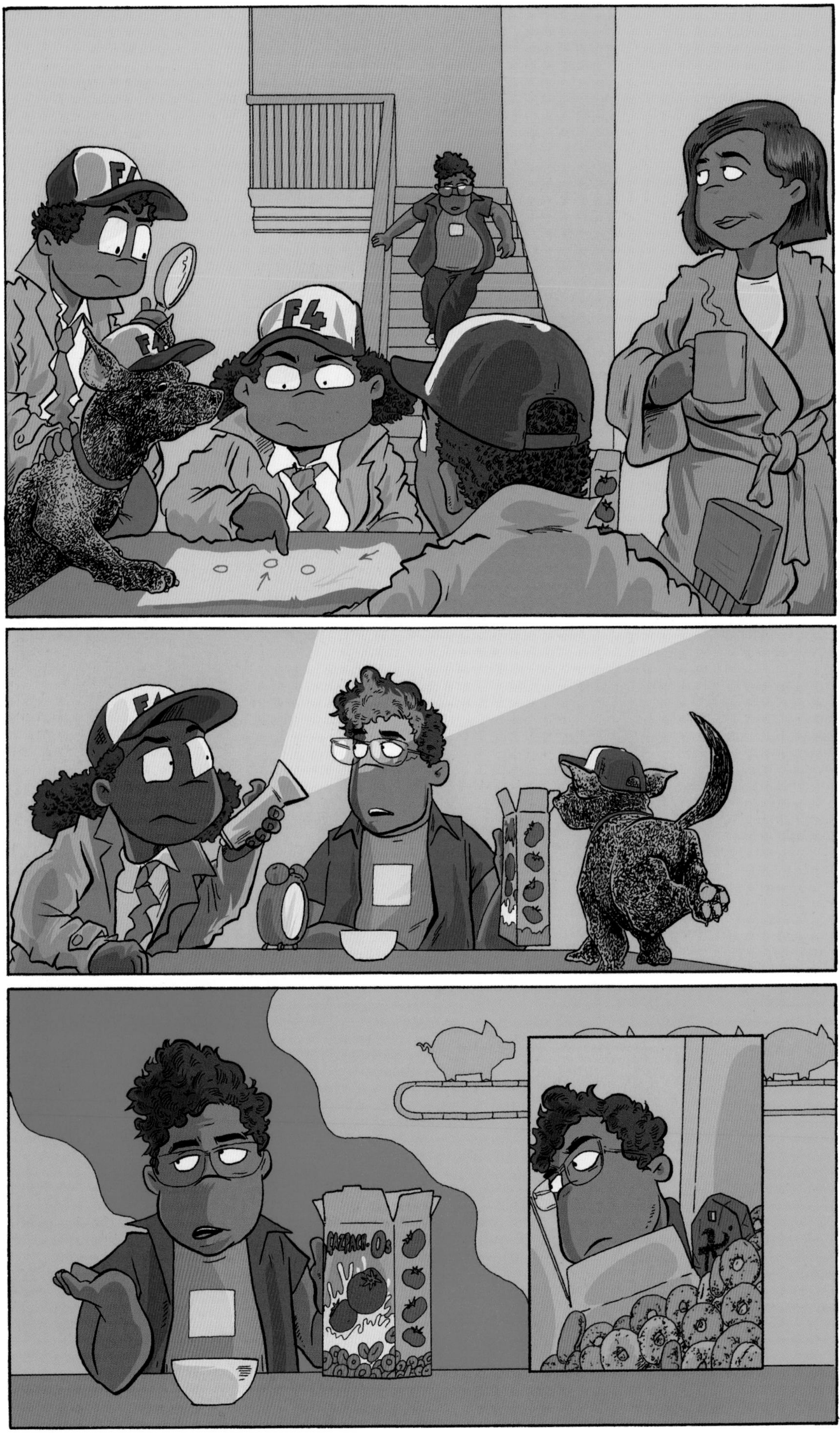
F4
GAZPACH-Os

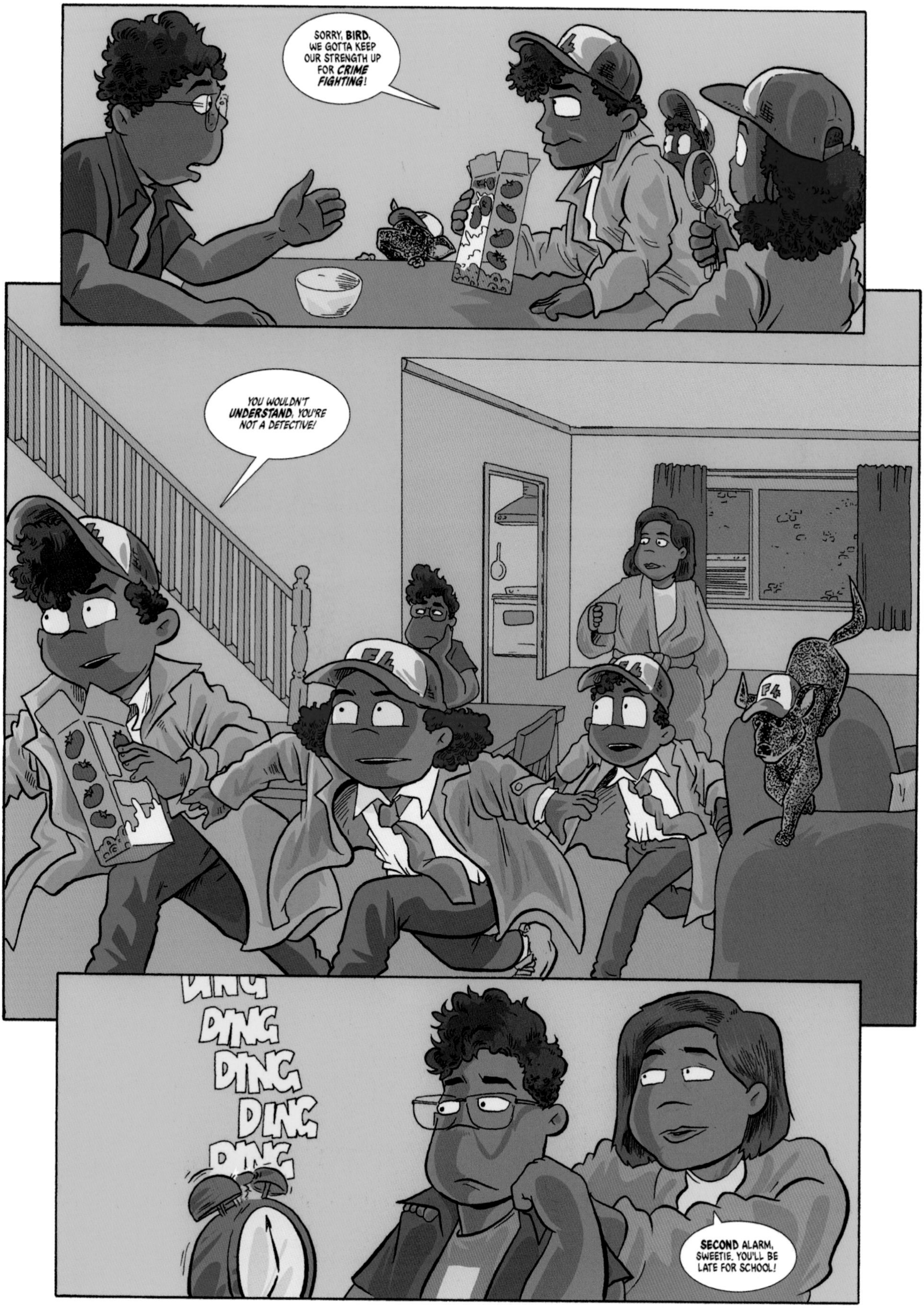
SORRY, BIRD, WE GOTTA KEEP OUR STRENGTH UP FOR CRIME FIGHTING!
YOU WOULDN'T UNDERSTAND, YOU'RE NOT A DETECTIVE!
DING DING DING DING DING
SECOND ALARM, SWEETIE, YOU'LL BE LATE FOR SCHOOL!

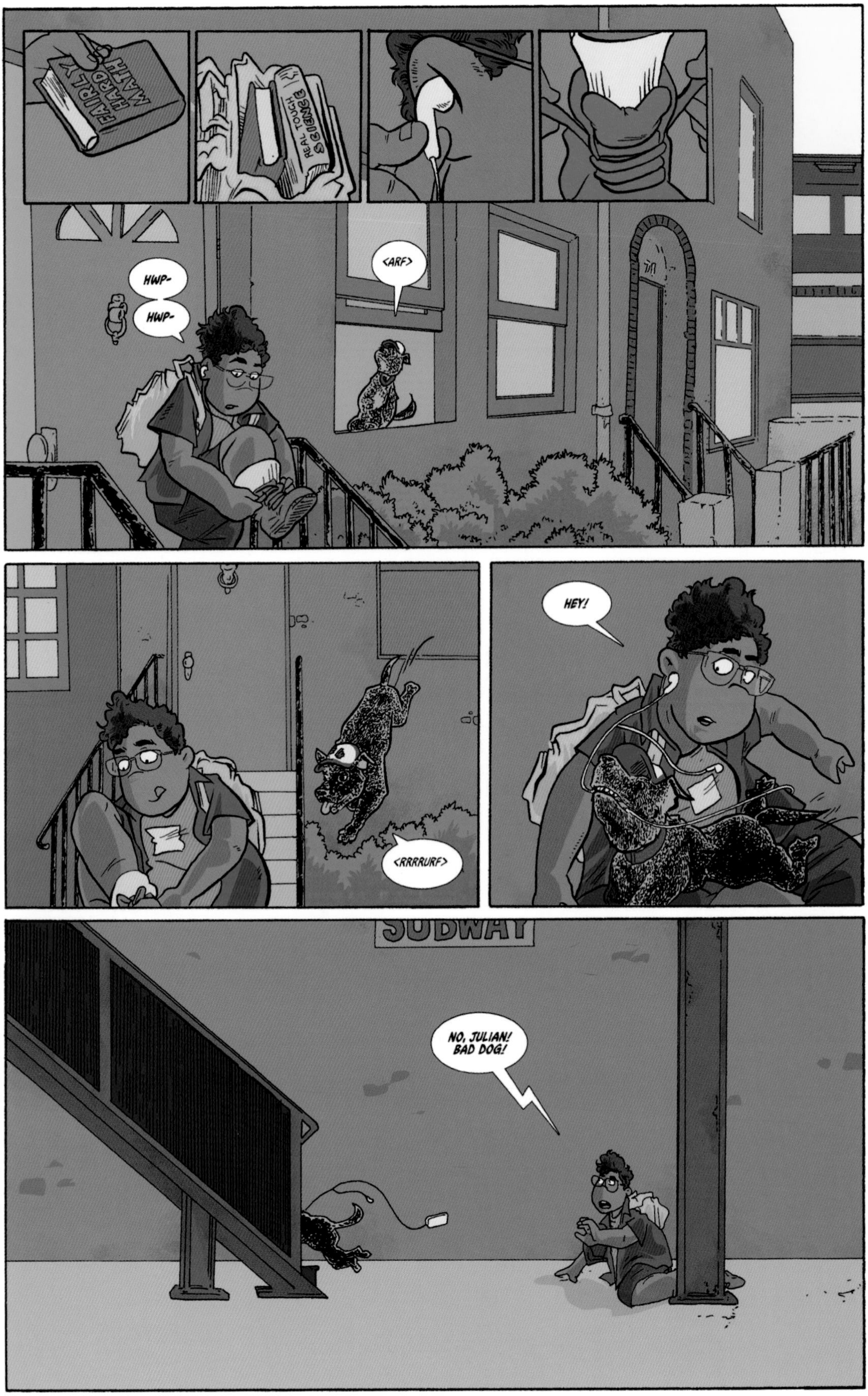
FAIRLY HARD MATH
REAL TOUGH SCIENCE
HWP-
HWP-
<ARF>
<RRRRURF>
HEY!
SUBWAY
NO, JULIAN! BAD DOG!

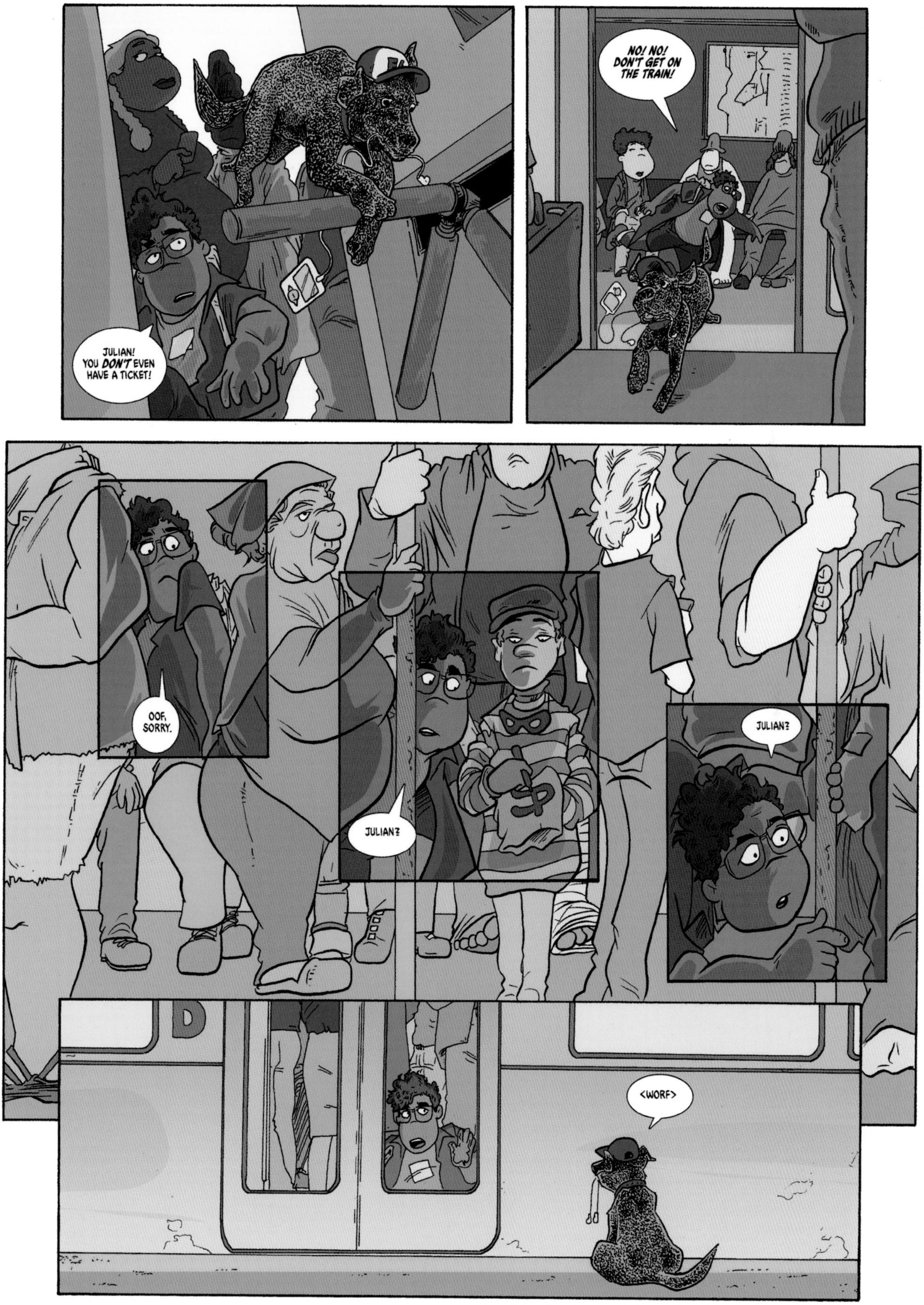
JULIAN! YOU DON'T EVEN HAVE A TICKET!
NO! NO! DON'T GET ON THE TRAIN!
OOF, SORRY.
JULIAN?
JULIAN?
<WORF>

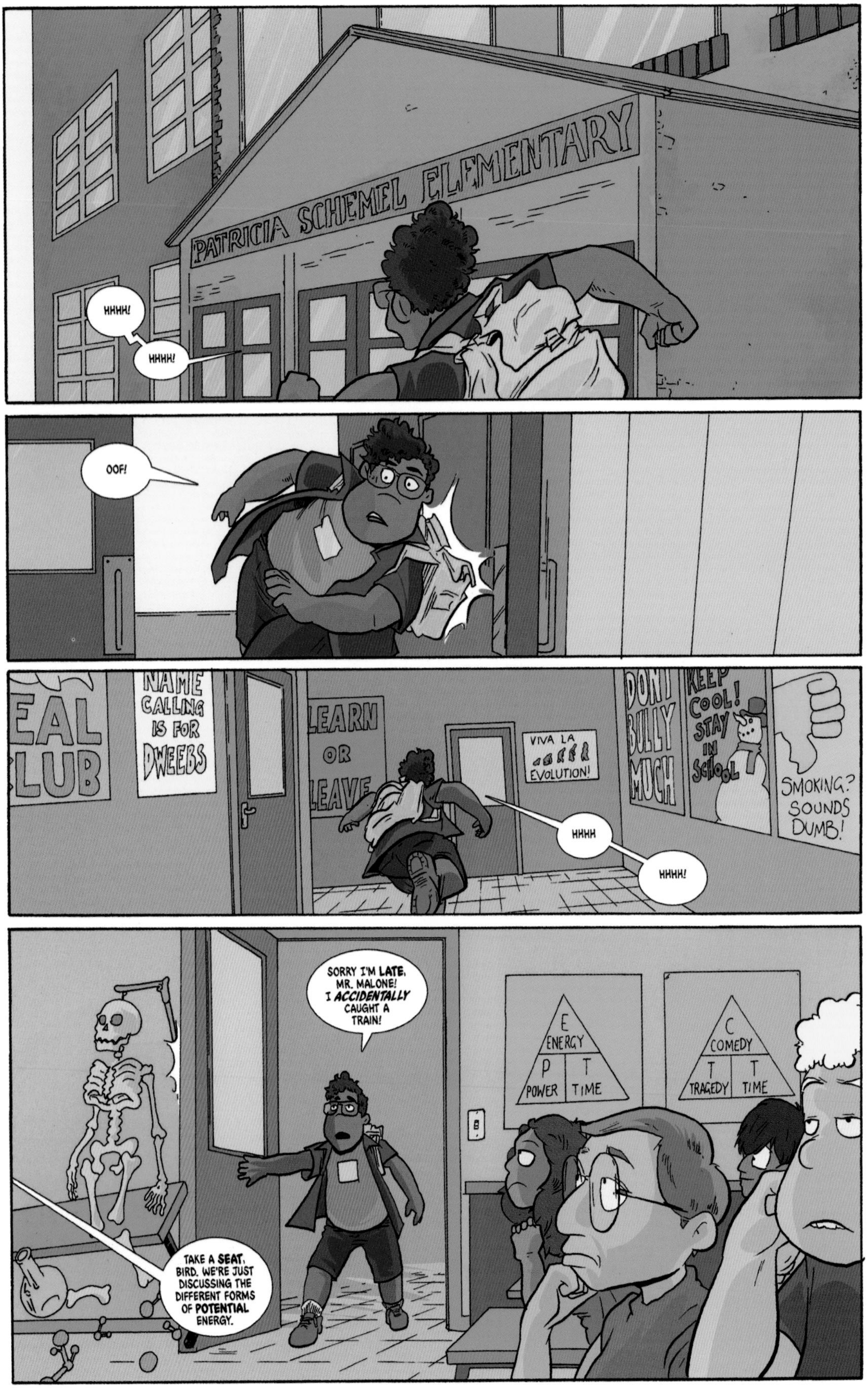
PATRICIA SCHEMEL ELEMENTARY
HHHH!
HHHH!
OOF!
NAME CALLING IS FOR DWEEBS
LEARN OR LEAVE
VIVA LA EVOLUTION!
DON'T BULLY MUCH
KEEP COOL! STAY IN SCHOOL
SMOKING? SOUNDS DUMB!
HHHH
HHHH!
SORRY I'M LATE, MR. MALONE! I ACCIDENTALLY CAUGHT A TRAIN!
E ENERGY P POWER T TIME
C COMEDY T TRAGEDY T TIME
TAKE A SEAT, BIRD. WE'RE JUST DISCUSSING THE DIFFERENT FORMS OF POTENTIAL ENERGY.

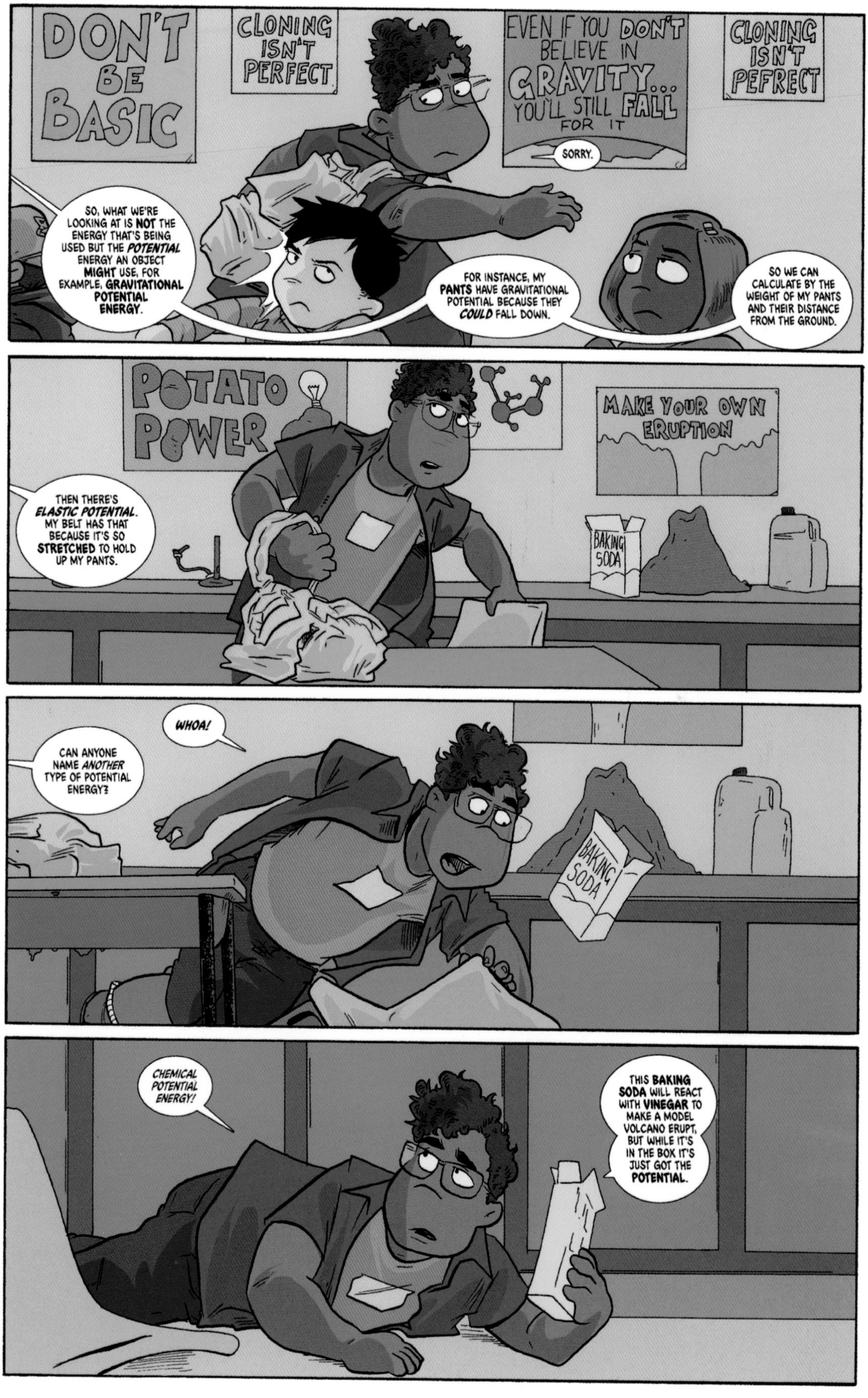
DON'T BE BASIC
CLONING ISN'T PERFECT
EVEN IF YOU DON'T BELIEVE IN GRAVITY... YOU'LL STILL FALL FOR IT
CLONING ISN'T PEFRECT
SORRY.
SO, WHAT WE'RE LOOKING AT IS NOT THE ENERGY THAT'S BEING USED BUT THE POTENTIAL ENERGY AN OBJECT MIGHT USE, FOR EXAMPLE, GRAVITATIONAL POTENTIAL ENERGY.
FOR INSTANCE, MY PANTS HAVE GRAVITATIONAL POTENTIAL BECAUSE THEY COULD FALL DOWN.
SO WE CAN CALCULATE BY THE WEIGHT OF MY PANTS AND THEIR DISTANCE FROM THE GROUND.
POTATO POWER
MAKE YOUR OWN ERUPTION
THEN THERE'S ELASTIC POTENTIAL. MY BELT HAS THAT BECAUSE IT'S SO STRETCHED TO HOLD UP MY PANTS.
BAKING SODA
CAN ANYONE NAME ANOTHER TYPE OF POTENTIAL ENERGY?
WHOA!
BAKING SODA
CHEMICAL POTENTIAL ENERGY!
THIS BAKING SODA WILL REACT WITH VINEGAR TO MAKE A MODEL VOLCANO ERUPT, BUT WHILE IT'S IN THE BOX IT'S JUST GOT THE POTENTIAL.

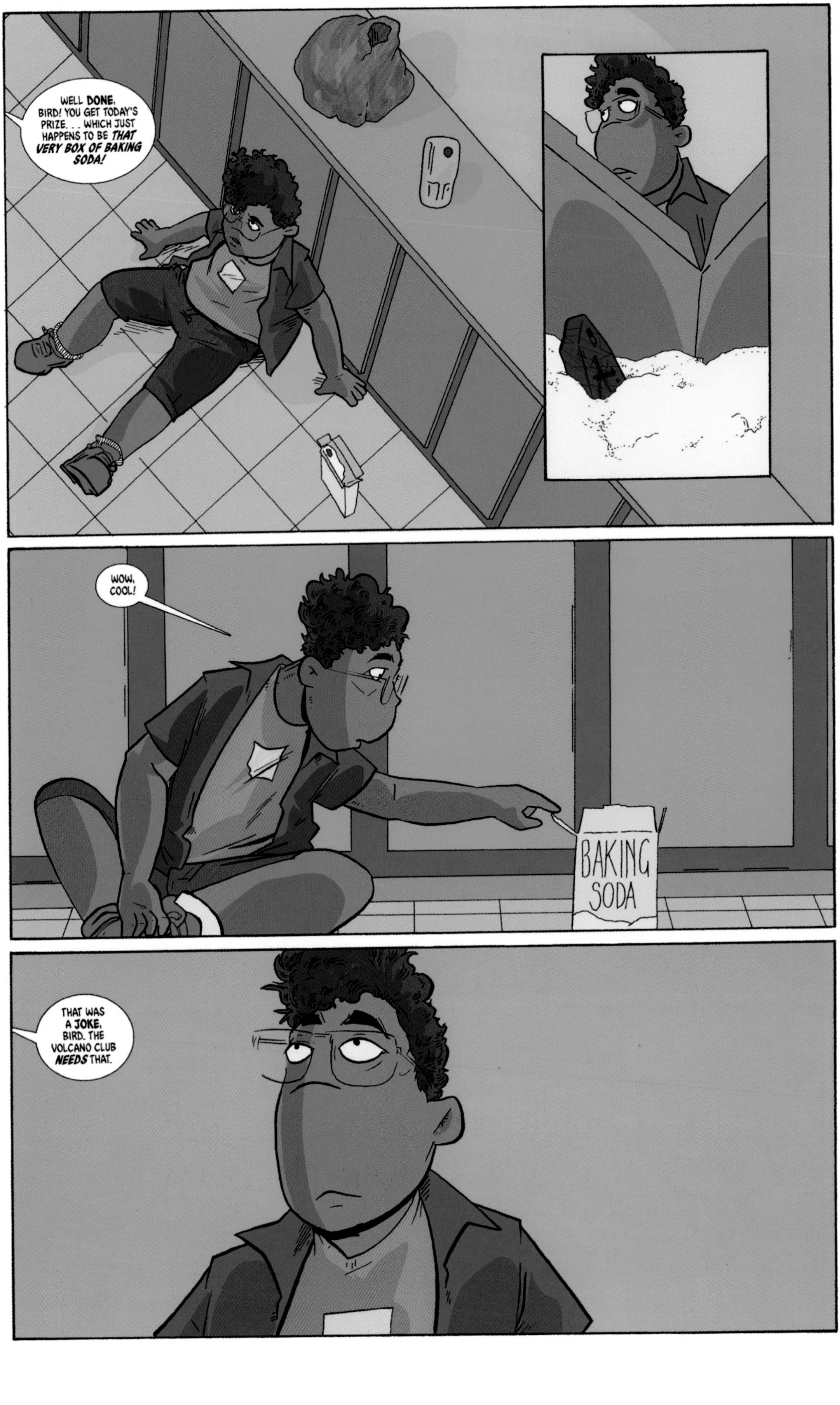
WELL DONE, BIRD! YOU GET TODAY'S PRIZE. . . WHICH JUST HAPPENS TO BE THAT VERY BOX OF BAKING SODA!
WOW, COOL!
BAKING SODA
THAT WAS A JOKE, BIRD. THE VOLCANO CLUB NEEDS THAT.

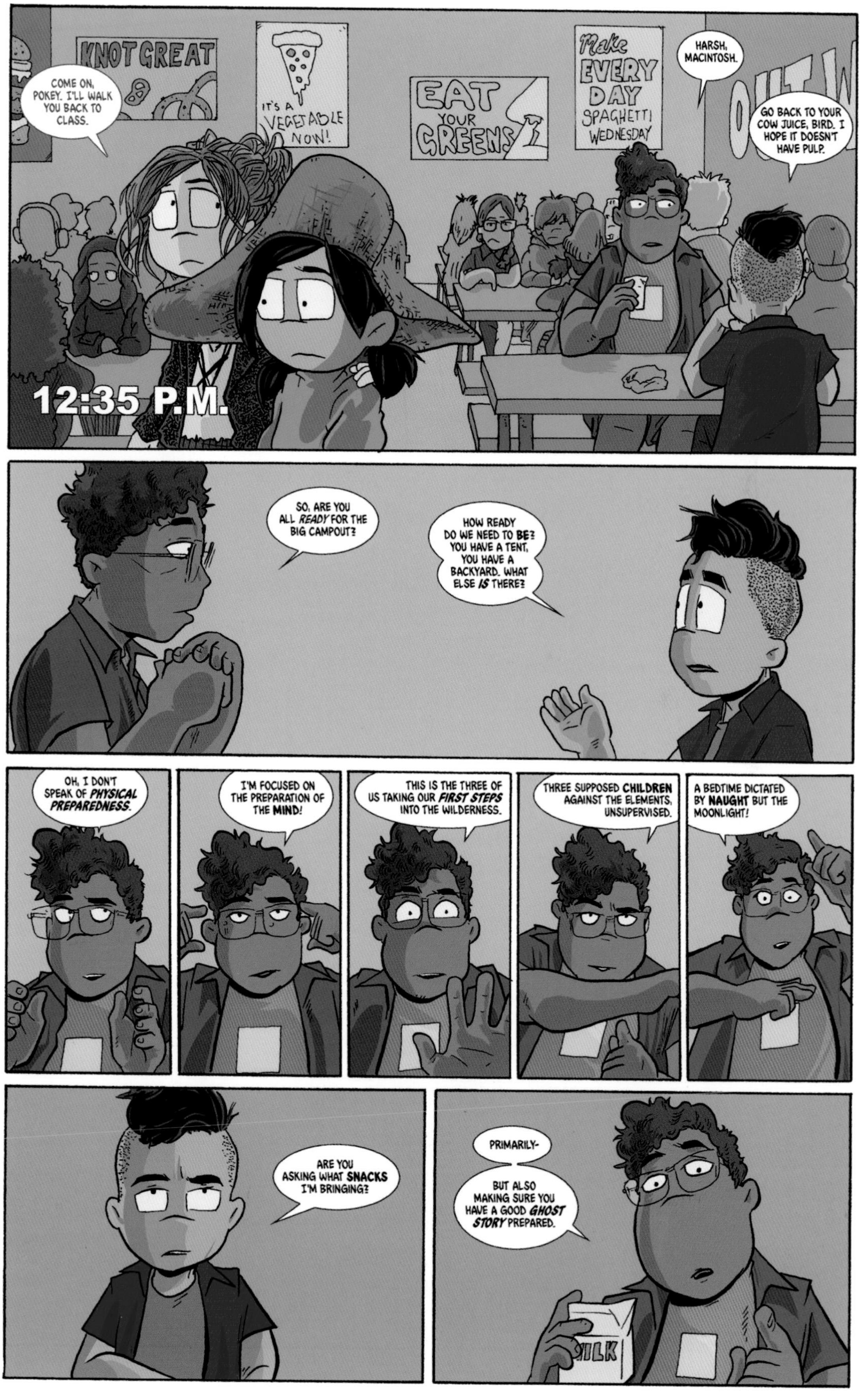
KNOT GREAT
COME ON, POKEY. I'LL WALK YOU BACK TO CLASS.
IT'S A VEGETABLE NOW!
EAT YOUR GREENS
Make EVERY DAY SPAGHETTI WEDNESDAY
HARSH, MACINTOSH.
GO BACK TO YOUR COW JUICE, BIRD. I HOPE IT DOESN'T HAVE PULP.
12:35 P.M.
SO, ARE YOU ALL READY FOR THE BIG CAMPOUT?
HOW READY DO WE NEED TO BE? YOU HAVE A TENT, YOU HAVE A BACKYARD. WHAT ELSE IS THERE?
OH, I DON'T SPEAK OF PHYSICAL PREPAREDNESS.
I'M FOCUSED ON THE PREPARATION OF THE MIND!
THIS IS THE THREE OF US TAKING OUR FIRST STEPS INTO THE WILDERNESS.
THREE SUPPOSED CHILDREN AGAINST THE ELEMENTS, UNSUPERVISED.
A BEDTIME DICTATED BY NAUGHT BUT THE MOONLIGHT!
ARE YOU ASKING WHAT SNACKS I'M BRINGING?
PRIMARILY-
BUT ALSO MAKING SURE YOU HAVE A GOOD GHOST STORY PREPARED.
MILK

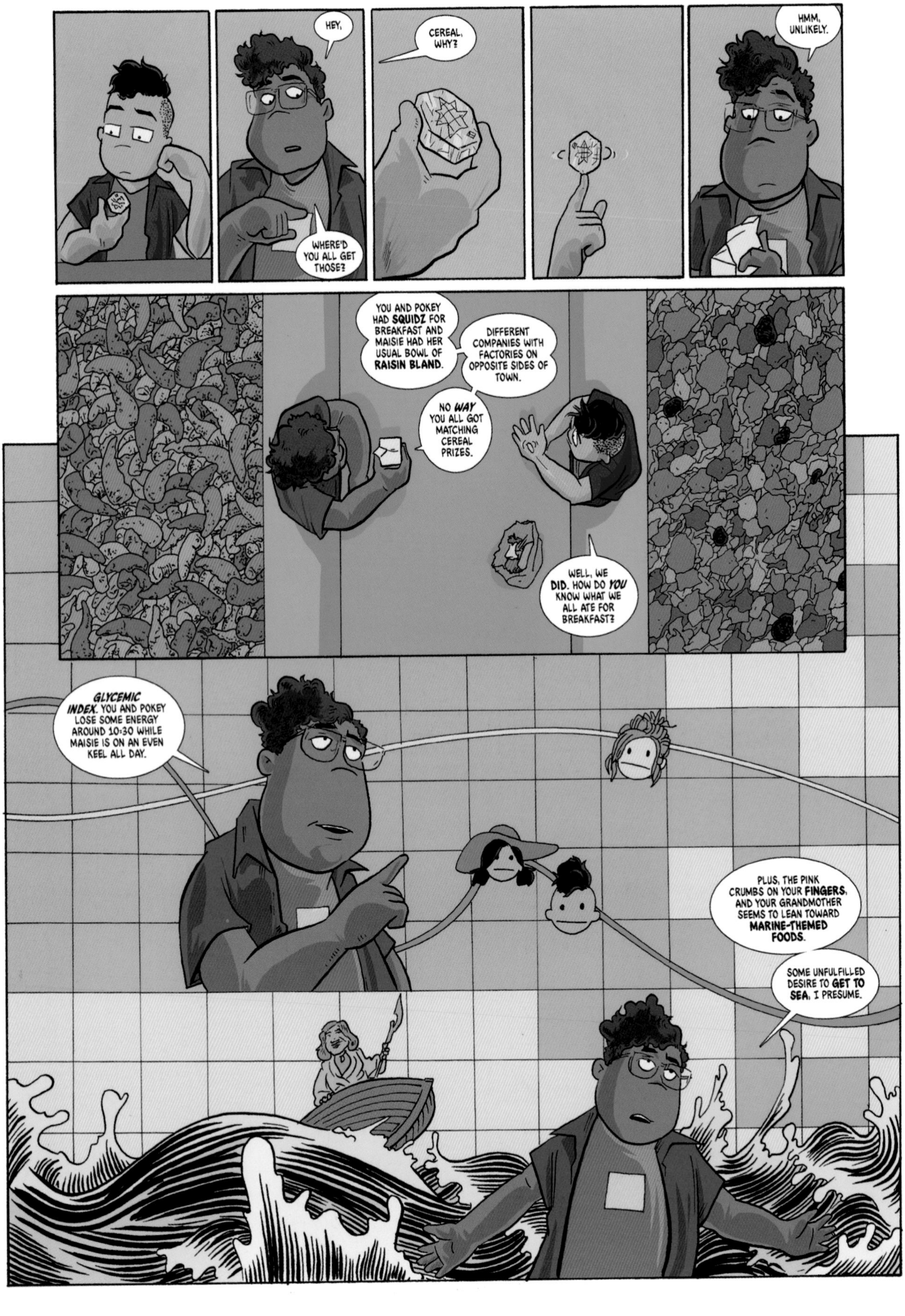

HEY,
WHERE'D YOU ALL GET THOSE?
CEREAL, WHY?
HMM, UNLIKELY.
YOU AND POKEY HAD SQUIDZ FOR BREAKFAST AND MAISIE HAD HER USUAL BOWL OF RAISIN BLAND.
DIFFERENT COMPANIES WITH FACTORIES ON OPPOSITE SIDES OF TOWN.
NO WAY YOU ALL GOT MATCHING CEREAL PRIZES.
WELL, WE DID. HOW DO YOU KNOW WHAT WE ALL ATE FOR BREAKFAST?
GLYCEMIC INDEX. YOU AND POKEY LOSE SOME ENERGY AROUND 10:30 WHILE MAISIE IS ON AN EVEN KEEL ALL DAY.
PLUS, THE PINK CRUMBS ON YOUR FINGERS, AND YOUR GRANDMOTHER SEEMS TO LEAN TOWARD MARINE-THEMED FOODS.
SOME UNFULFILLED DESIRE TO GET TO SEA, I PRESUME.

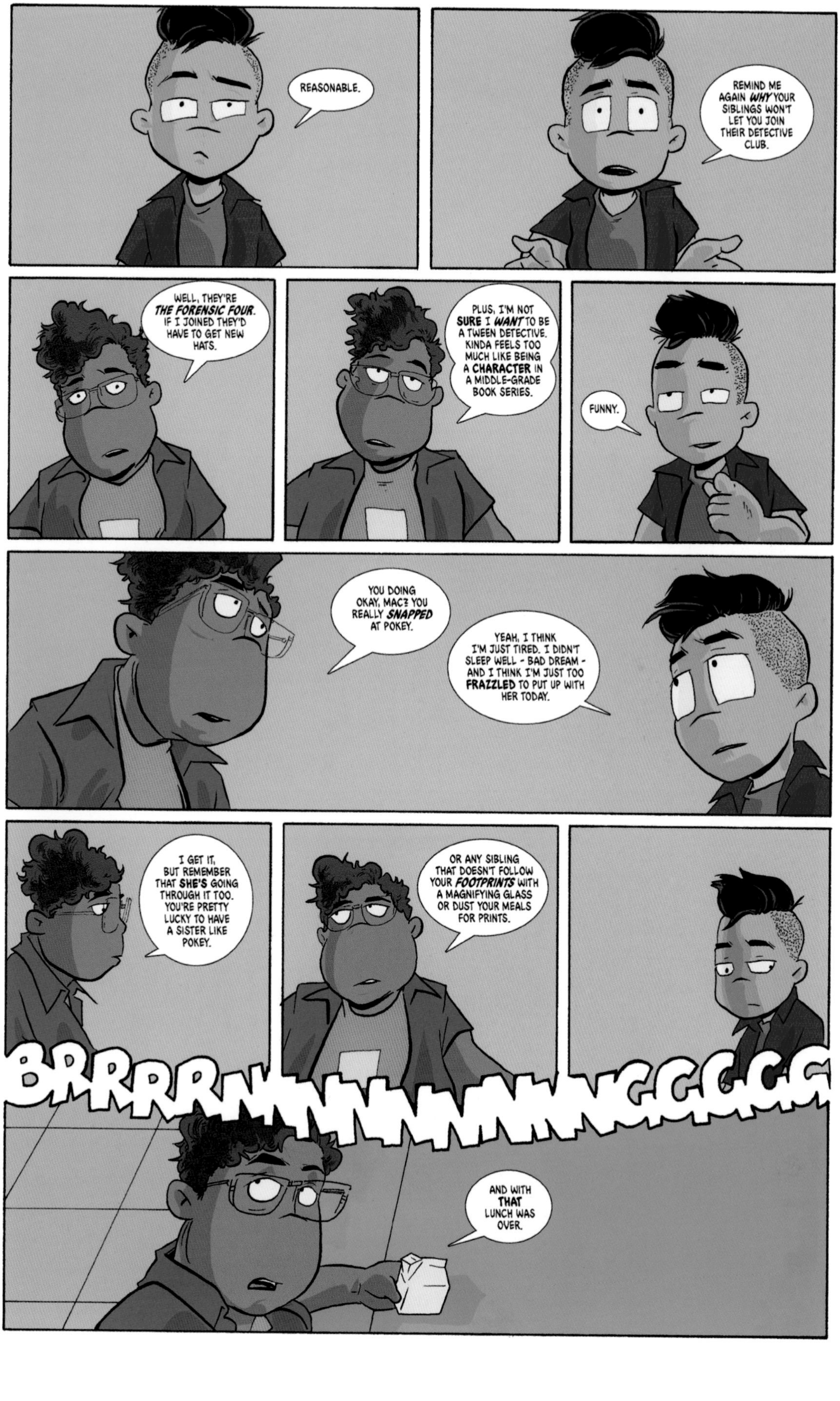
REASONABLE.
REMIND ME AGAIN WHY YOUR SIBLINGS WON'T LET YOU JOIN THEIR DETECTIVE CLUB.
WELL, THEY'RE THE FORENSIC FOUR. IF I JOINED THEY'D HAVE TO GET NEW HATS.
PLUS, I'M NOT SURE I WANT TO BE A TWEEN DETECTIVE. KINDA FEELS TOO MUCH LIKE BEING A CHARACTER IN A MIDDLE-GRADE BOOK SERIES.
FUNNY.
YOU DOING OKAY, MAC? YOU REALLY SNAPPED AT POKEY.
YEAH, I THINK I'M JUST TIRED. I DIDN'T SLEEP WELL - BAD DREAM - AND I THINK I'M JUST TOO FRAZZLED TO PUT UP WITH HER TODAY.
I GET IT, BUT REMEMBER THAT SHE'S GOING THROUGH IT TOO. YOU'RE PRETTY LUCKY TO HAVE A SISTER LIKE POKEY.
OR ANY SIBLING THAT DOESN'T FOLLOW YOUR FOOTPRINTS WITH A MAGNIFYING GLASS OR DUST YOUR MEALS FOR PRINTS.
BRRRRNNNNNNNNNGGGG
AND WITH THAT LUNCH WAS OVER.

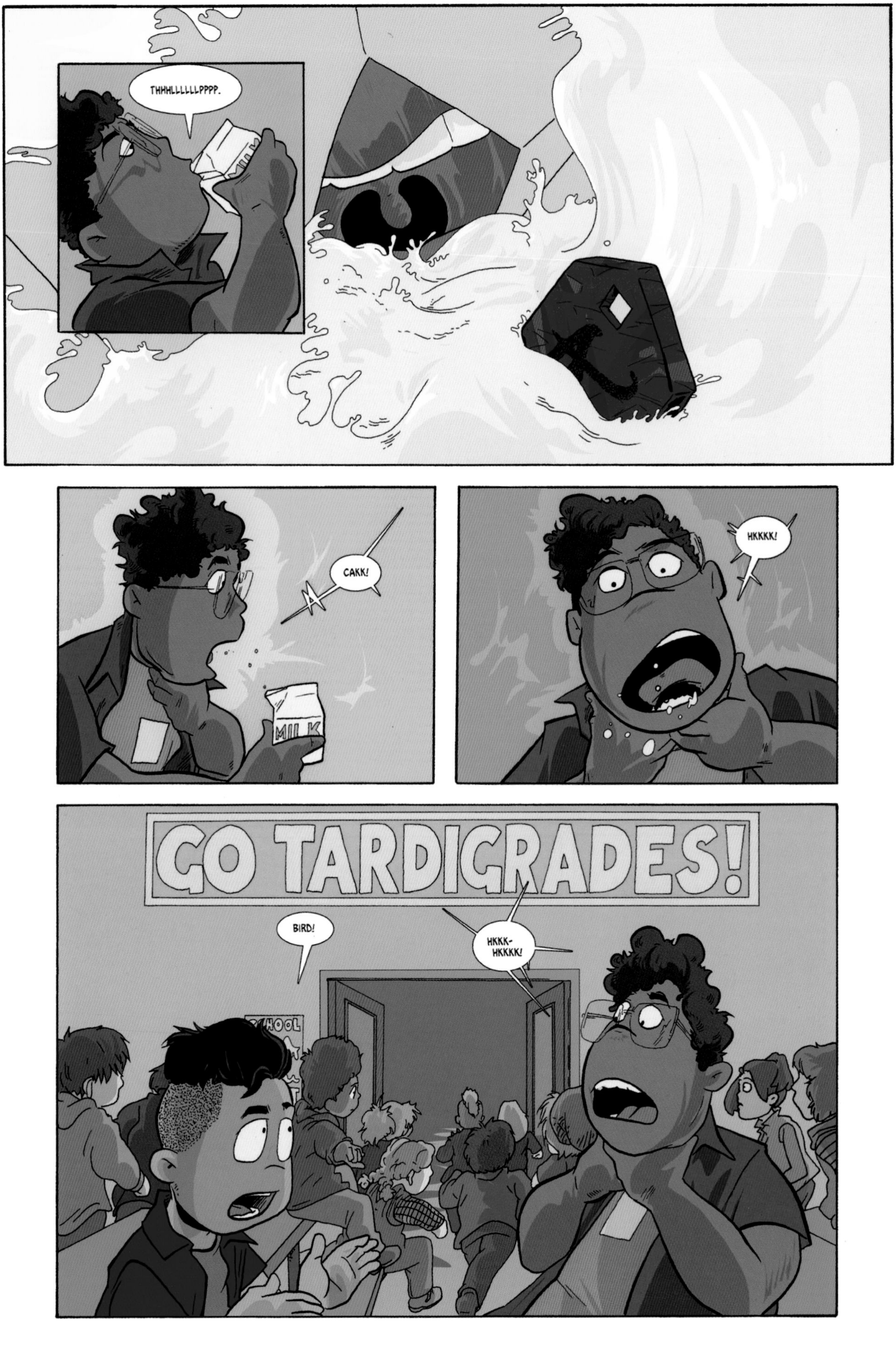
THHHLLLLLLPPPP.
CAKK!
HKKKK!
GO TARDIGRADES!
BIRD!
HKKK-
HKKKK!

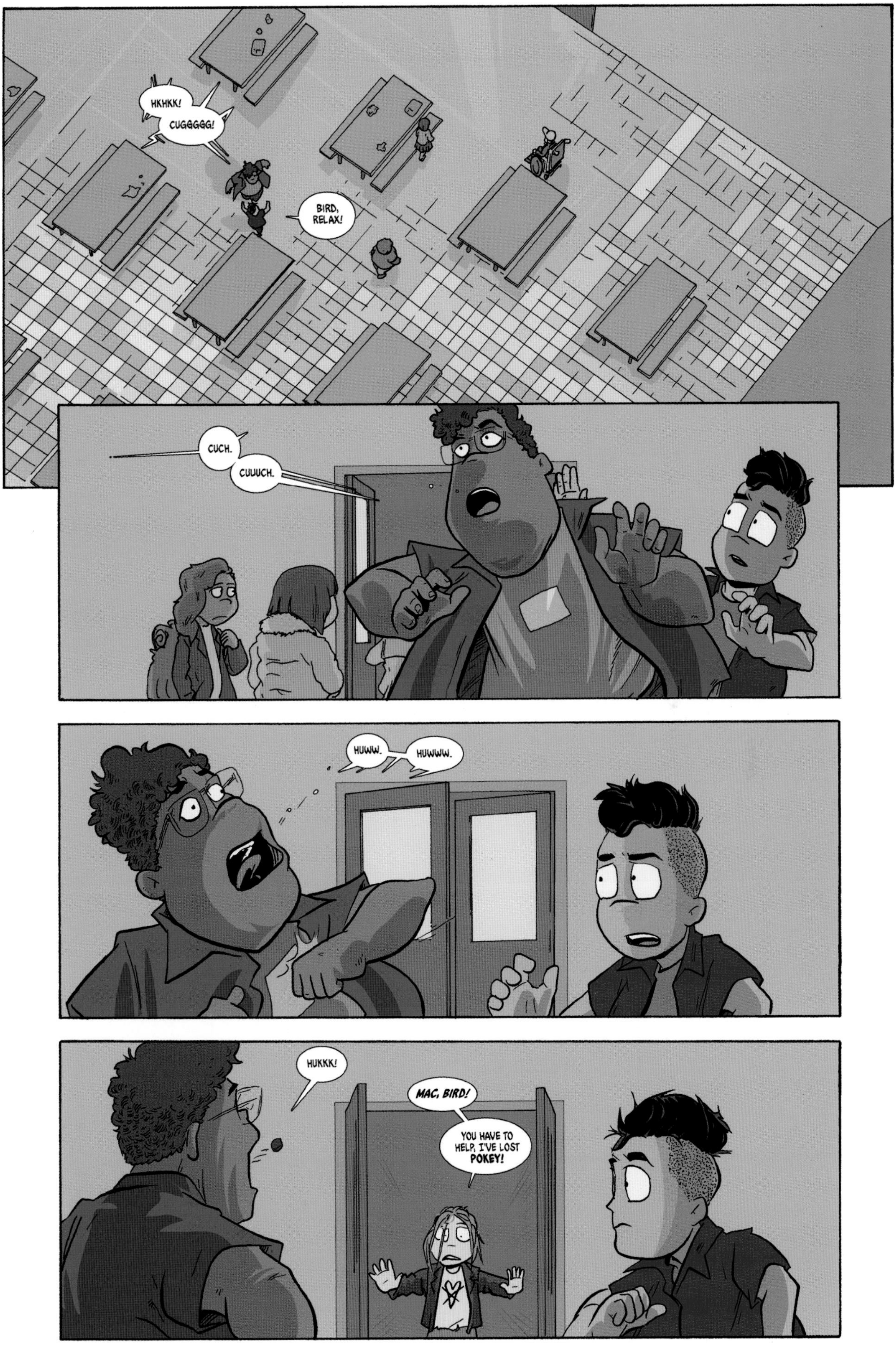
HKHKK!
CUGGGGG!
BIRD, RELAX!
CUCH.
CUUUCH.
HUWW.
HUWWW.
HUKKK!
MAC, BIRD!
YOU HAVE TO HELP, I'VE LOST POKEY!

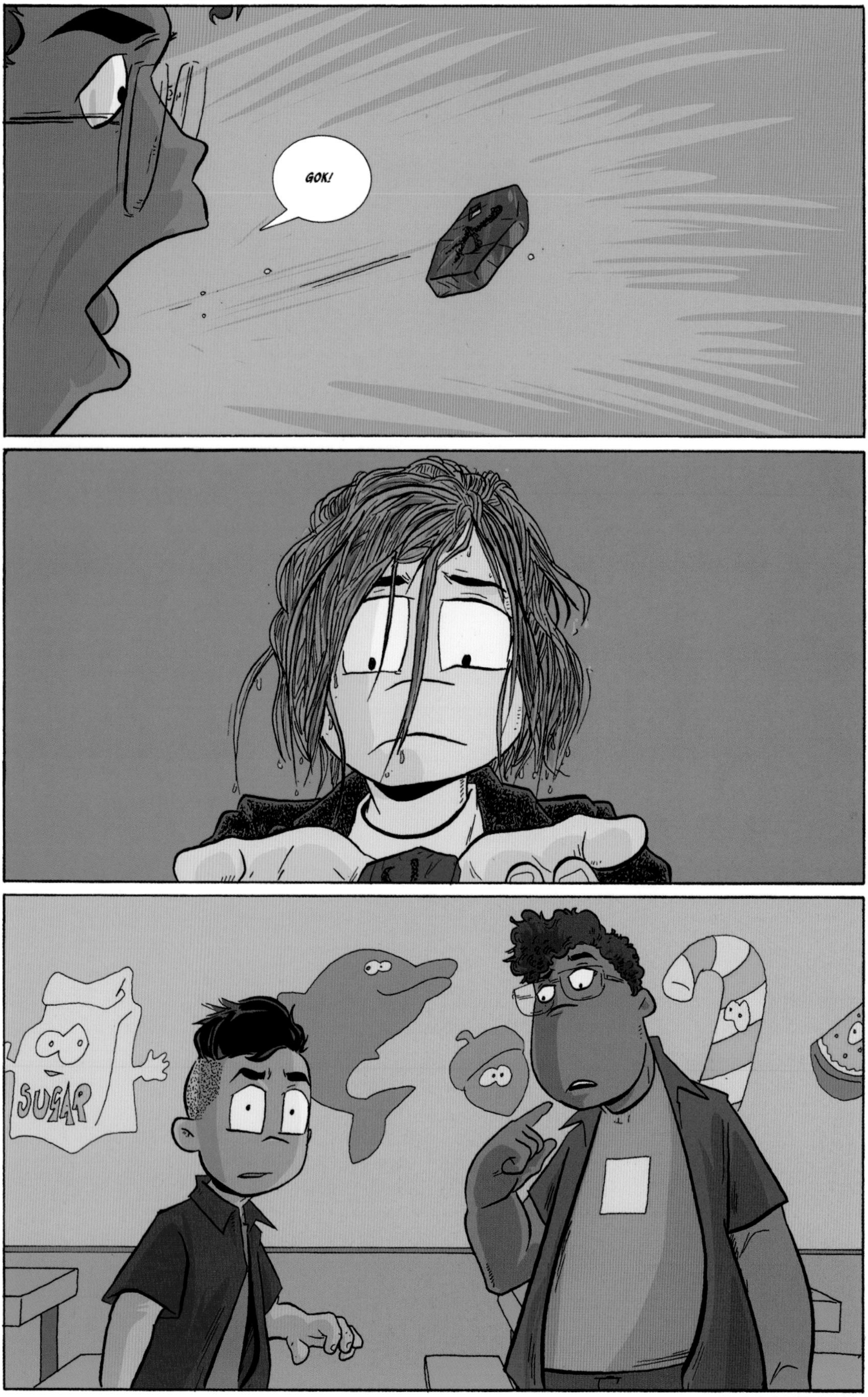
GOK!
SUGAR

TO BE CONTINUED.

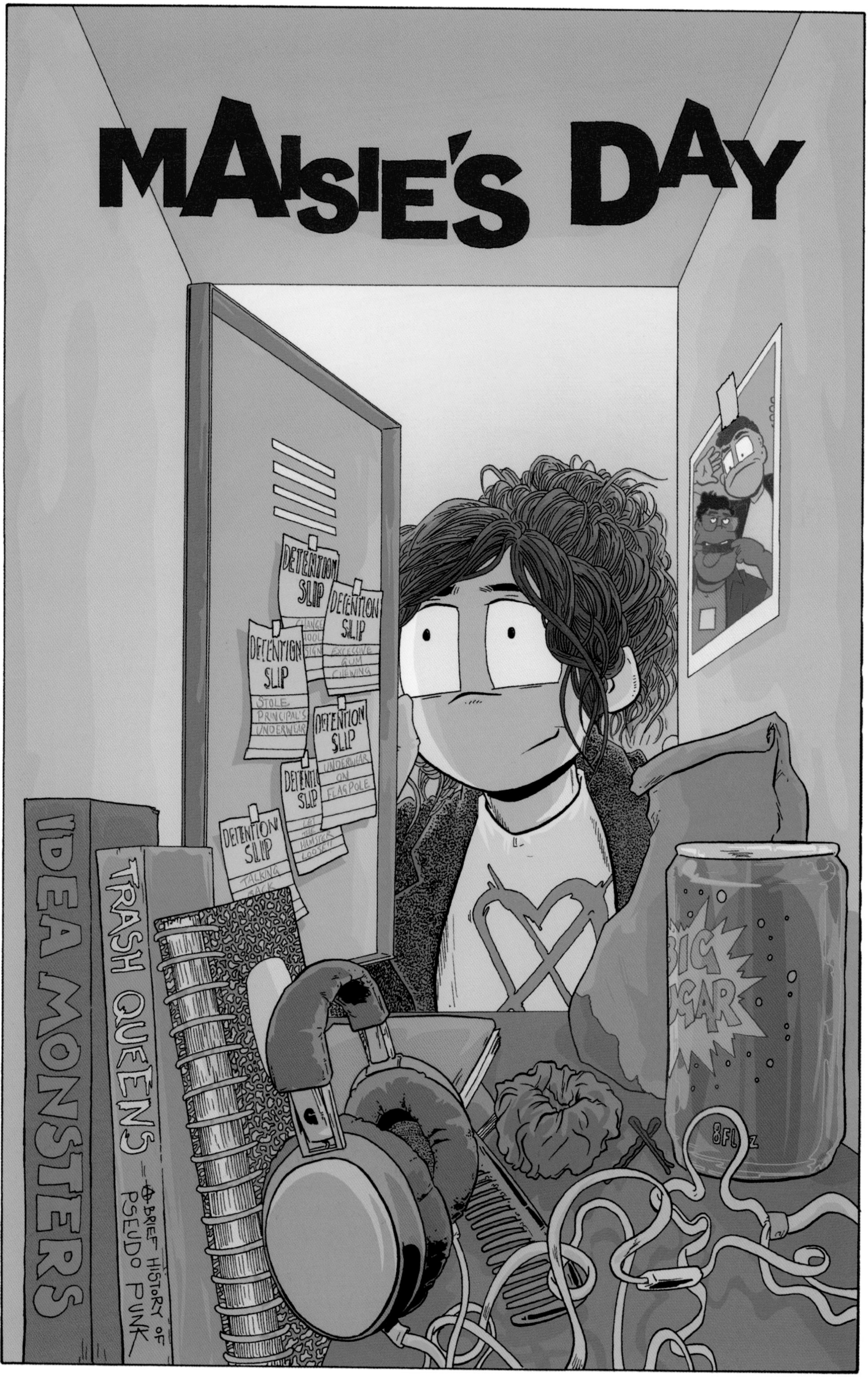
MAISIE'S DAY
DETENTION SLIP
DETENTION SLIP
EXCESSIVE GUM CHEWING
DETENTION SLIP
STOLE PRINCIPAL'S UNDERWEAR
DETENTION SLIP
UNDERWEAR ON FLAGPOLE
DETENTION SLIP
TALKING BACK
IDEA MONSTERS
TRASH QUEENS
A BRIEF HISTORY OF PSEUDO PUNK

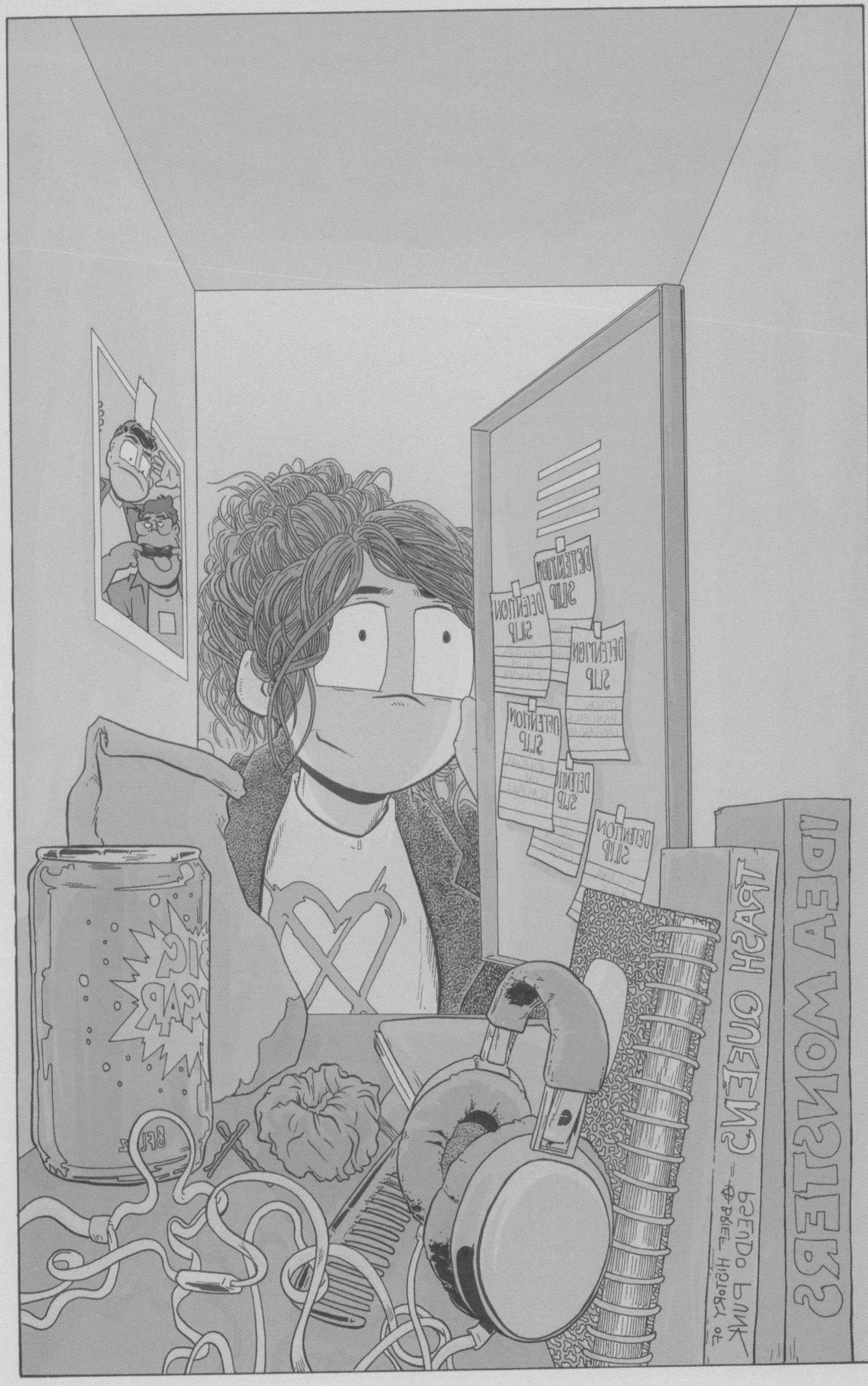
DETENTION SLIP
DETENTION SLIP
DETENTION SLIP
DETENTION SLIP
DETENTION SLIP
DETENTION SLIP
IDEA MONSTERS
TRASH QUEENS
A BRIEF HISTORY OF PSEUDO PUNK

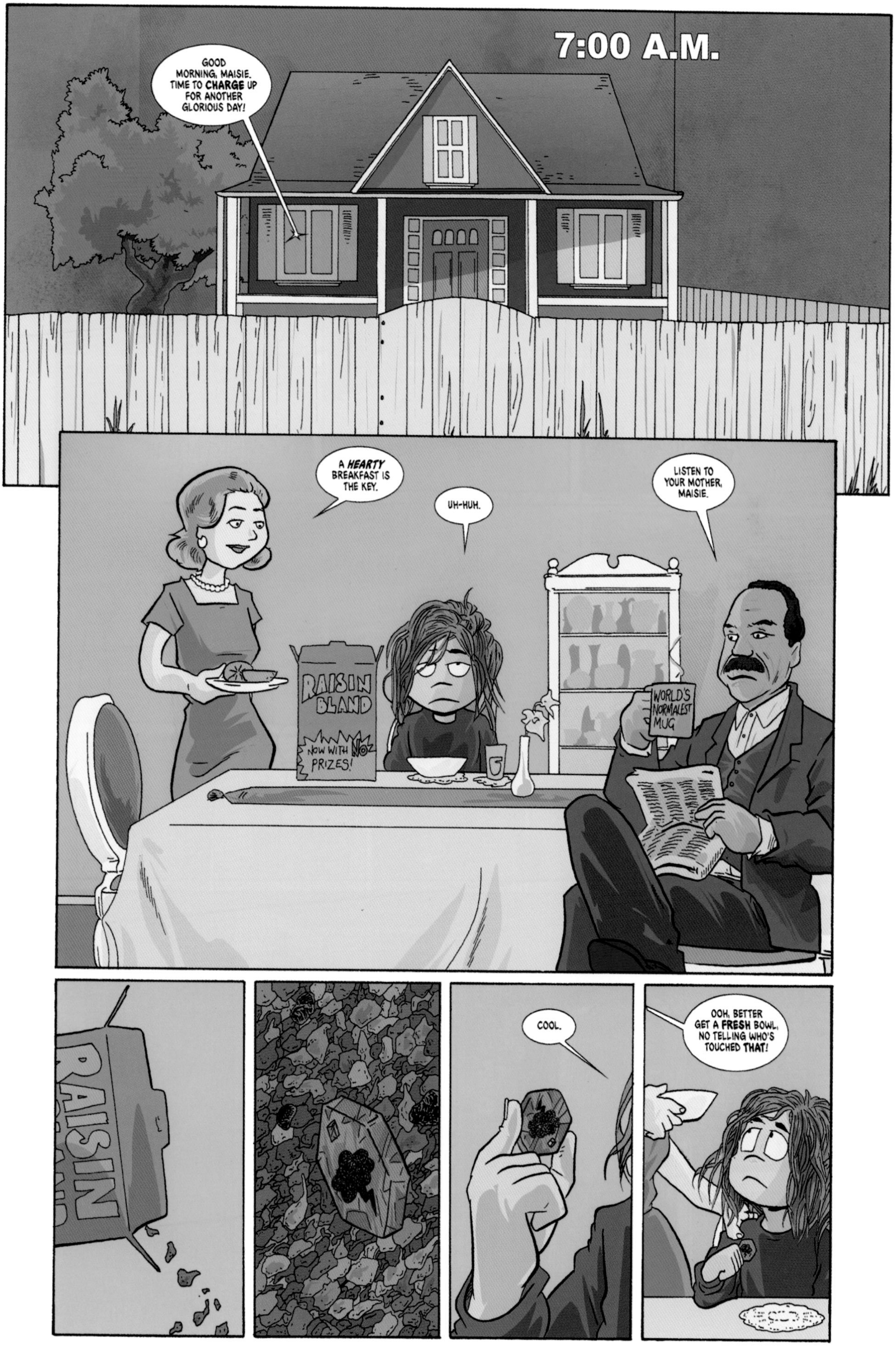
7:00 A.M.
GOOD MORNING, MAISIE. TIME TO **CHARGE** UP FOR ANOTHER GLORIOUS DAY!
A ***HEARTY*** BREAKFAST IS THE KEY.
UH-HUH.
LISTEN TO YOUR MOTHER, MAISIE.
RAISIN BLAND
NOW WITH NO PRIZES!
WORLD'S NORMALEST MUG
RAISIN
COOL.
OOH, BETTER GET A **FRESH** BOWL, NO TELLING WHO'S TOUCHED **THAT**!

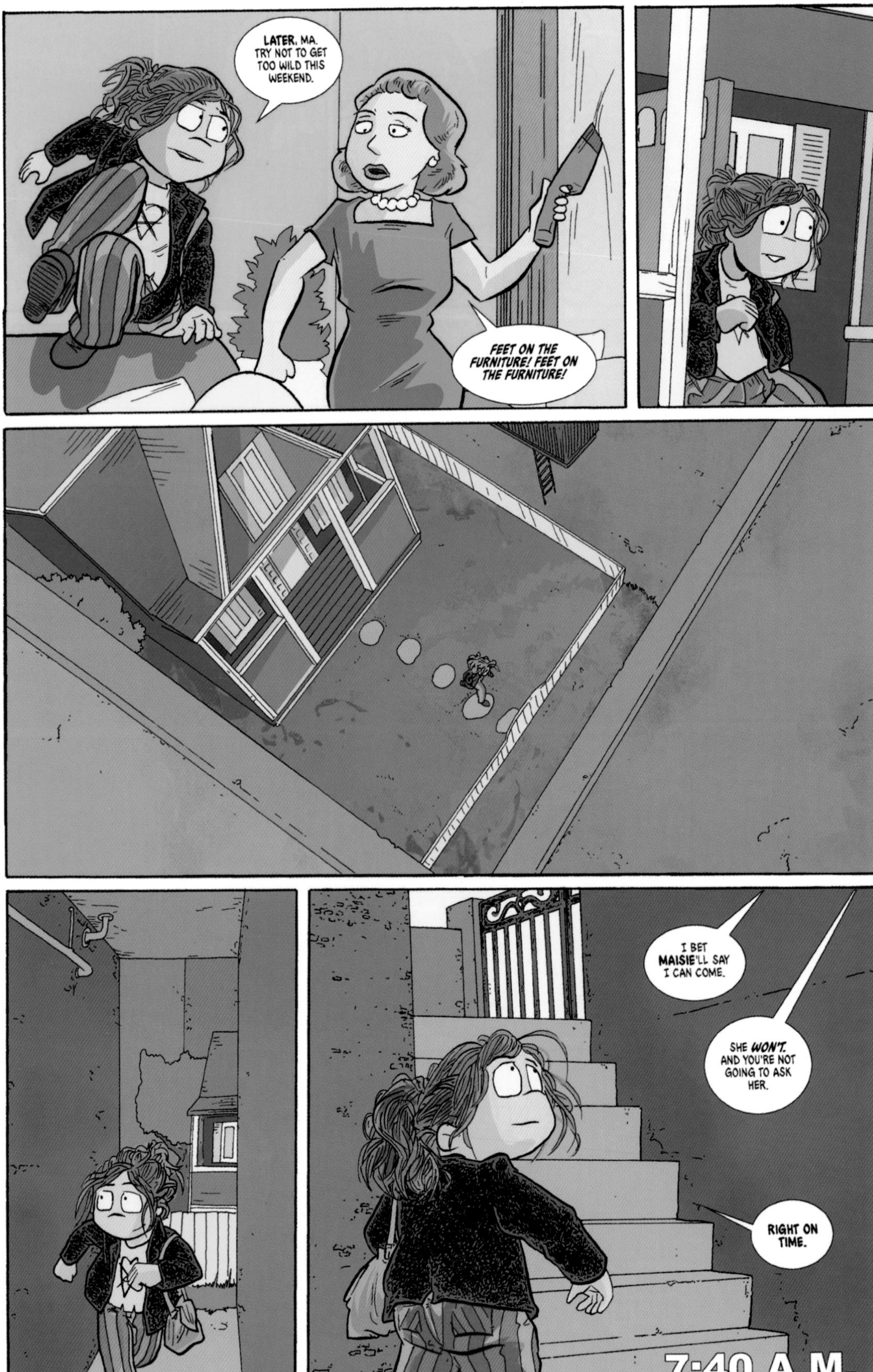
LATER, MA. TRY NOT TO GET TOO WILD THIS WEEKEND.
FEET ON THE FURNITURE! FEET ON THE FURNITURE!
I BET MAISIE'LL SAY I CAN COME.
SHE WON'T. AND YOU'RE NOT GOING TO ASK HER.
RIGHT ON TIME.
7:40 A.M.

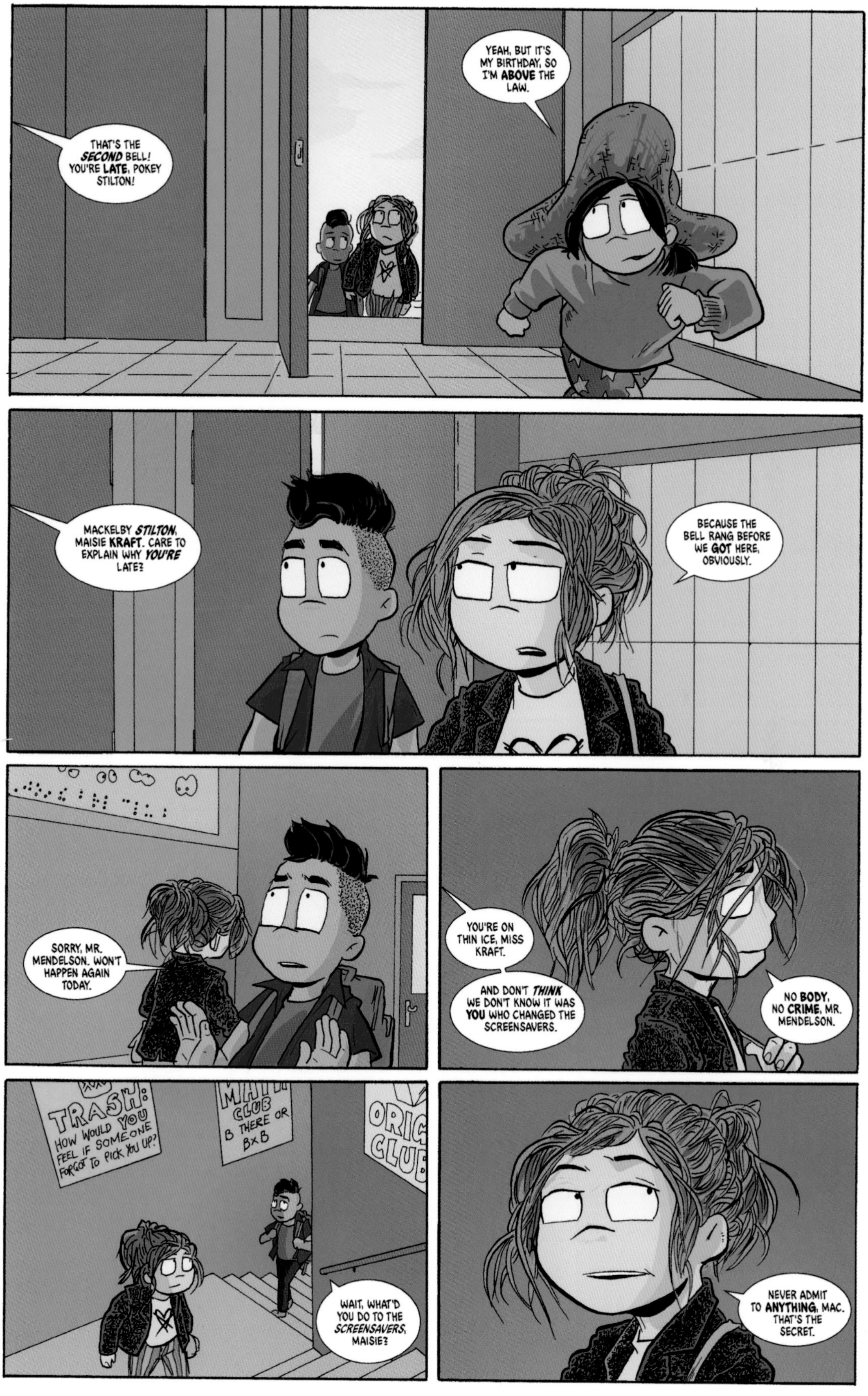
THAT'S THE SECOND BELL! YOU'RE LATE, POKEY STILTON!
YEAH, BUT IT'S MY BIRTHDAY, SO I'M ABOVE THE LAW.
MACKELBY STILTON, MAISIE KRAFT. CARE TO EXPLAIN WHY YOU'RE LATE?
BECAUSE THE BELL RANG BEFORE WE GOT HERE, OBVIOUSLY.
SORRY, MR. MENDELSON. WON'T HAPPEN AGAIN TODAY.
YOU'RE ON THIN ICE, MISS KRAFT.
AND DON'T THINK WE DON'T KNOW IT WAS YOU WHO CHANGED THE SCREENSAVERS.
NO BODY, NO CRIME, MR. MENDELSON.
TRASH: HOW WOULD YOU FEEL IF SOMEONE FORGOT TO PICK YOU UP?
MATH CLUB B THERE OR B×B
WAIT, WHAT'D YOU DO TO THE SCREENSAVERS, MAISIE?
NEVER ADMIT TO ANYTHING, MAC. THAT'S THE SECRET.

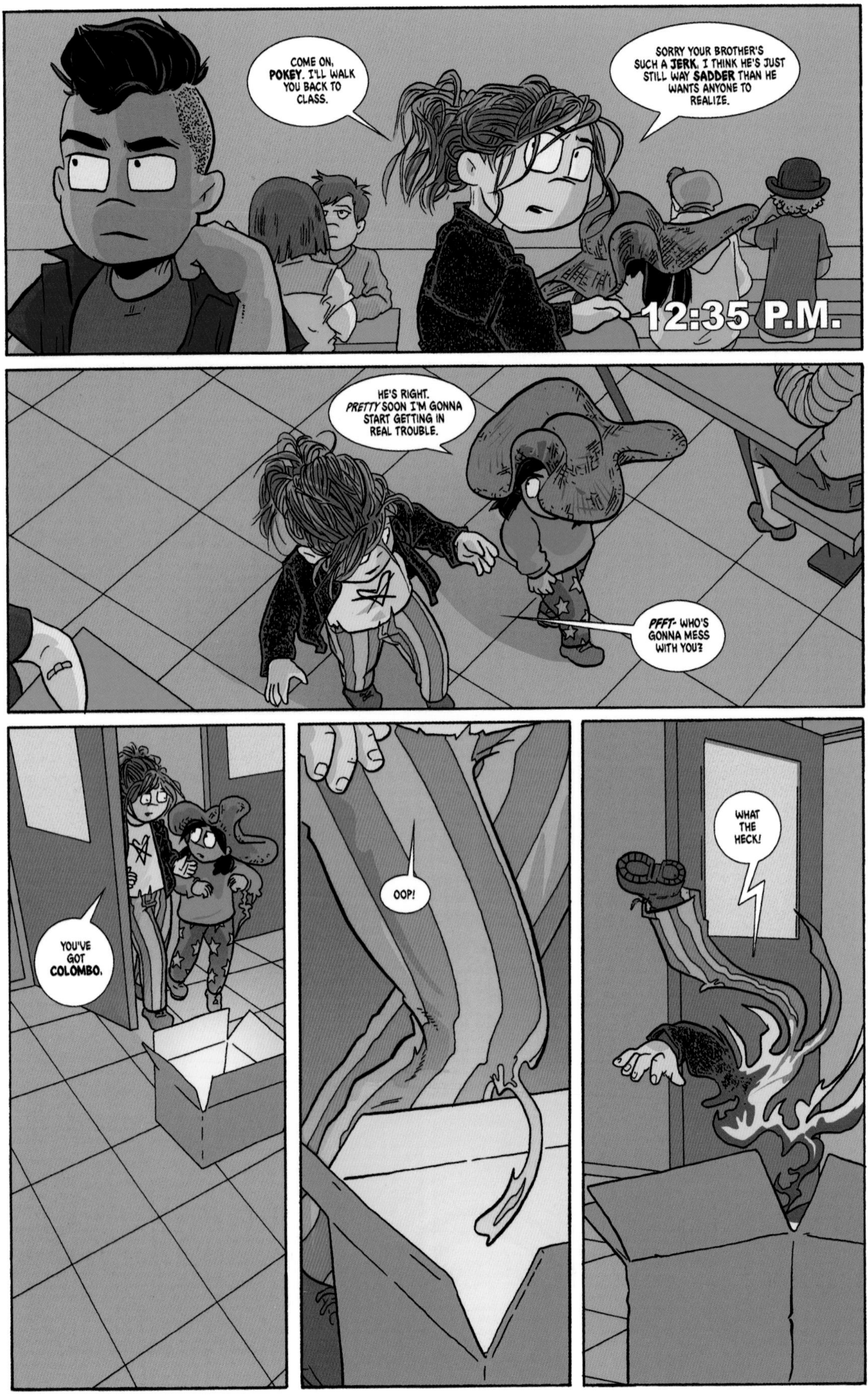
COME ON, POKEY. I'LL WALK YOU BACK TO CLASS.
SORRY YOUR BROTHER'S SUCH A JERK. I THINK HE'S JUST STILL WAY SADDER THAN HE WANTS ANYONE TO REALIZE.
12:35 P.M.
HE'S RIGHT. PRETTY SOON I'M GONNA START GETTING IN REAL TROUBLE.
PFFT- WHO'S GONNA MESS WITH YOU?
YOU'VE GOT COLOMBO.
OOP!
WHAT THE HECK!

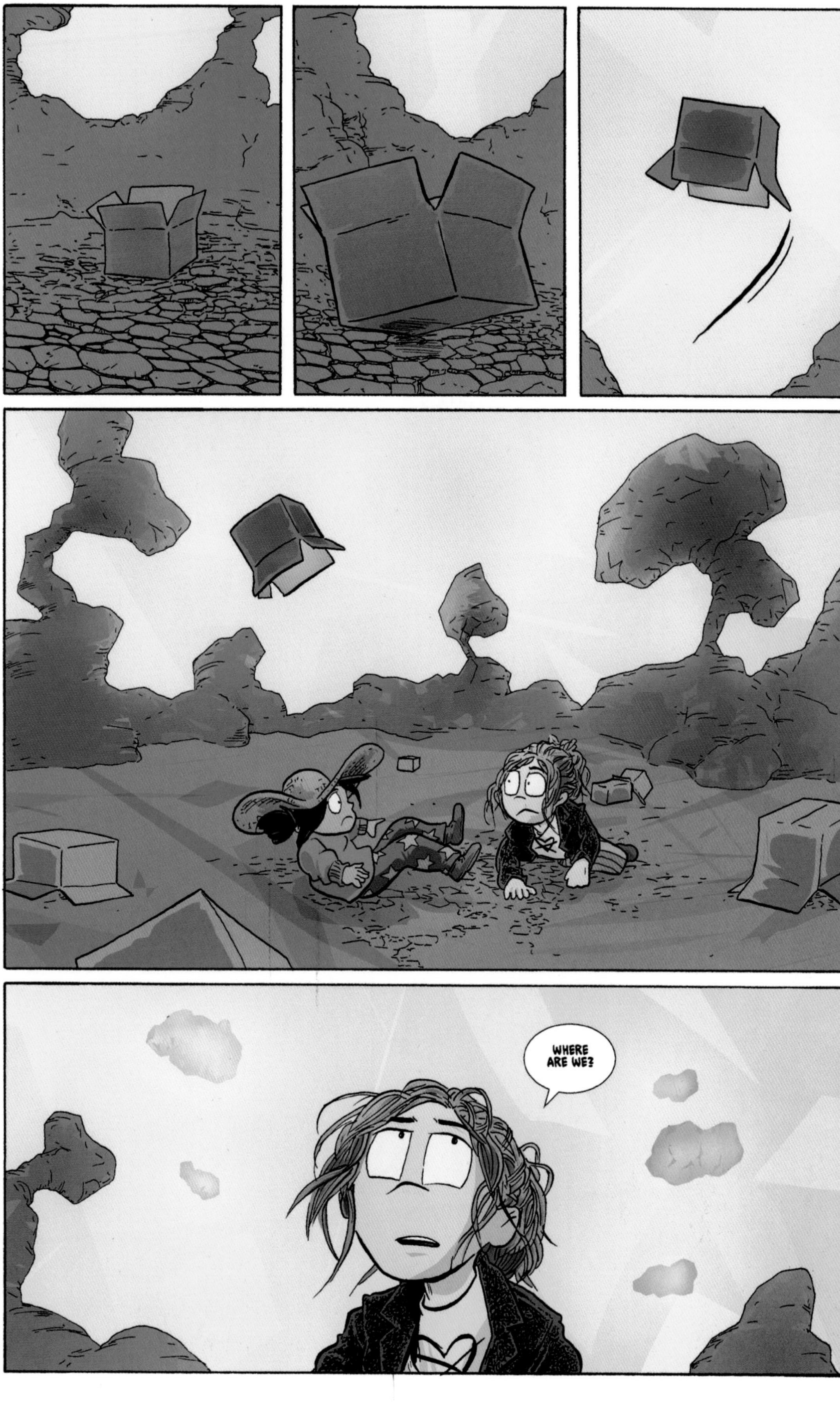
WHERE ARE WE?

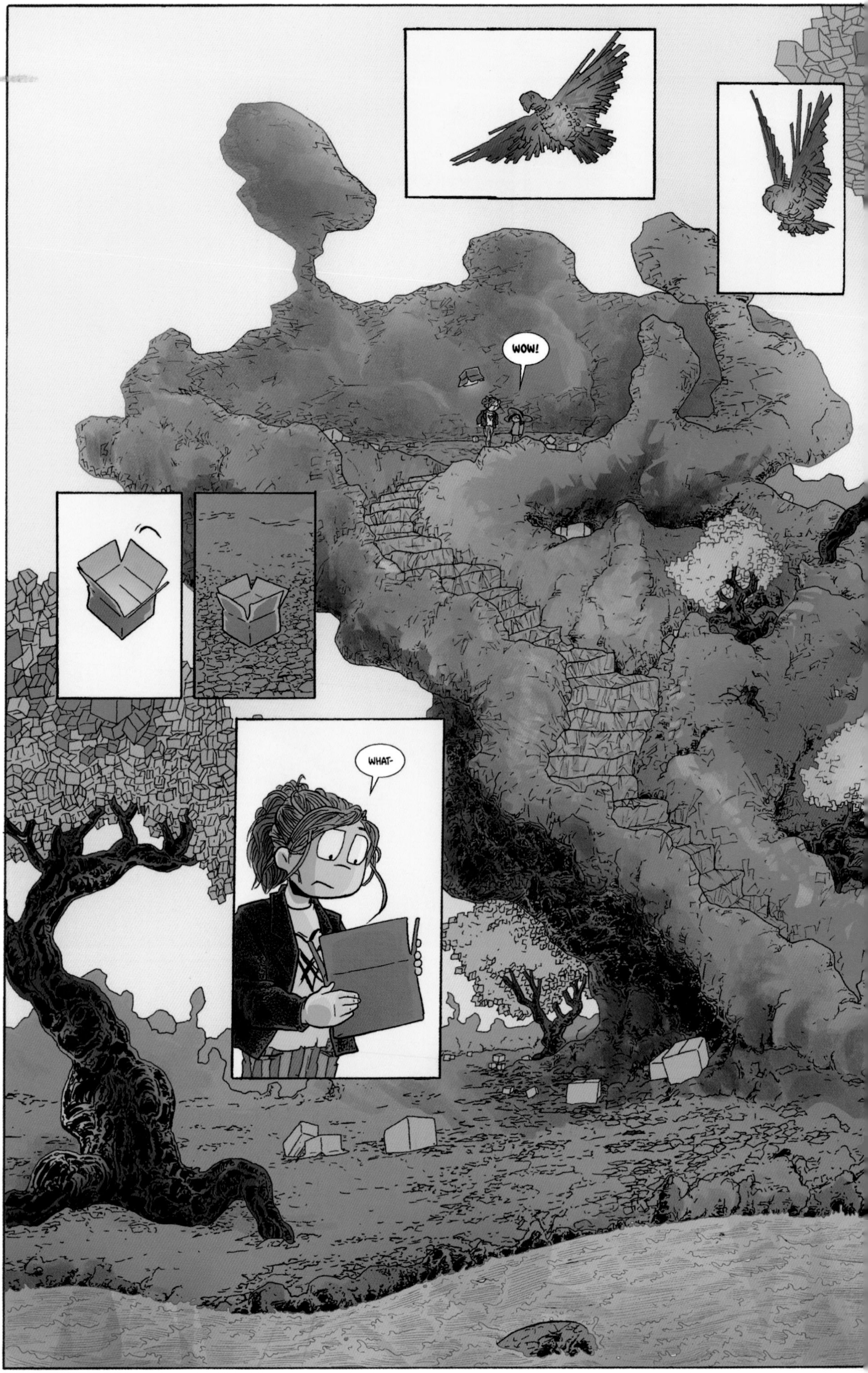
WOW!
WHAT-

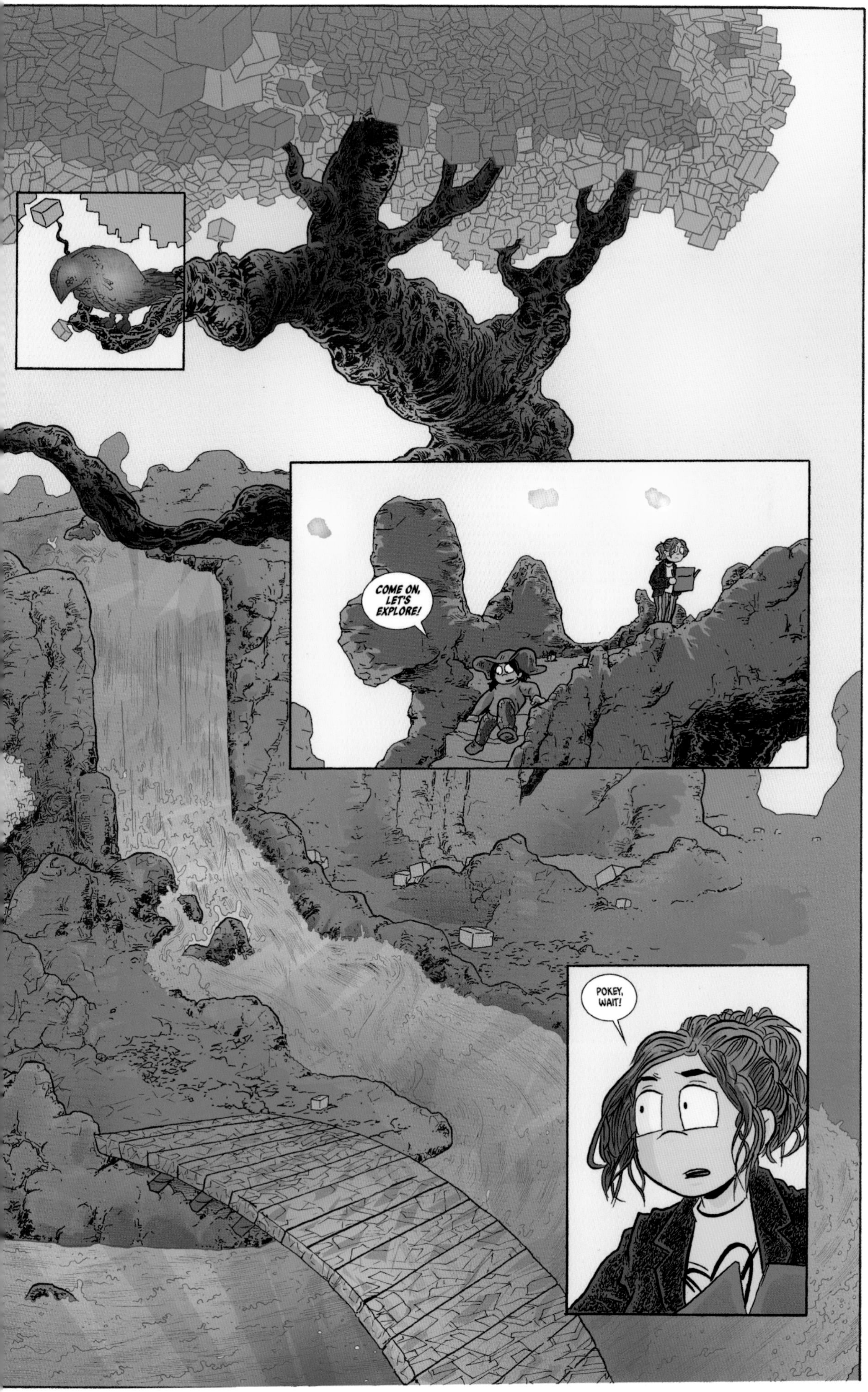
COME ON, LET'S EXPLORE!
POKEY, WAIT!

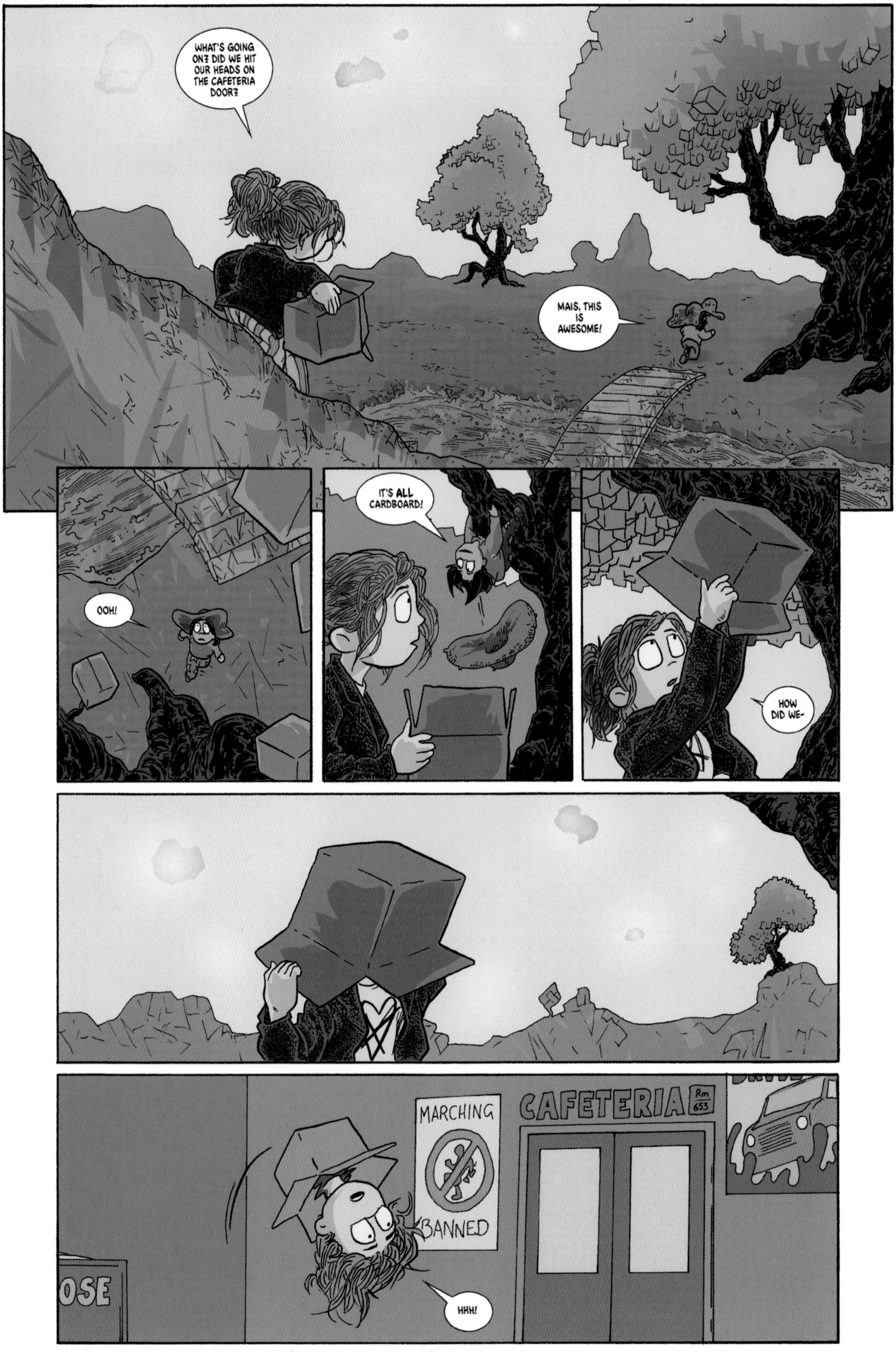
WHAT'S GOING ON? DID WE HIT OUR HEADS ON THE CAFETERIA DOOR?
MAIS, THIS IS AWESOME!
OOH!
IT'S ALL CARDBOARD!
HOW DID WE-
MARCHING BANNED
CAFETERIA
Rm 653
OSE
HHH!

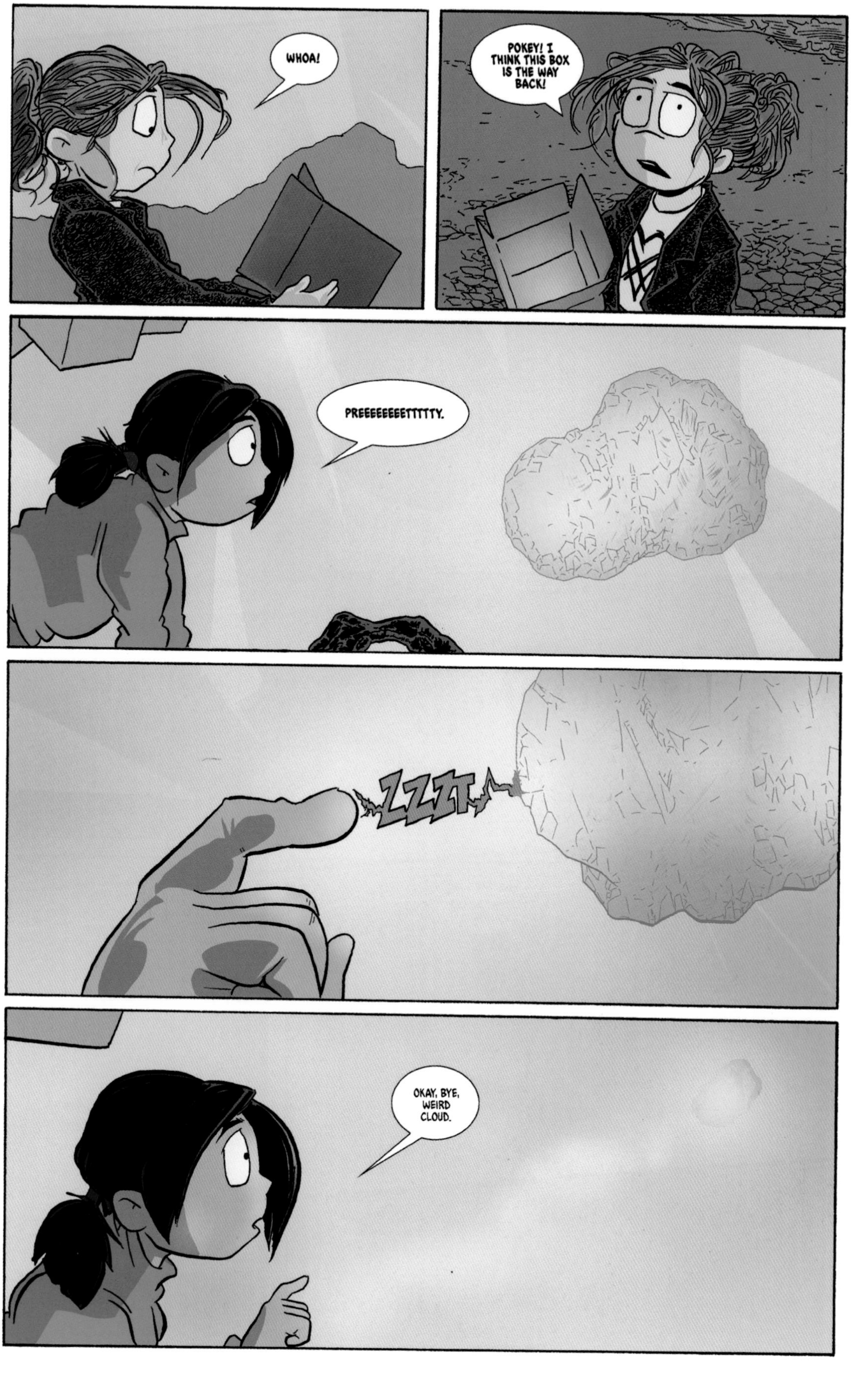
WHOA!
POKEY! I THINK THIS BOX IS THE WAY BACK!
PREEEEEEEETTTTTY.
ZZZT
OKAY, BYE, WEIRD CLOUD.

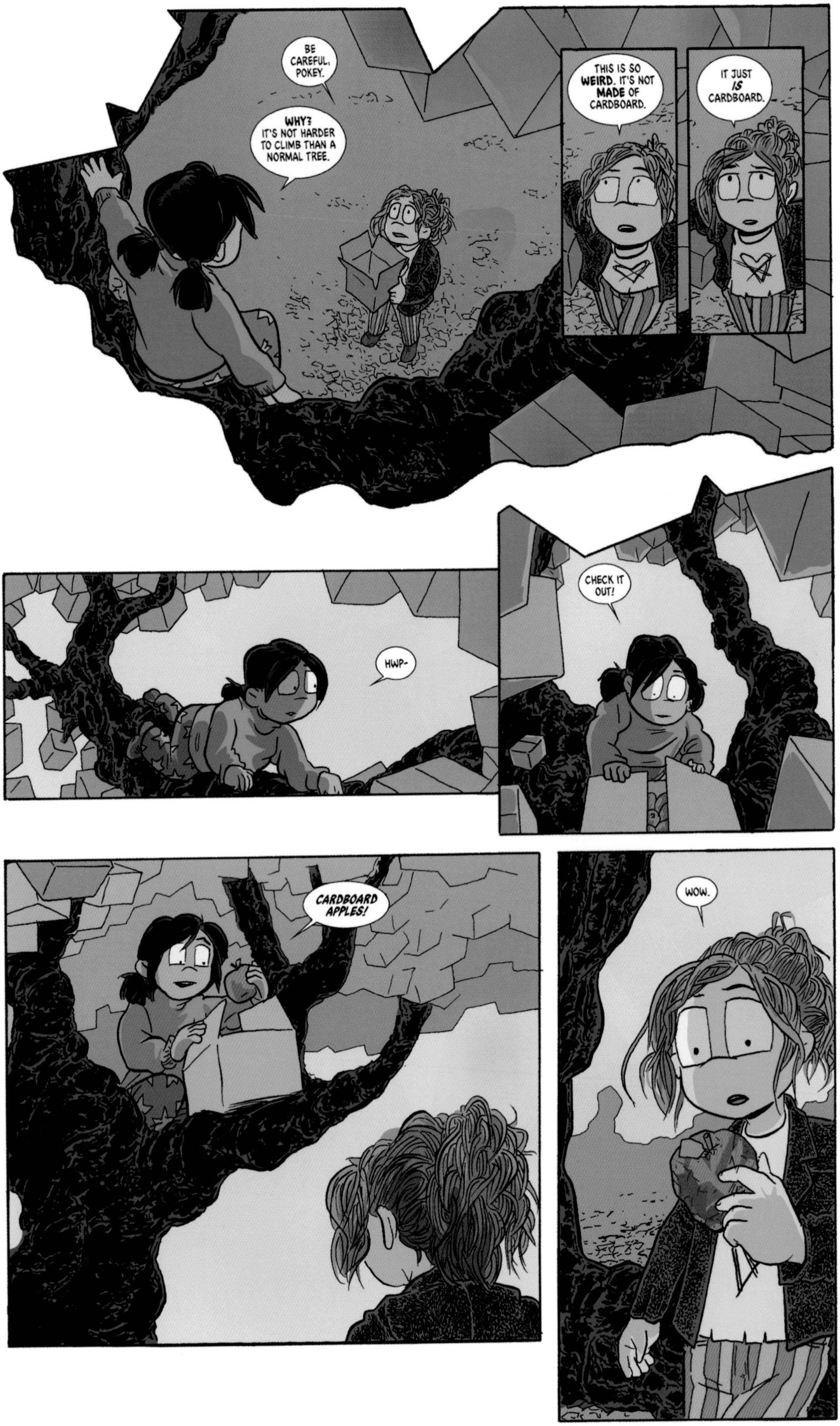
BE CAREFUL, POKEY.
WHY? IT'S NOT HARDER TO CLIMB THAN A NORMAL TREE.
THIS IS SO WEIRD. IT'S NOT MADE OF CARDBOARD.
IT JUST IS CARDBOARD.
HWP-
CHECK IT OUT!
CARDBOARD APPLES!
WOW.

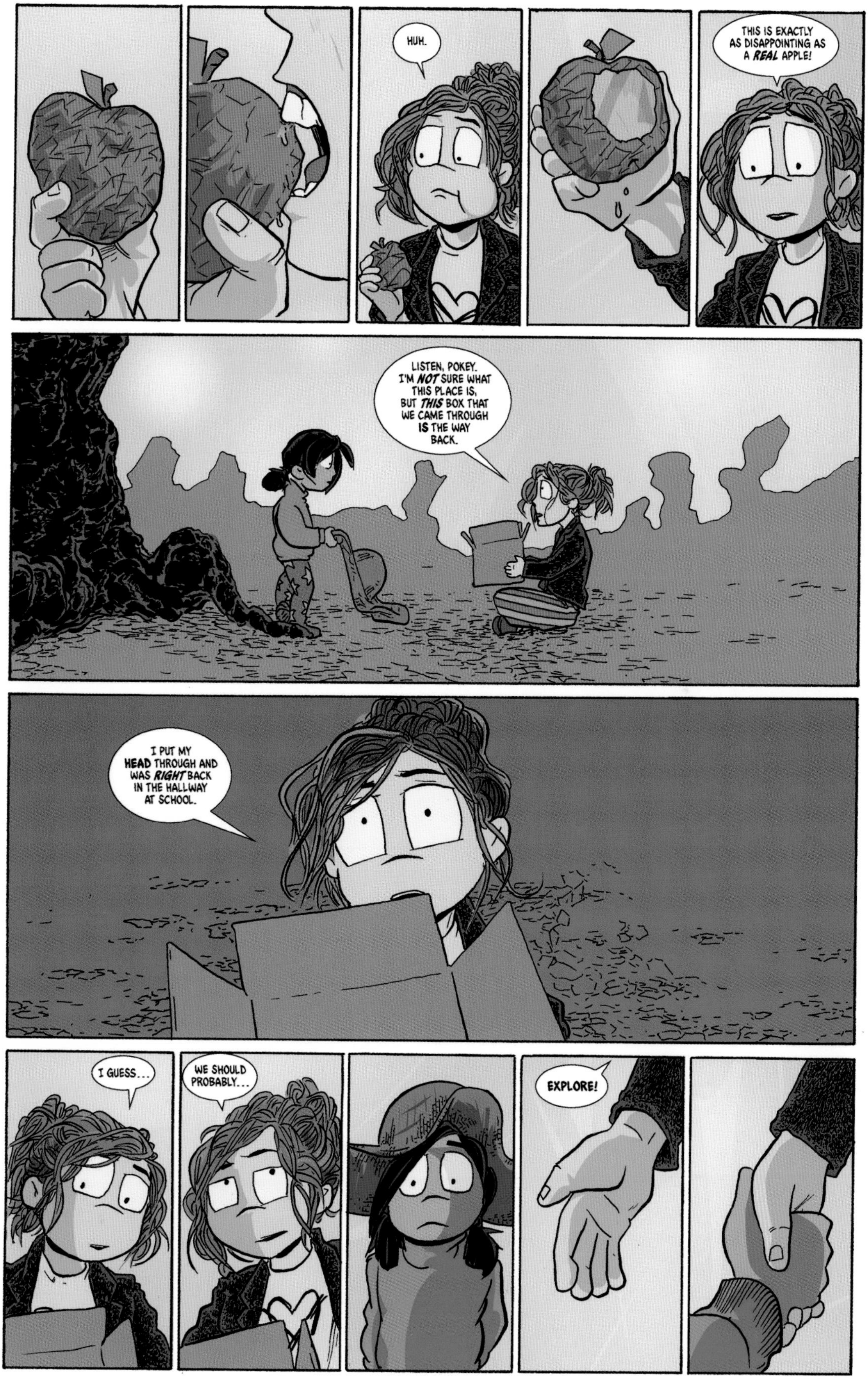
HUH.
THIS IS EXACTLY AS DISAPPOINTING AS A *REAL* APPLE!
LISTEN, POKEY. I'M *NOT* SURE WHAT THIS PLACE IS, BUT *THIS* BOX THAT WE CAME THROUGH **IS** THE WAY BACK.
I PUT MY **HEAD** THROUGH AND WAS *RIGHT* BACK IN THE HALLWAY AT SCHOOL.
I GUESS...
WE SHOULD PROBABLY...
EXPLORE!

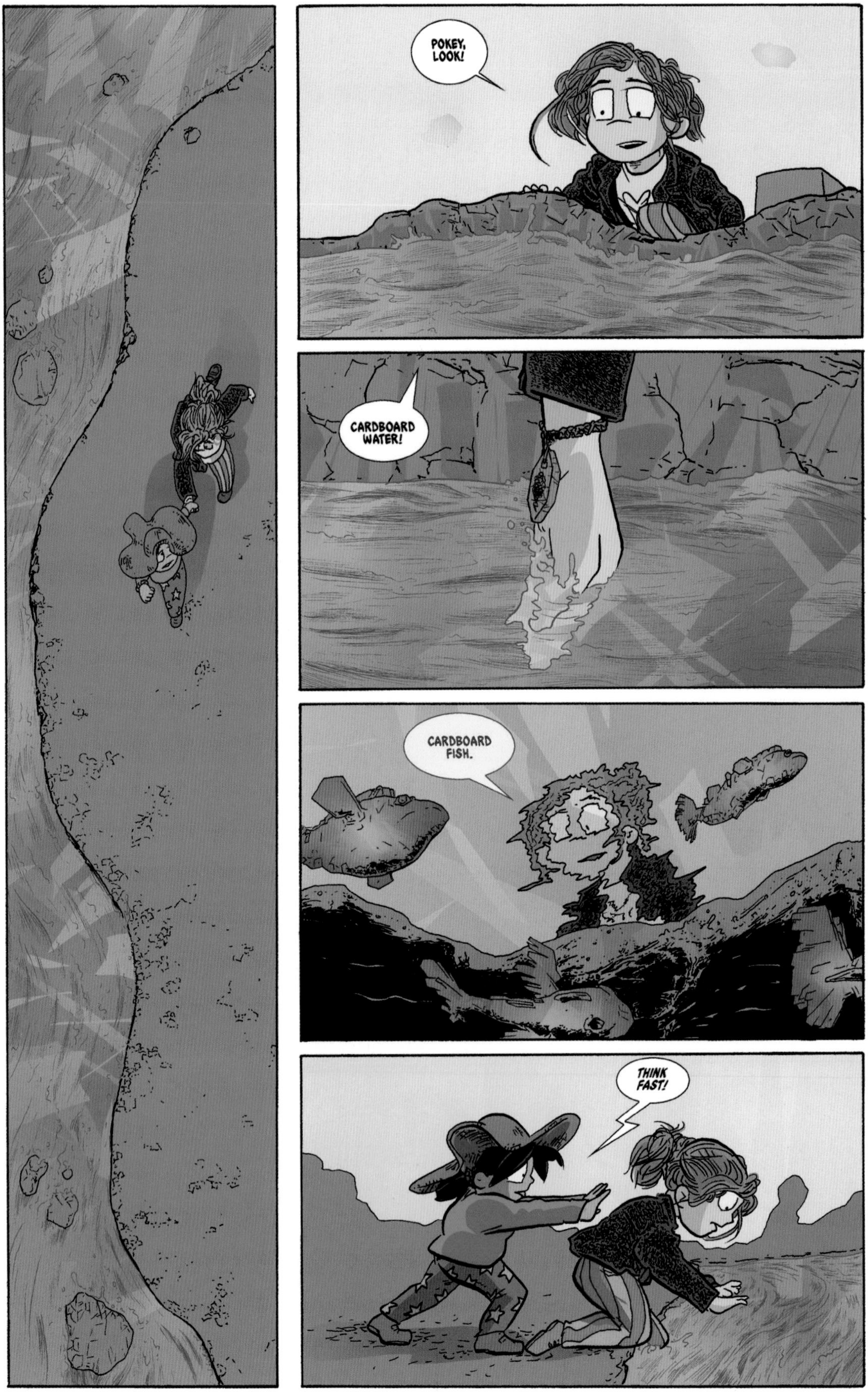
POKEY, LOOK!
CARDBOARD WATER!
CARDBOARD FISH.
THINK FAST!

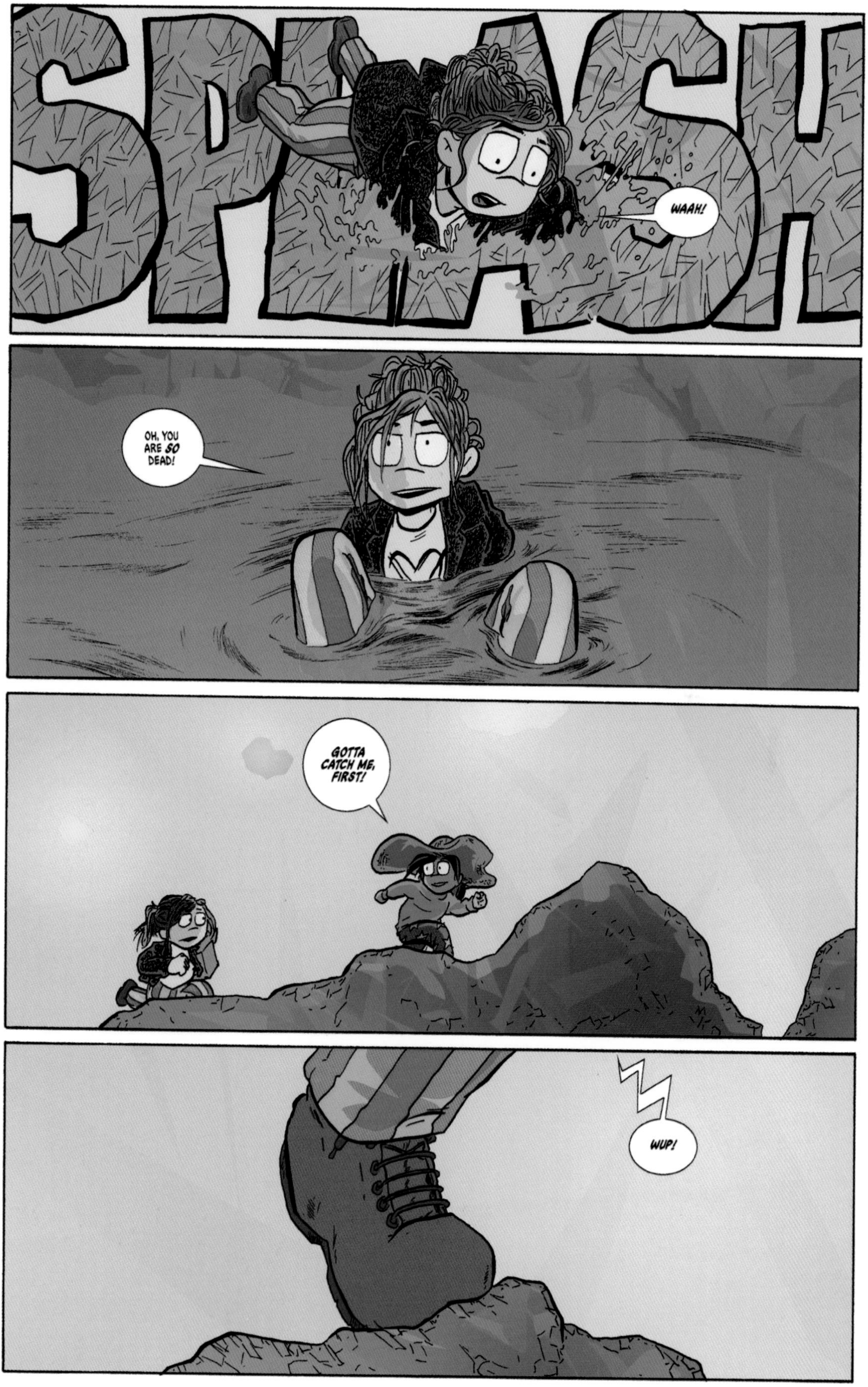
SPLASH
WAAH!
OH, YOU ARE SO DEAD!
GOTTA CATCH ME, FIRST!
WUP!

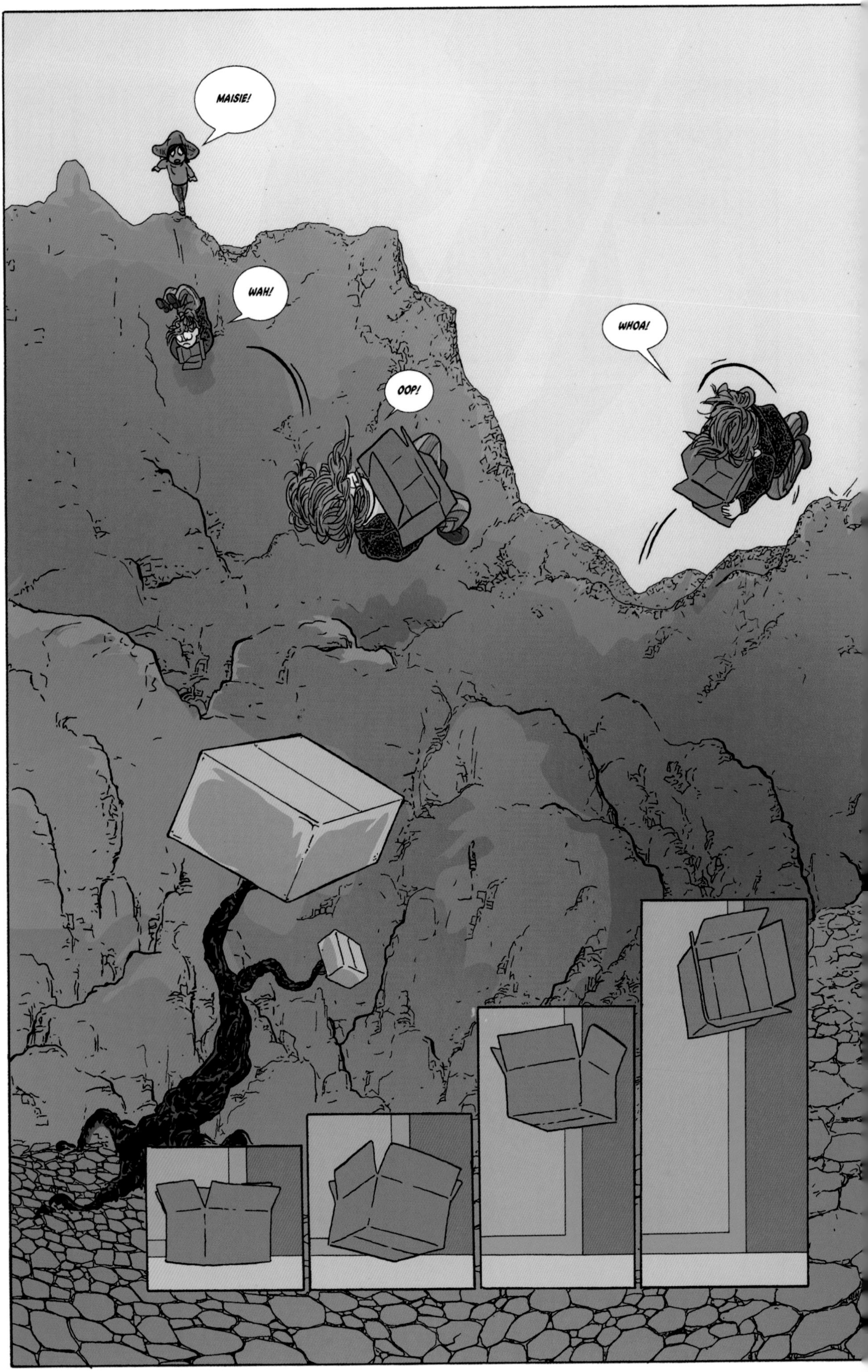
MAISIE!
WAH!
OOP!
WHOA!

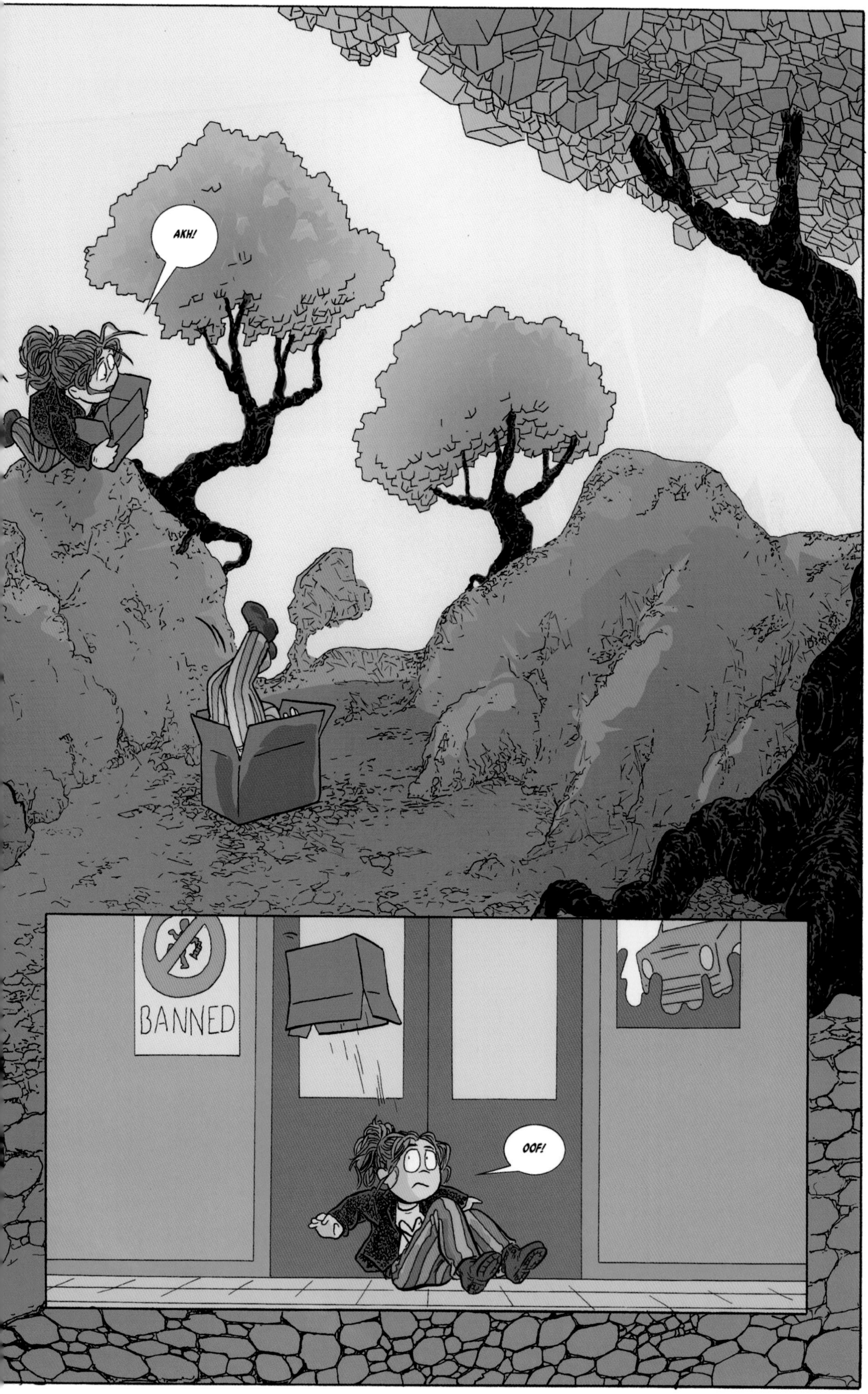
AKH!
BANNED
OOF!

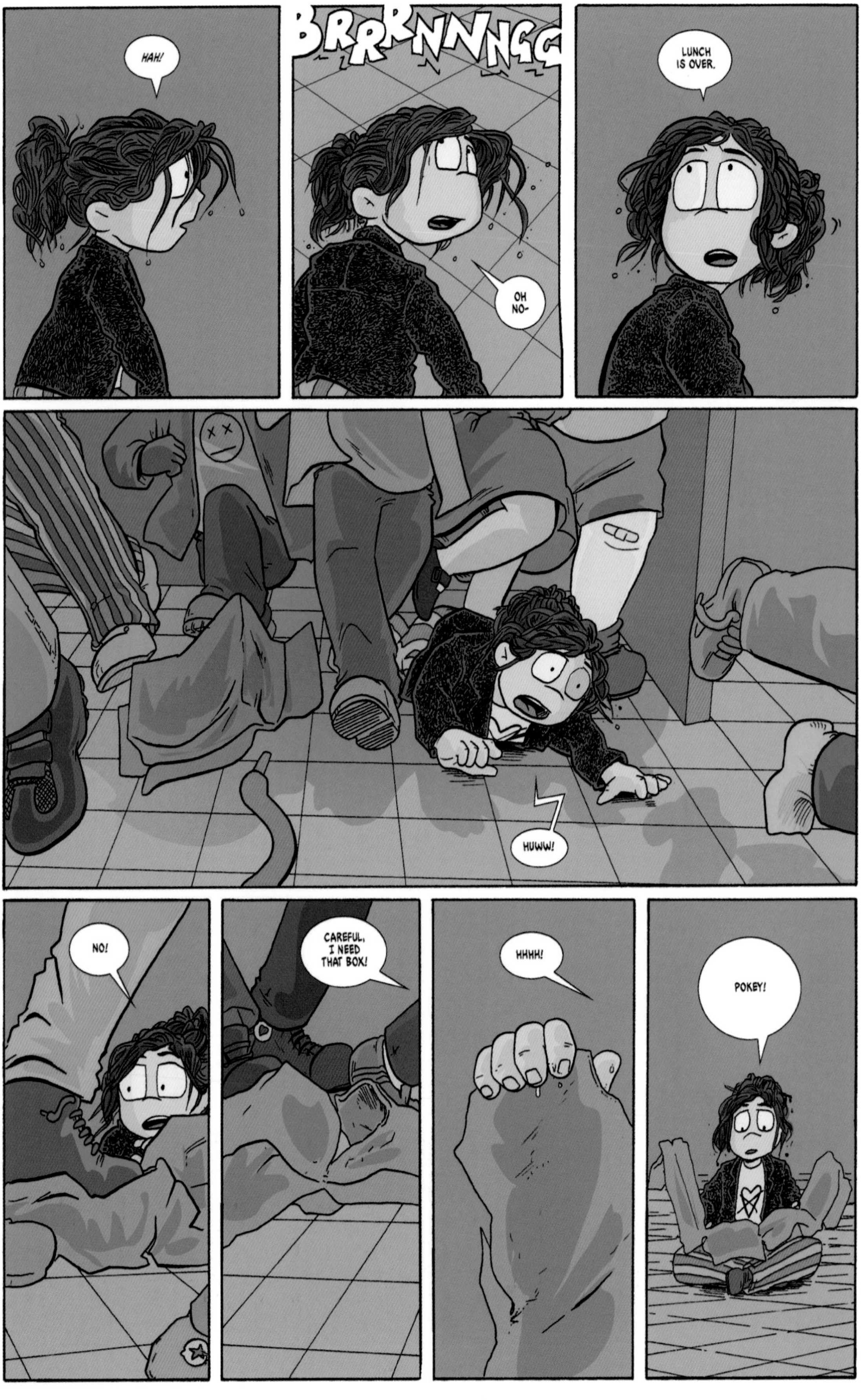
HAH!
BRRRNNNGG
OH NO-
LUNCH IS OVER.
HUWW!
NO!
CAREFUL, I NEED THAT BOX!
HHHH!
POKEY!

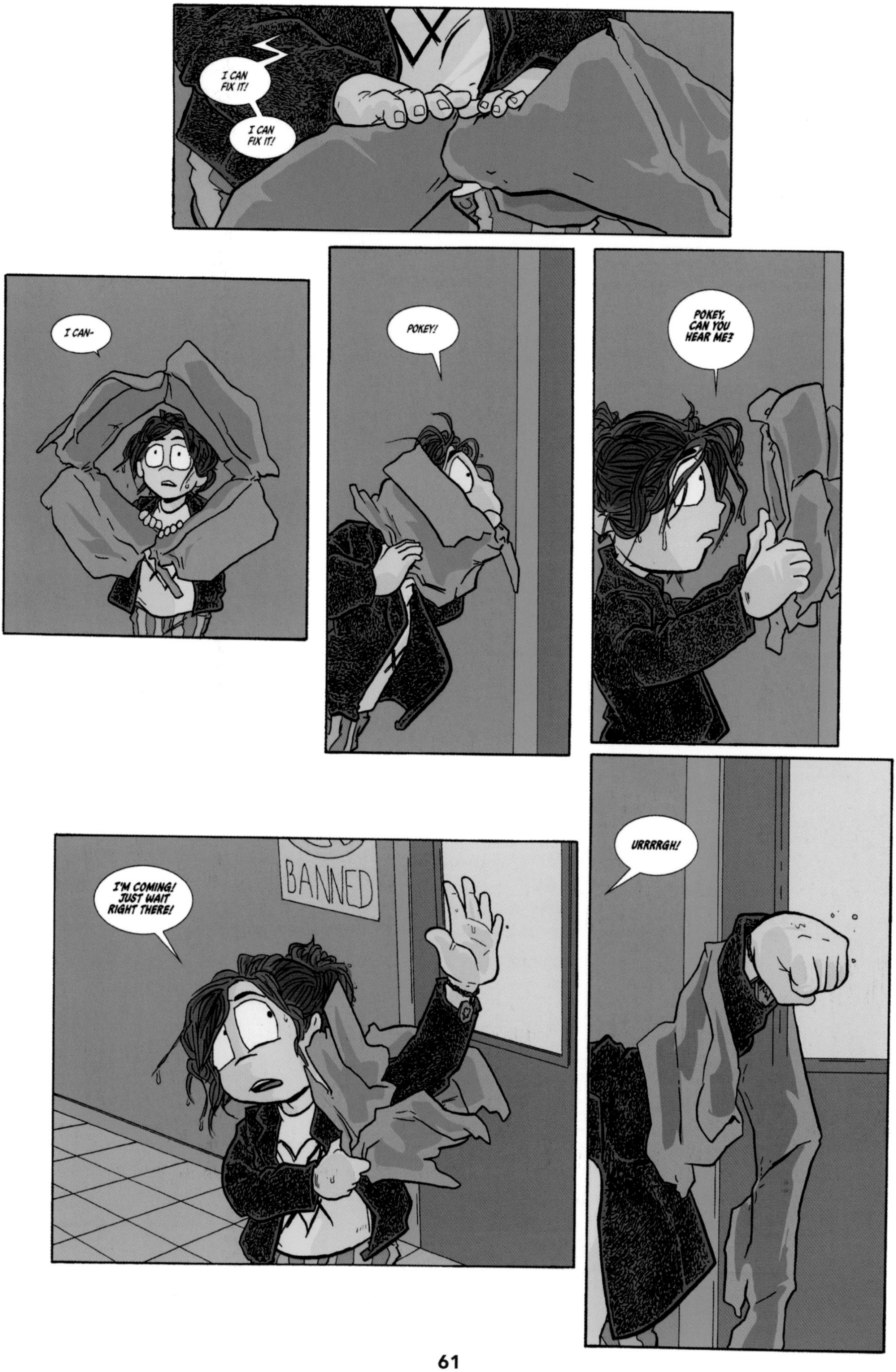
I CAN FIX IT!
I CAN FIX IT!
I CAN-
POKEY!
POKEY, CAN YOU HEAR ME?
I'M COMING! JUST WAIT RIGHT THERE!
BANNED
URRRRGH!

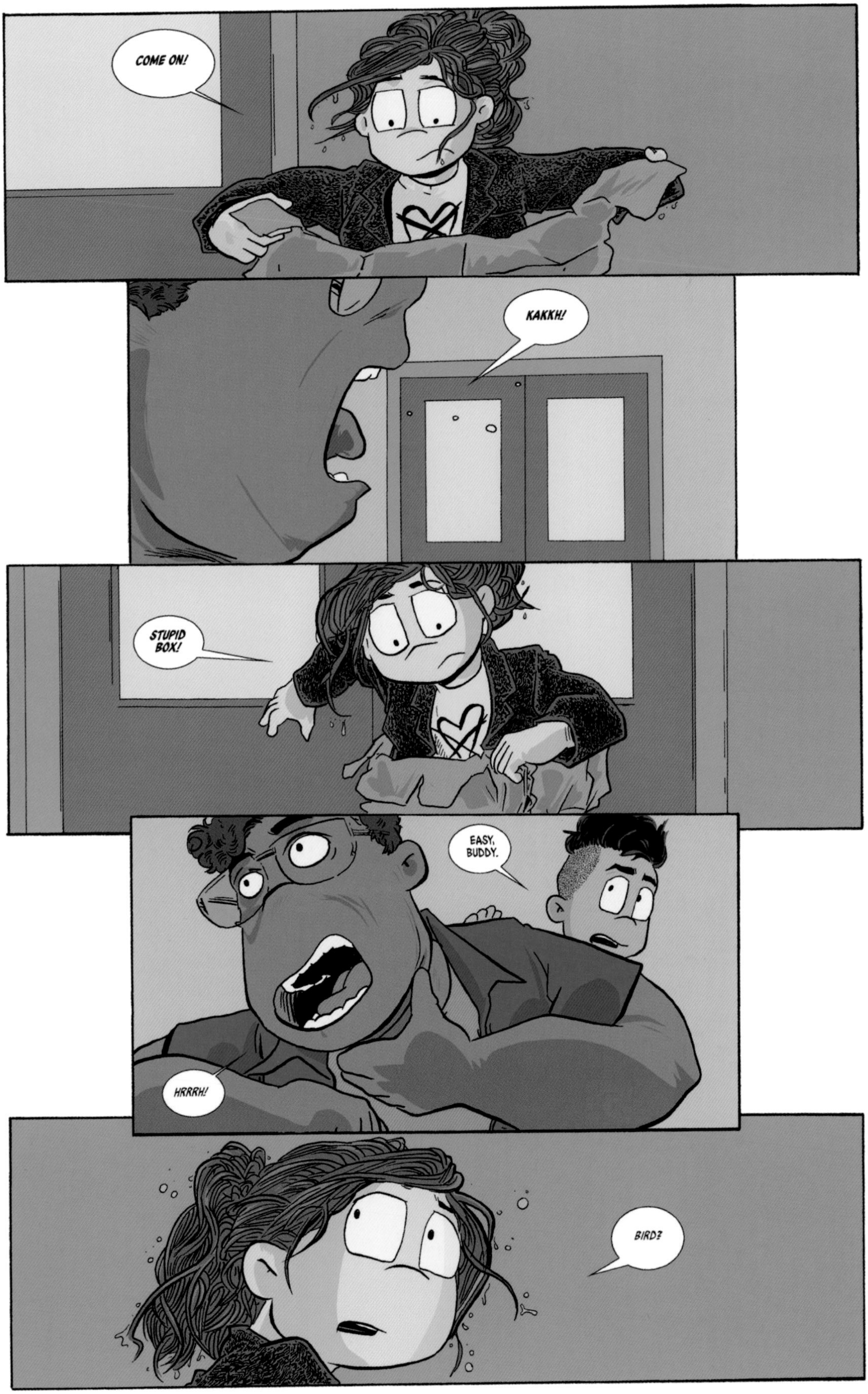
COME ON!
KAKKH!
STUPID BOX!
EASY, BUDDY.
HRRRH!
BIRD?

MAC, BIRD!

YOU HAVE TO HELP, I'VE LOST POKEY!

HOKK!

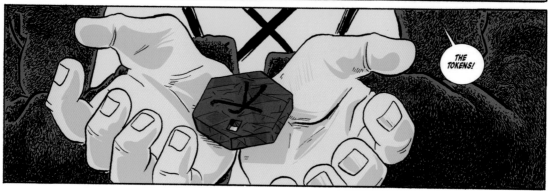

THE TOKENS!

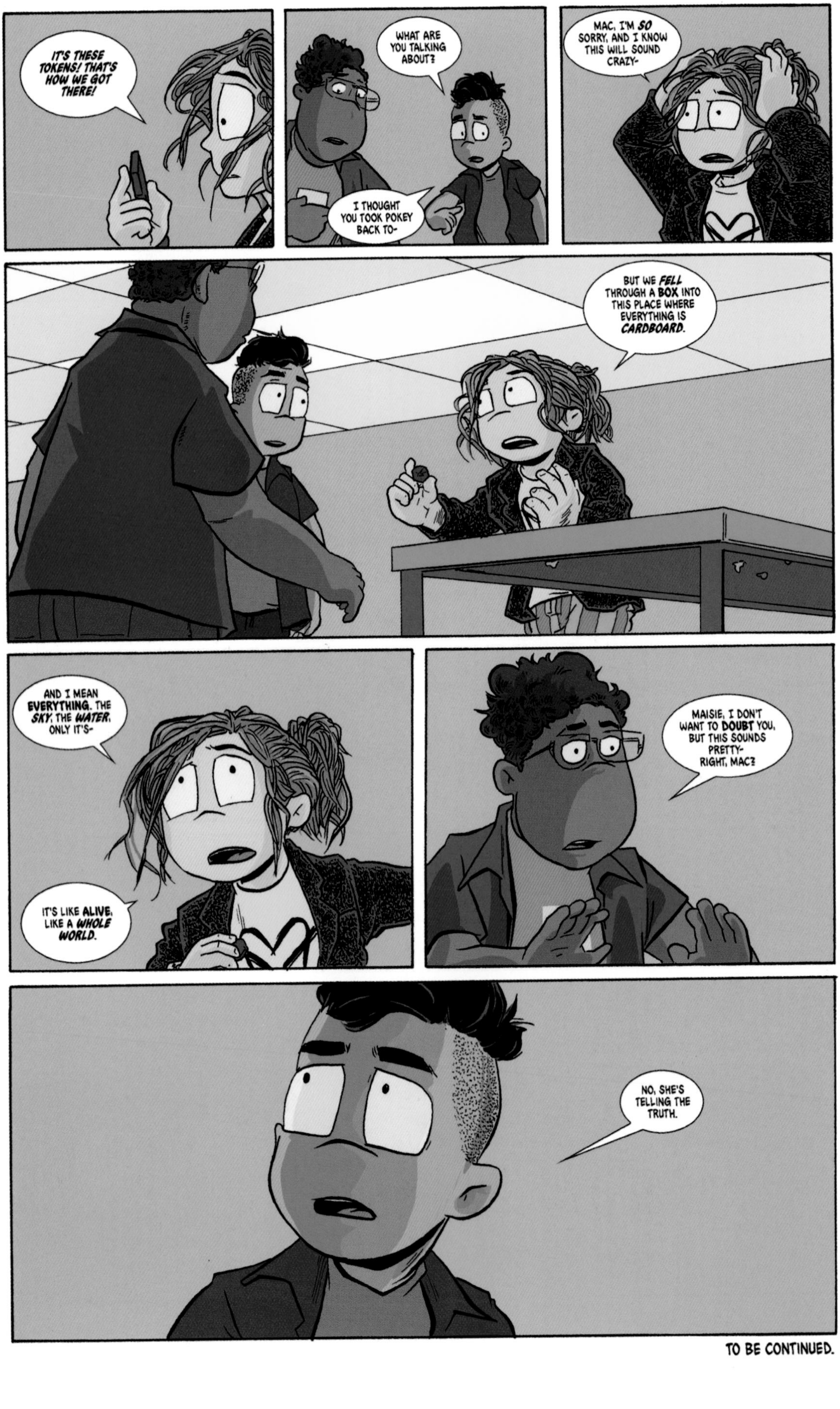
IT'S THESE TOKENS! THAT'S HOW WE GOT THERE!
WHAT ARE YOU TALKING ABOUT?
I THOUGHT YOU TOOK POKEY BACK TO-
MAC, I'M SO SORRY, AND I KNOW THIS WILL SOUND CRAZY-
BUT WE FELL THROUGH A BOX INTO THIS PLACE WHERE EVERYTHING IS CARDBOARD.
AND I MEAN EVERYTHING. THE SKY, THE WATER, ONLY IT'S-
IT'S LIKE ALIVE, LIKE A WHOLE WORLD.
MAISIE, I DON'T WANT TO DOUBT YOU, BUT THIS SOUNDS PRETTY-
RIGHT, MAC?
NO, SHE'S TELLING THE TRUTH.

TO BE CONTINUED.

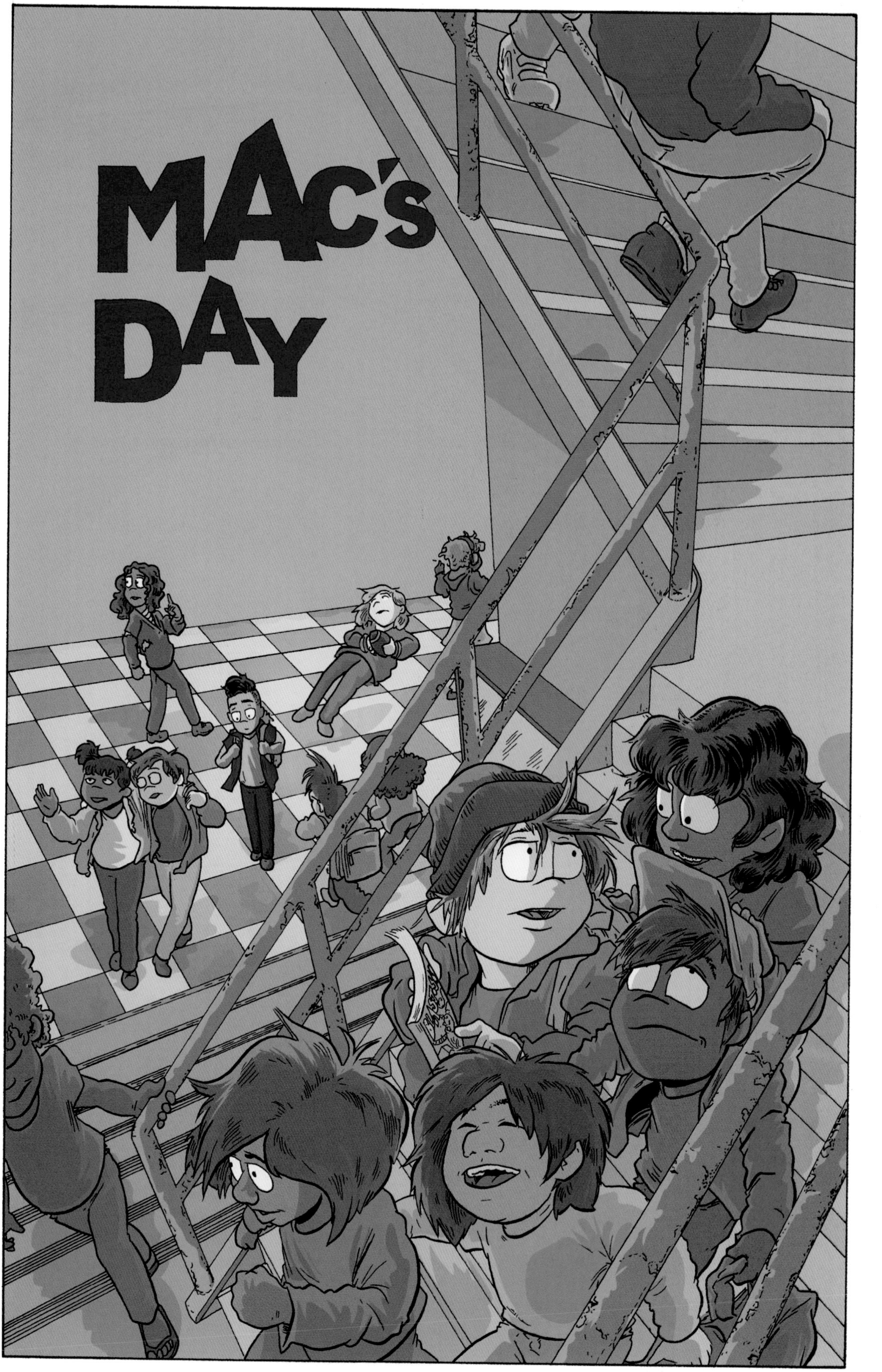
MAC'S DAY

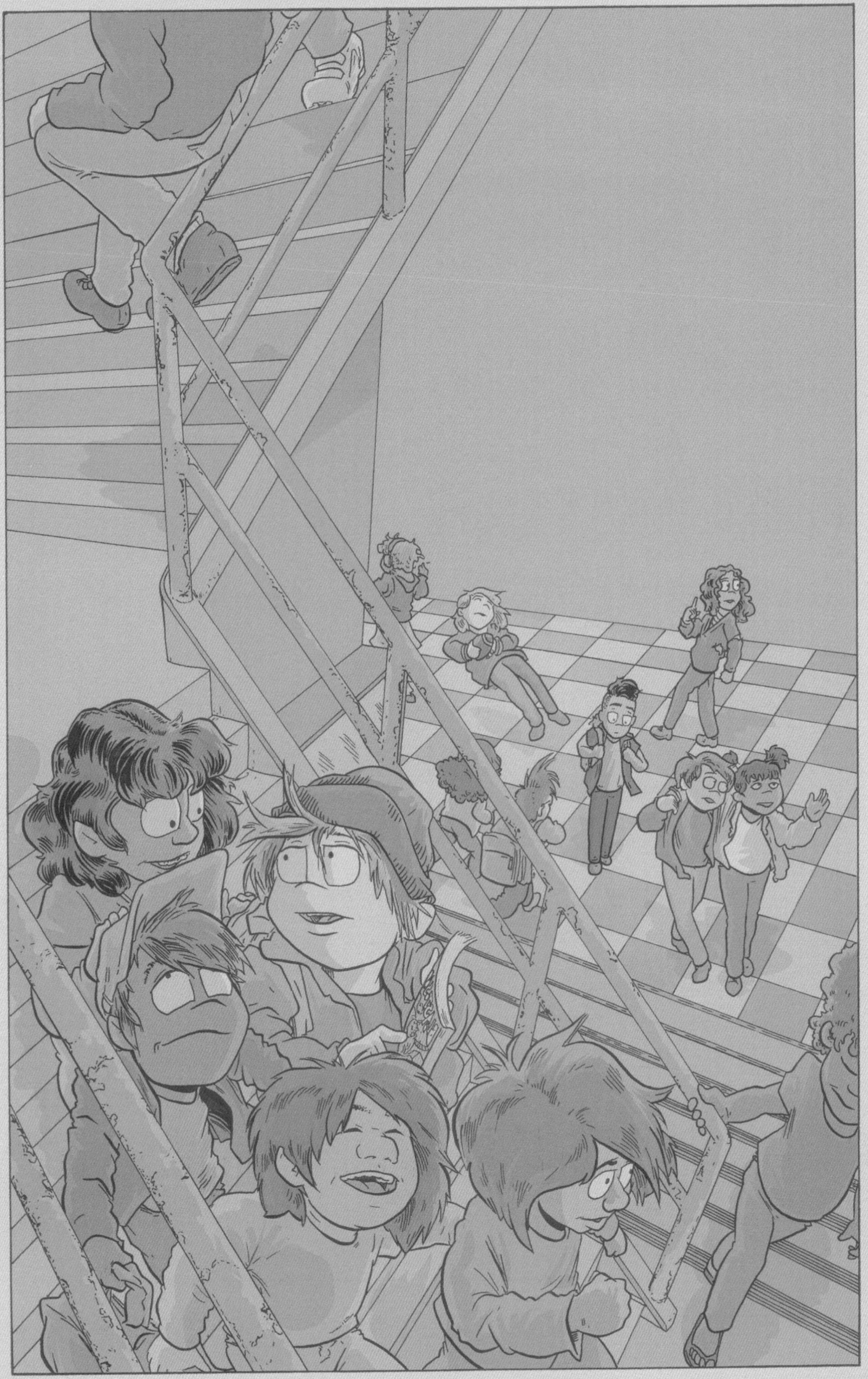

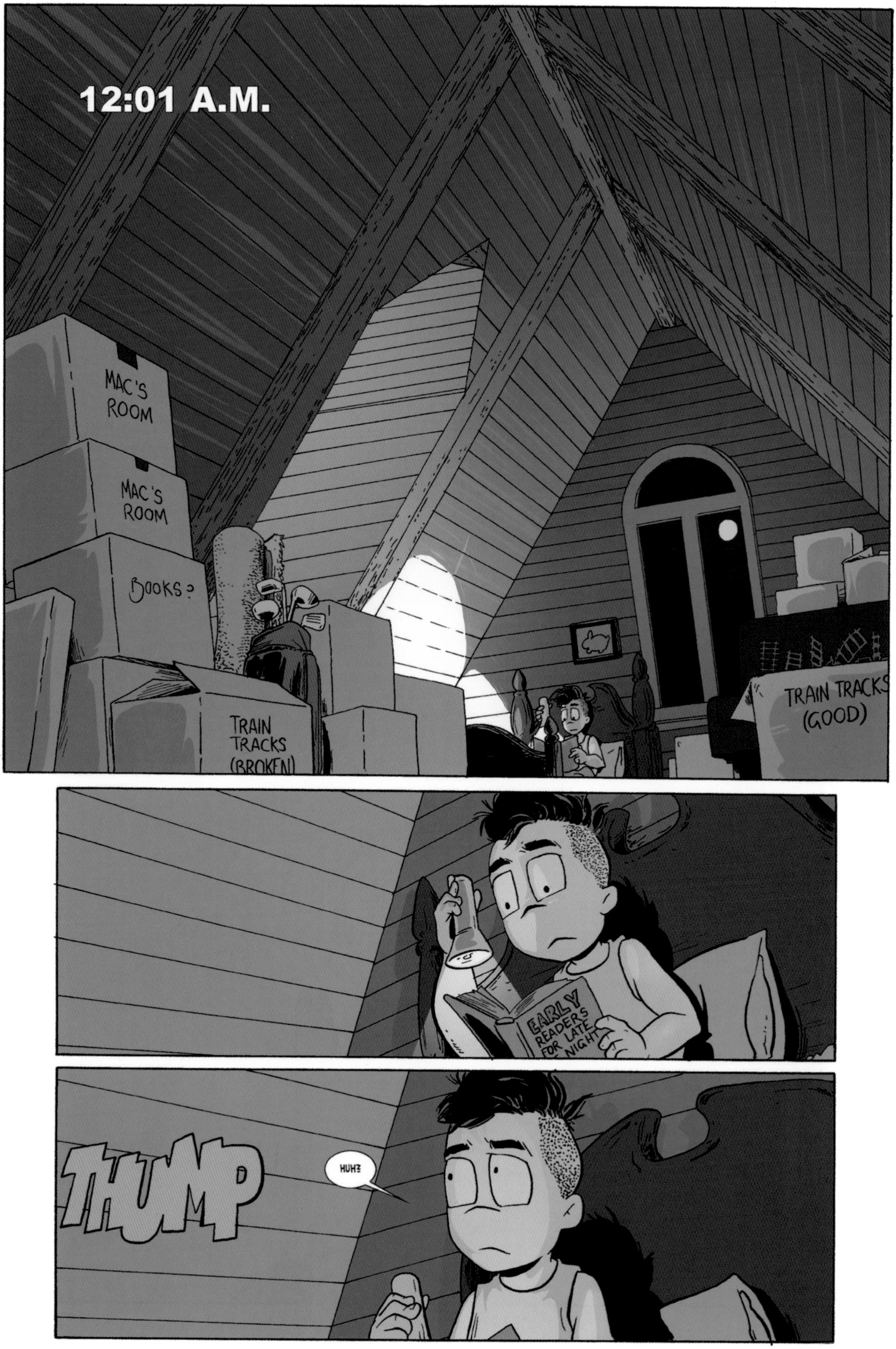

12:01 A.M.
MAC'S ROOM
MAC'S ROOM
BOOKS?
TRAIN TRACKS (BROKEN)
TRAIN TRACKS (GOOD)
EARLY READERS FOR LATE NIGHT
THUMP
HUH?

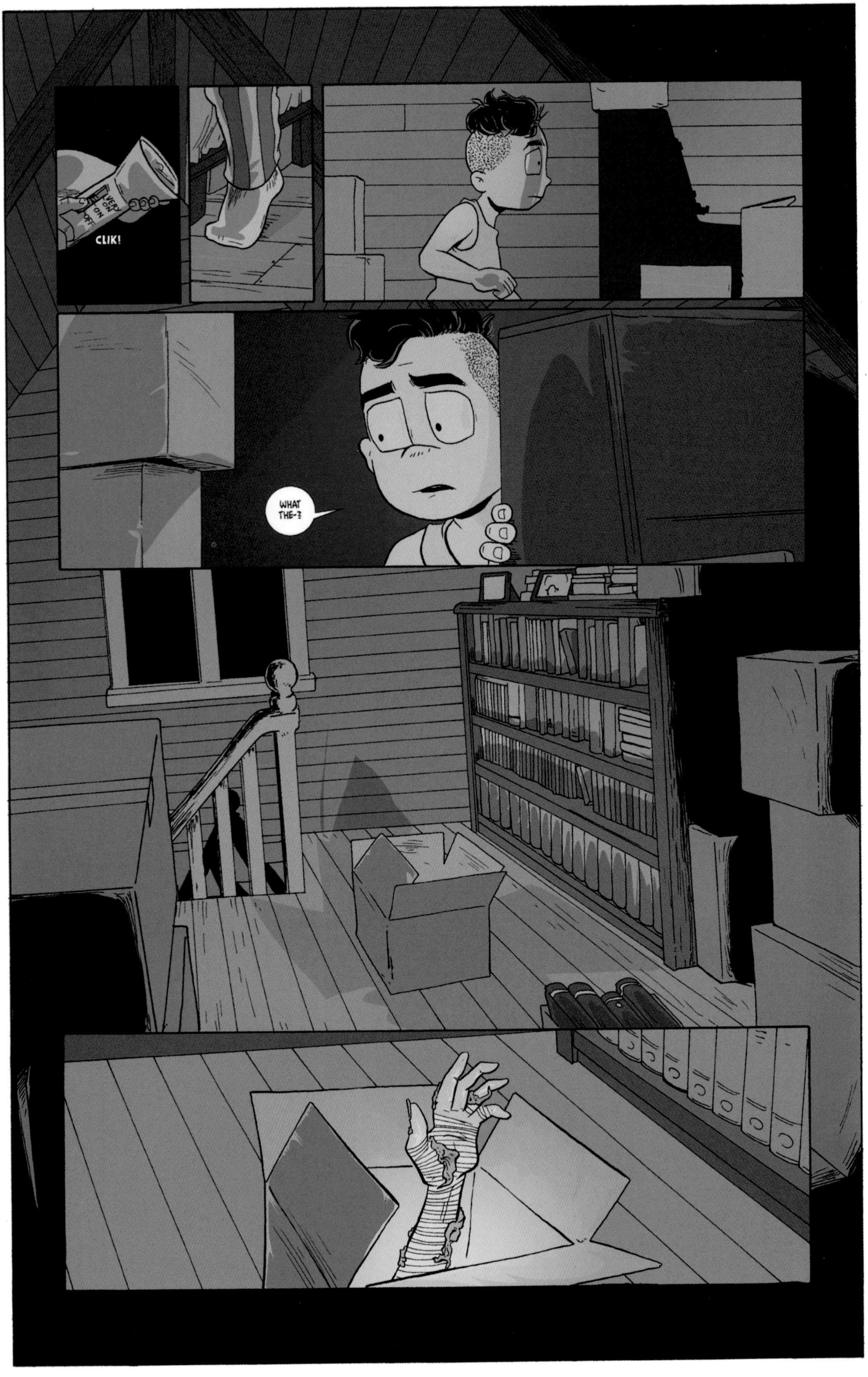
VERY ON
ON
OFF
CLIK!
WHAT THE-?

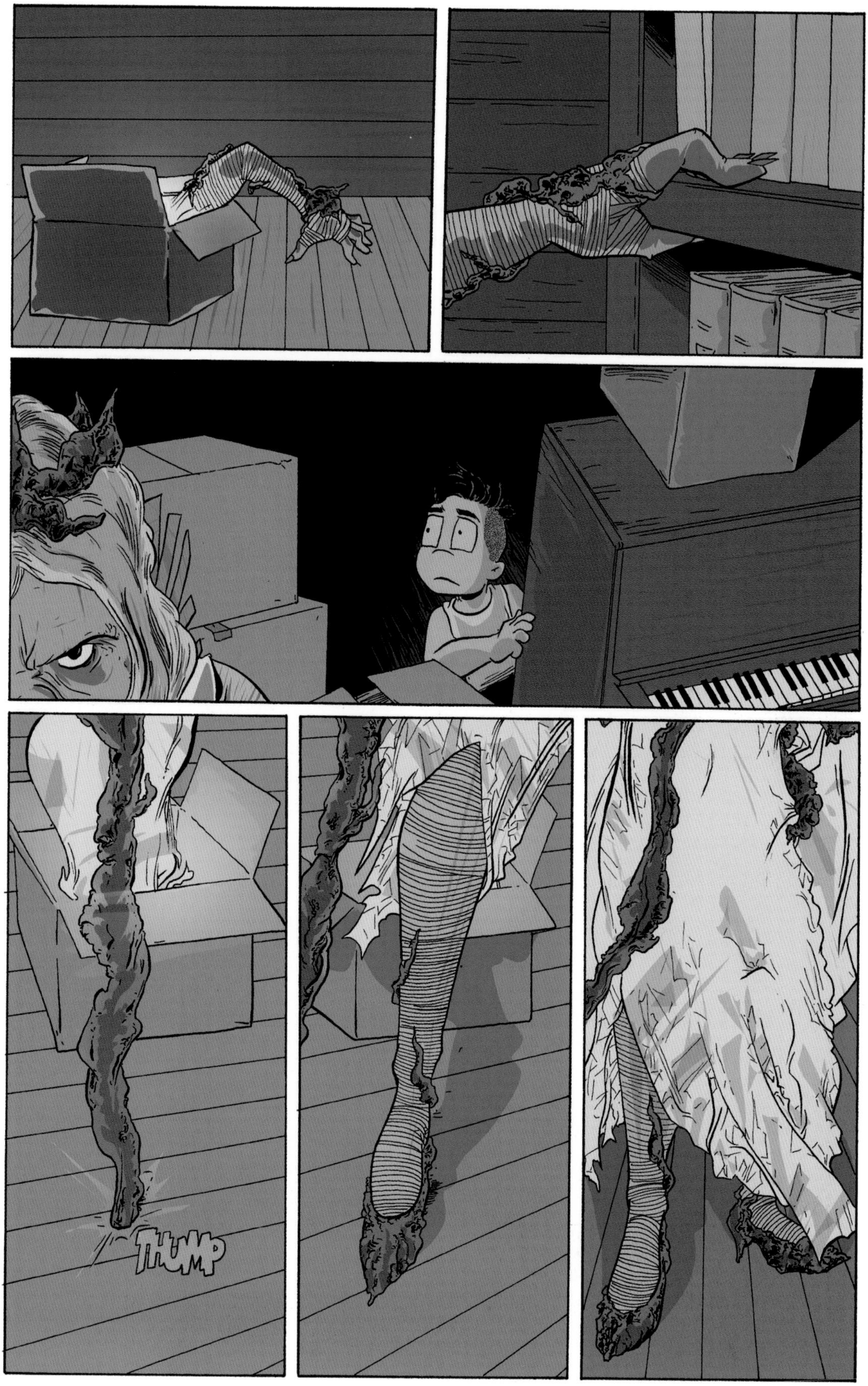
THUMP

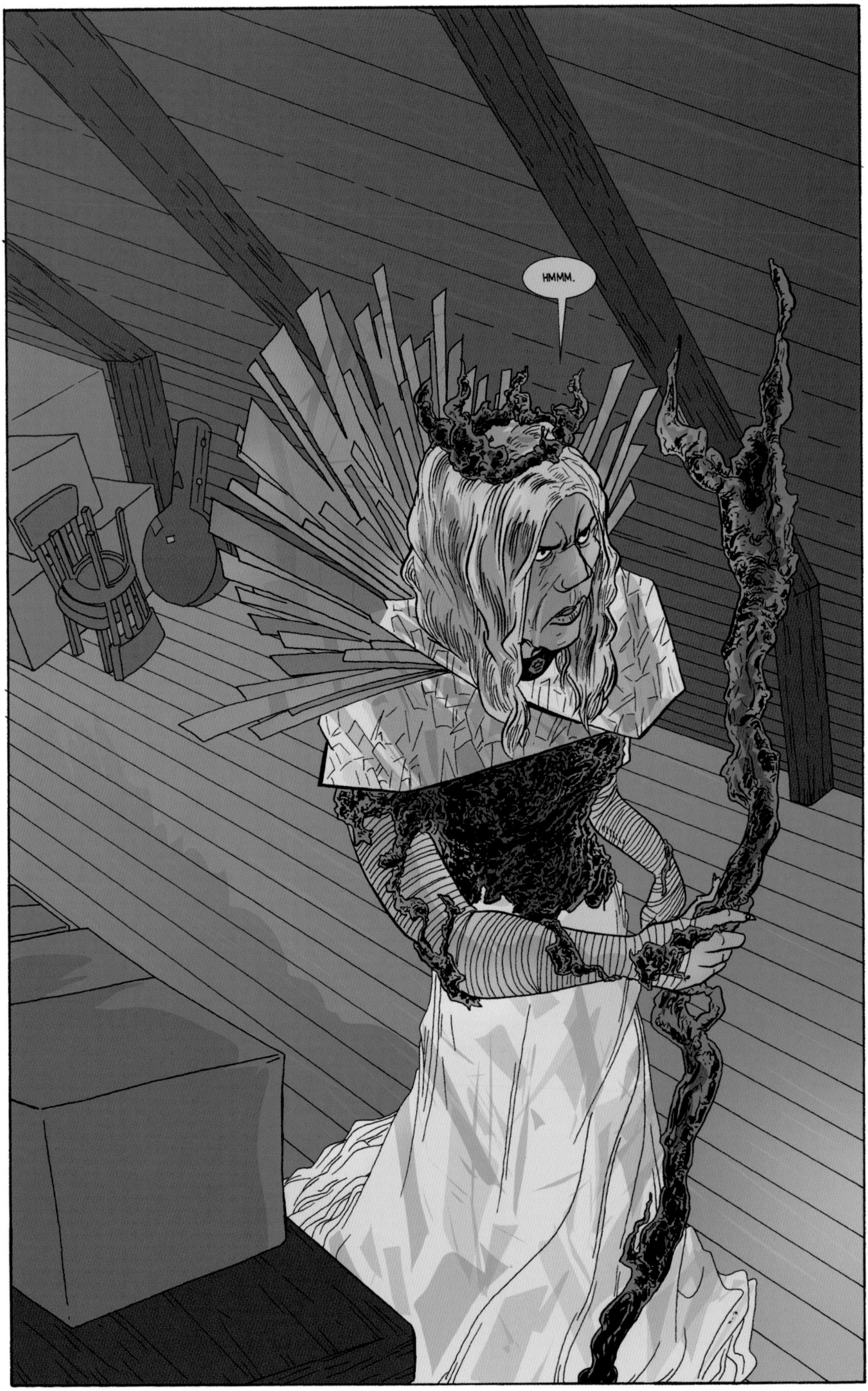
HMMM.

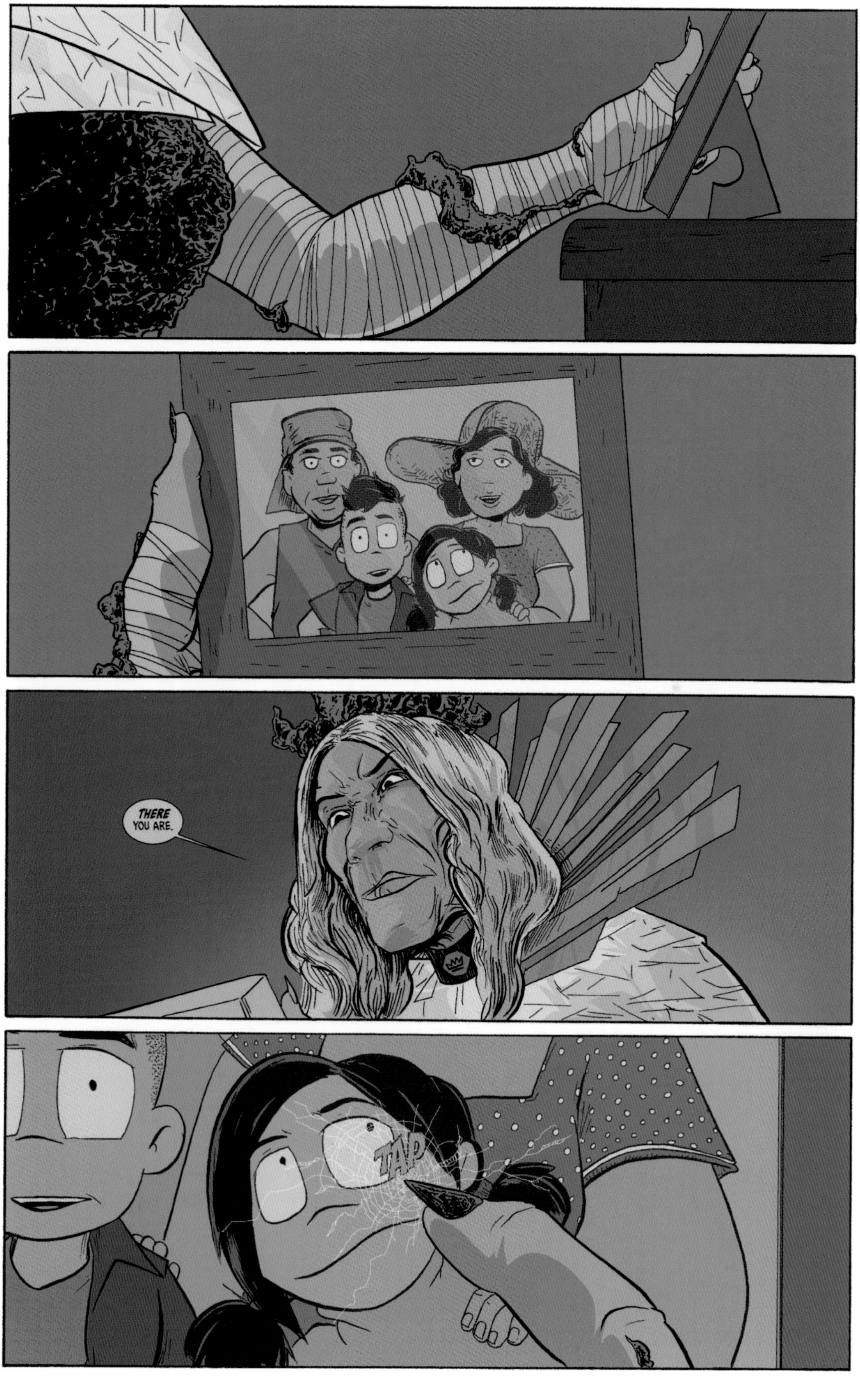
THERE YOU ARE.
TAP

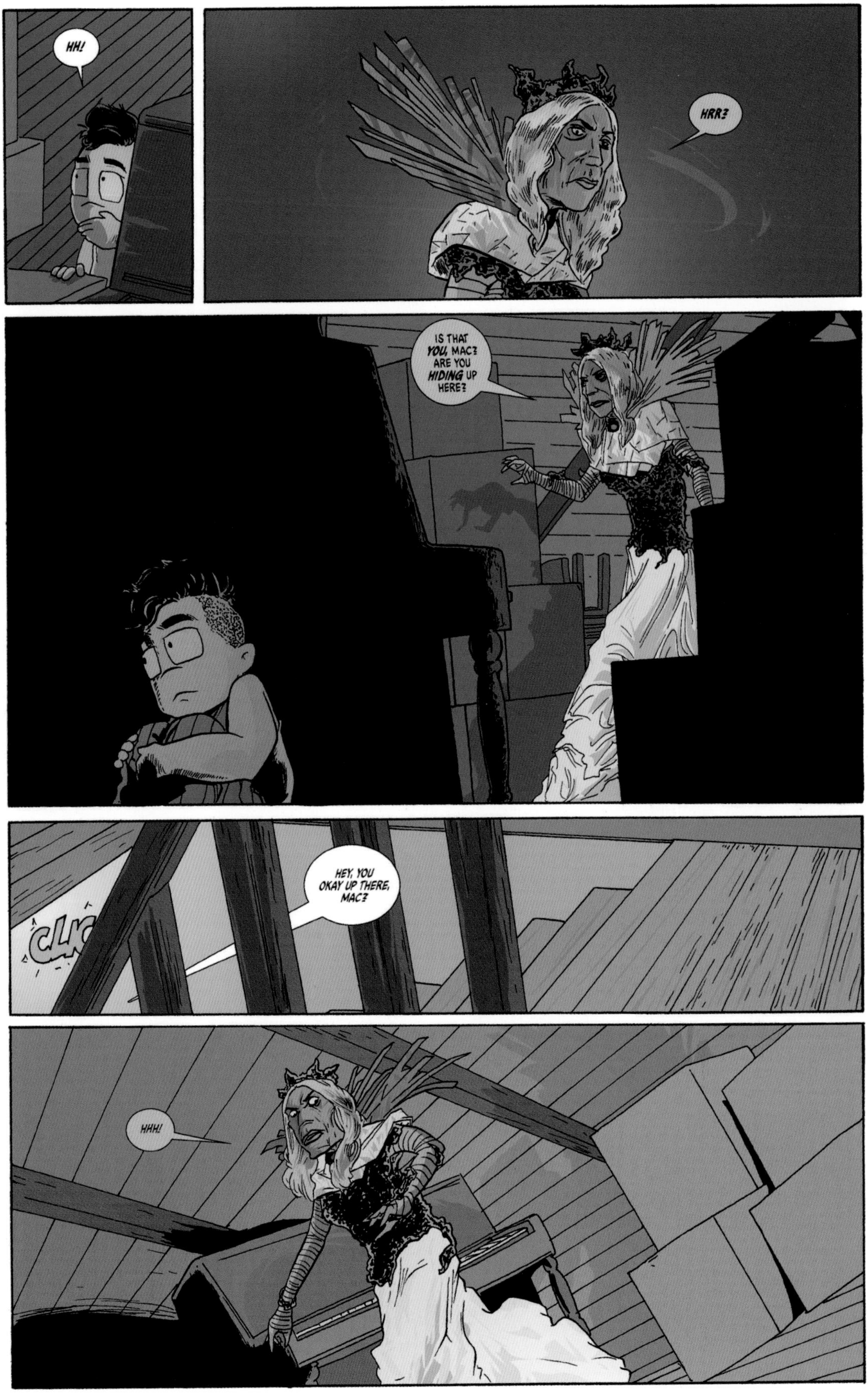
HH!
HRR?
IS THAT YOU, MAC? ARE YOU HIDING UP HERE?
CLIC
HEY, YOU OKAY UP THERE, MAC?
HHH!

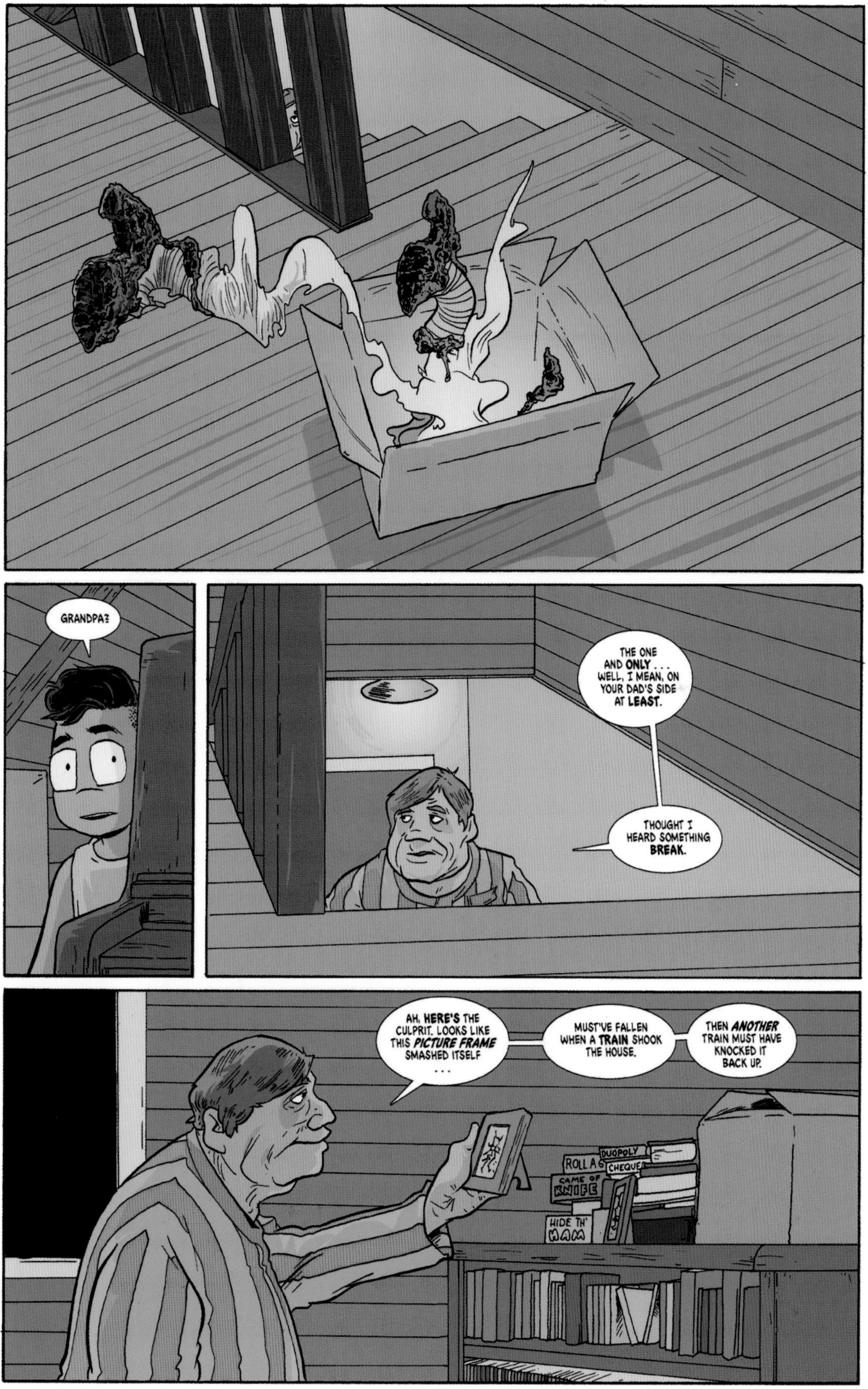
GRANDPA?
THE ONE AND ONLY . . . WELL, I MEAN, ON YOUR DAD'S SIDE AT LEAST.
THOUGHT I HEARD SOMETHING BREAK.
AH, HERE'S THE CULPRIT. LOOKS LIKE THIS PICTURE FRAME SMASHED ITSELF . . .
MUST'VE FALLEN WHEN A TRAIN SHOOK THE HOUSE.
THEN ANOTHER TRAIN MUST HAVE KNOCKED IT BACK UP.
ROLL A
DUOPOLY
CHEQUE
GAME OF KNIFE
HIDE TH' HAM

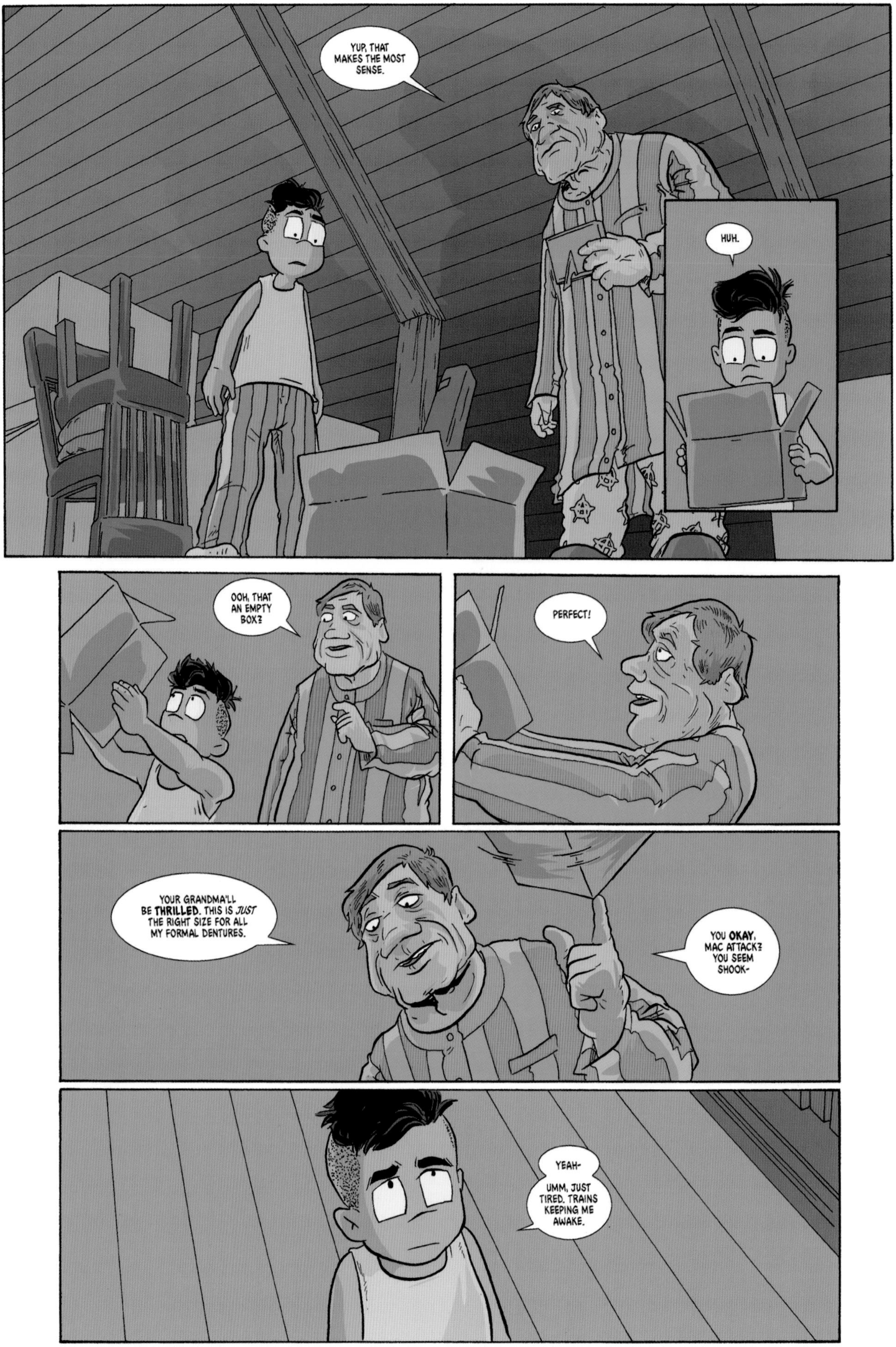
YUP, THAT MAKES THE MOST SENSE.
HUH.
OOH, THAT AN EMPTY BOX?
PERFECT!
YOUR GRANDMA'LL BE **THRILLED**. THIS IS *JUST* THE RIGHT SIZE FOR ALL MY FORMAL DENTURES.
YOU **OKAY**, MAC ATTACK? YOU SEEM SHOOK-
YEAH-
UMM, JUST TIRED. TRAINS KEEPING ME AWAKE.

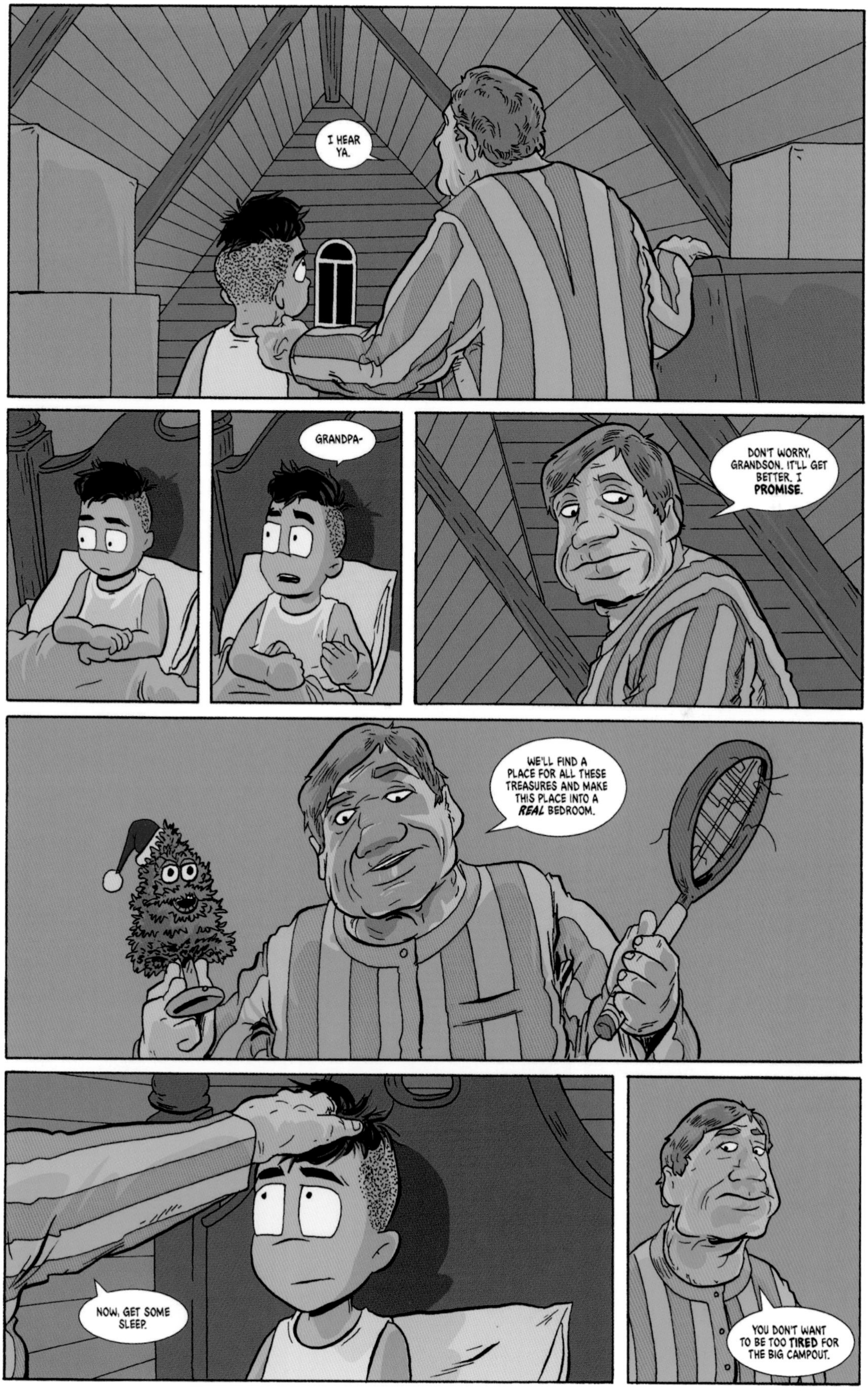
I HEAR YA.
GRANDPA-
DON'T WORRY, GRANDSON. IT'LL GET BETTER. I **PROMISE**.
WE'LL FIND A PLACE FOR ALL THESE TREASURES AND MAKE THIS PLACE INTO A ***REAL*** BEDROOM.
NOW, GET SOME SLEEP.
YOU DON'T WANT TO BE TOO **TIRED** FOR THE BIG CAMPOUT.

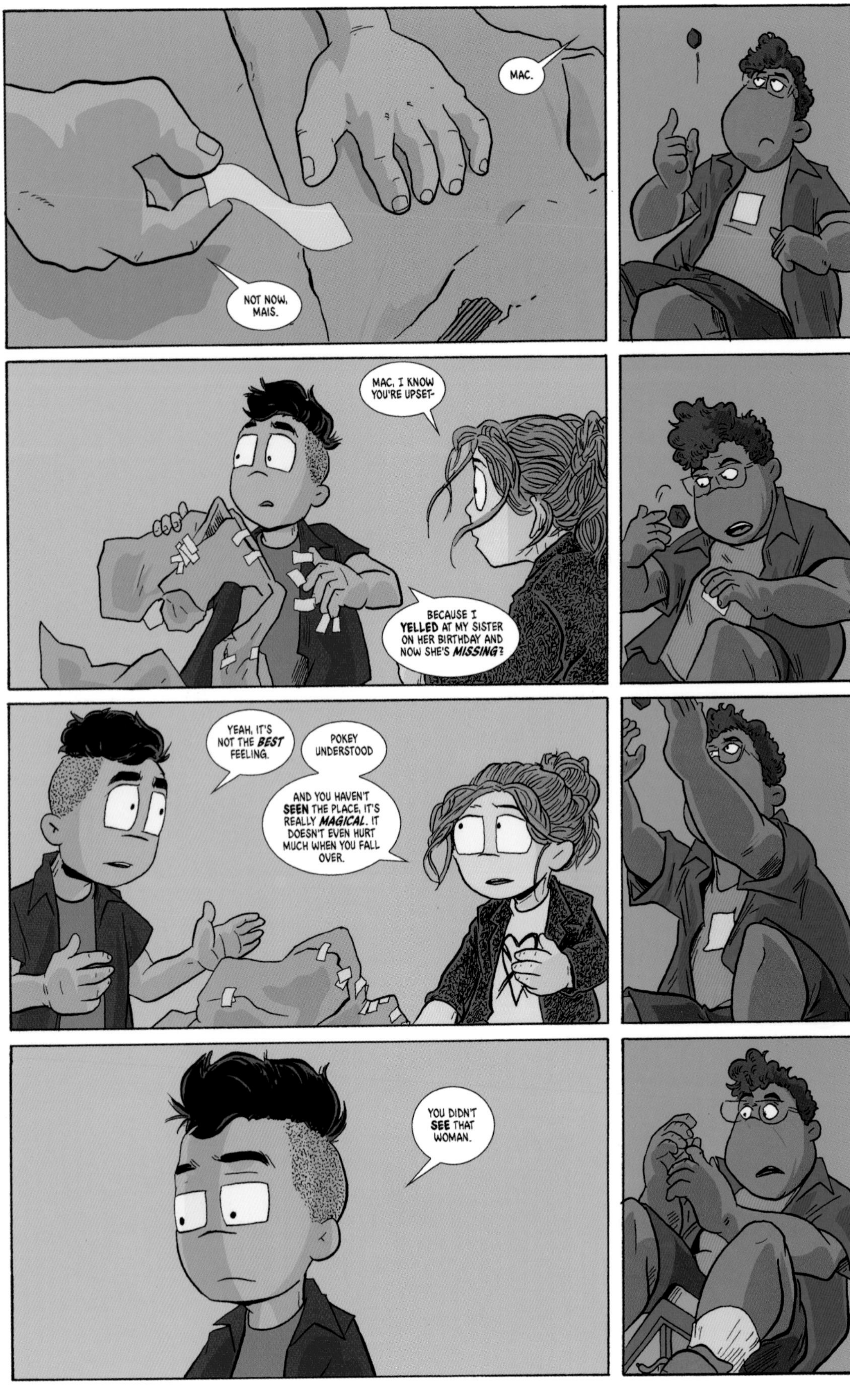
MAC.
NOT NOW, MAIS.
MAC, I KNOW YOU'RE UPSET-
BECAUSE I **YELLED** AT MY SISTER ON HER BIRTHDAY AND NOW SHE'S ***MISSING***?
YEAH, IT'S NOT THE ***BEST*** FEELING.
POKEY UNDERSTOOD
AND YOU HAVEN'T **SEEN** THE PLACE, IT'S REALLY ***MAGICAL***. IT DOESN'T EVEN HURT MUCH WHEN YOU FALL OVER.
YOU DIDN'T **SEE** THAT WOMAN.

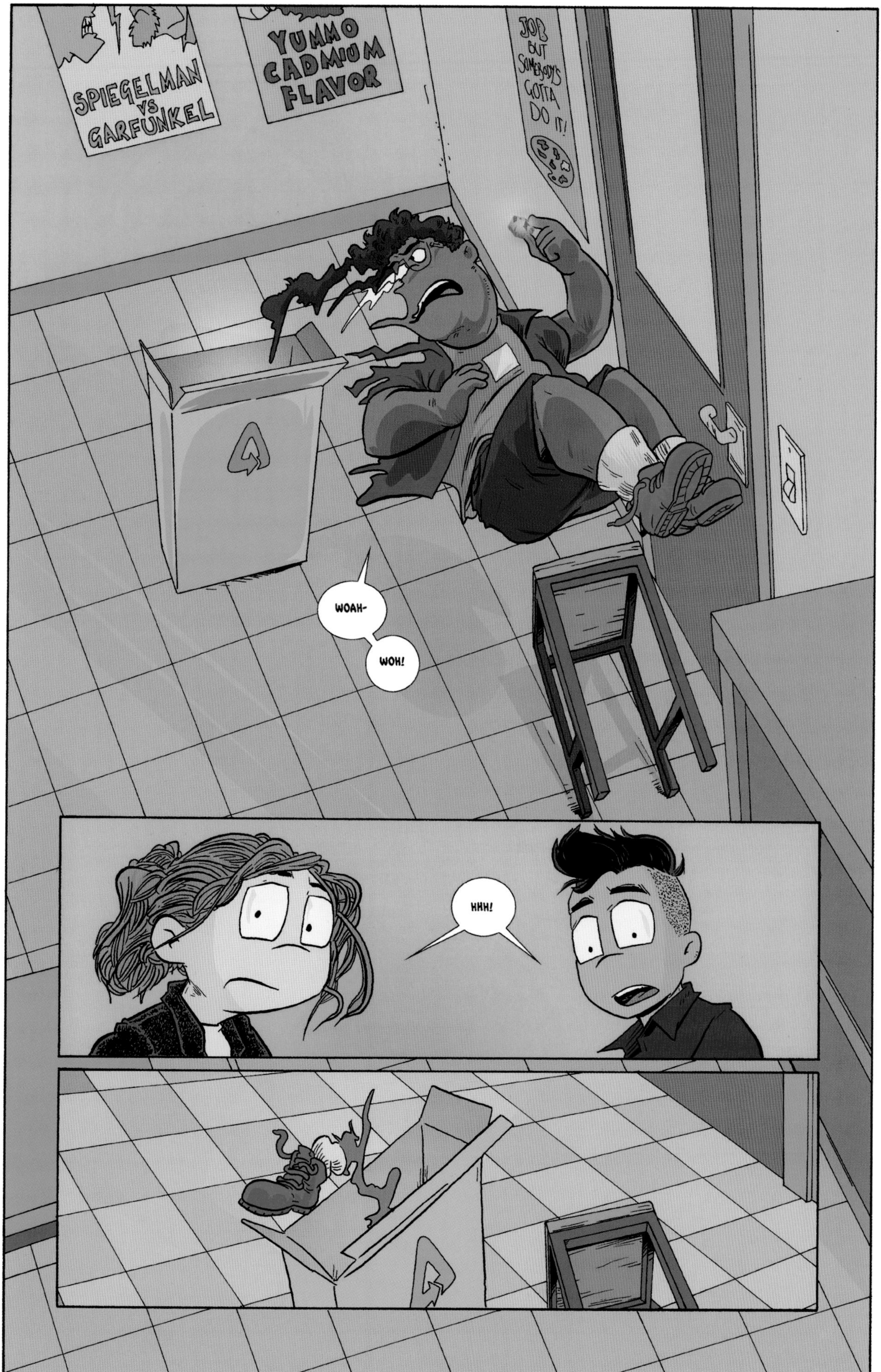
SPIEGELMAN VS GARFUNKEL
YUMMO CADMIUM FLAVOR
JOB BUT SOMEBODY'S GOTTA DO IT!
WOAH-
WOH!
HHH!

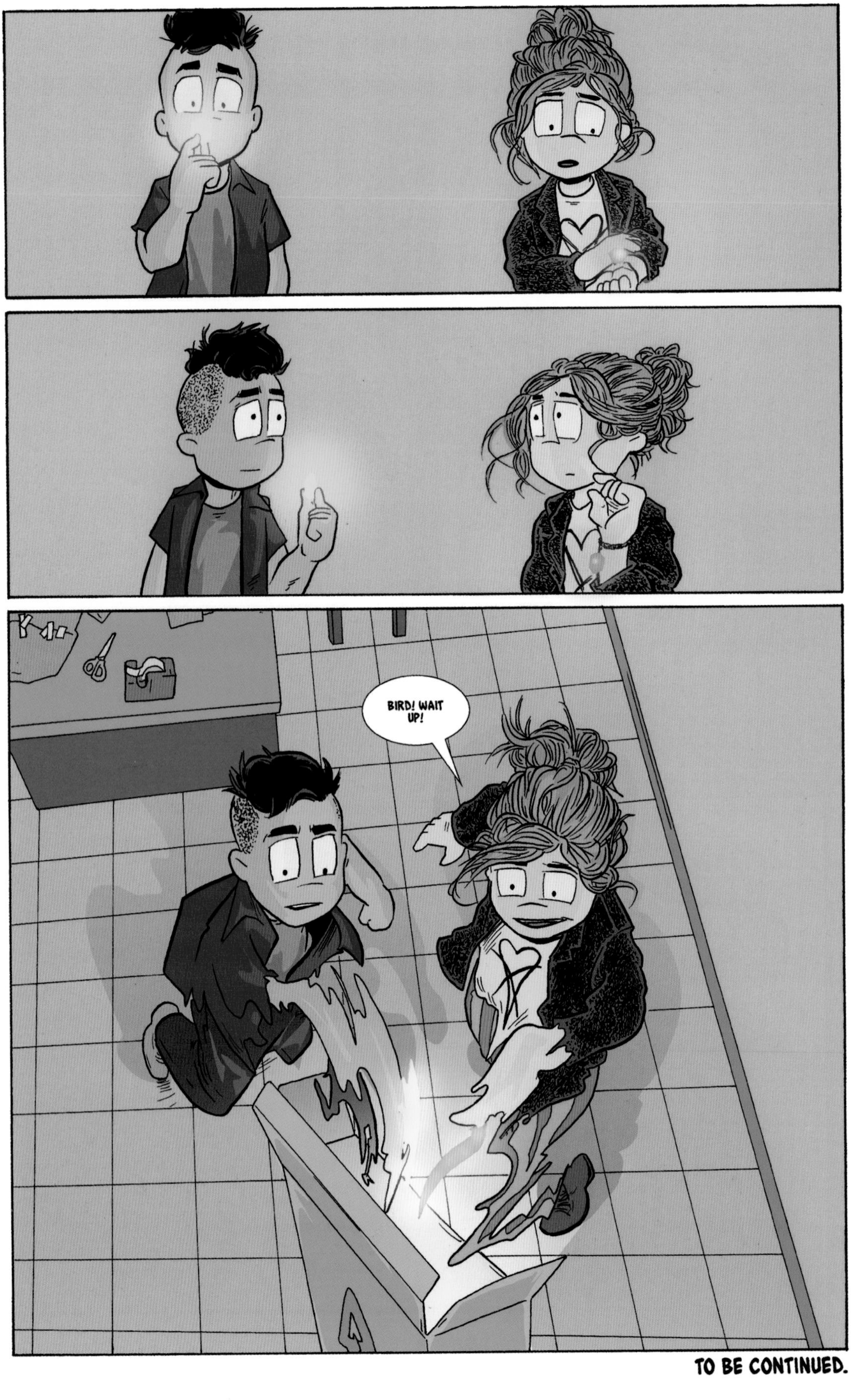
BIRD! WAIT UP!

TO BE CONTINUED.

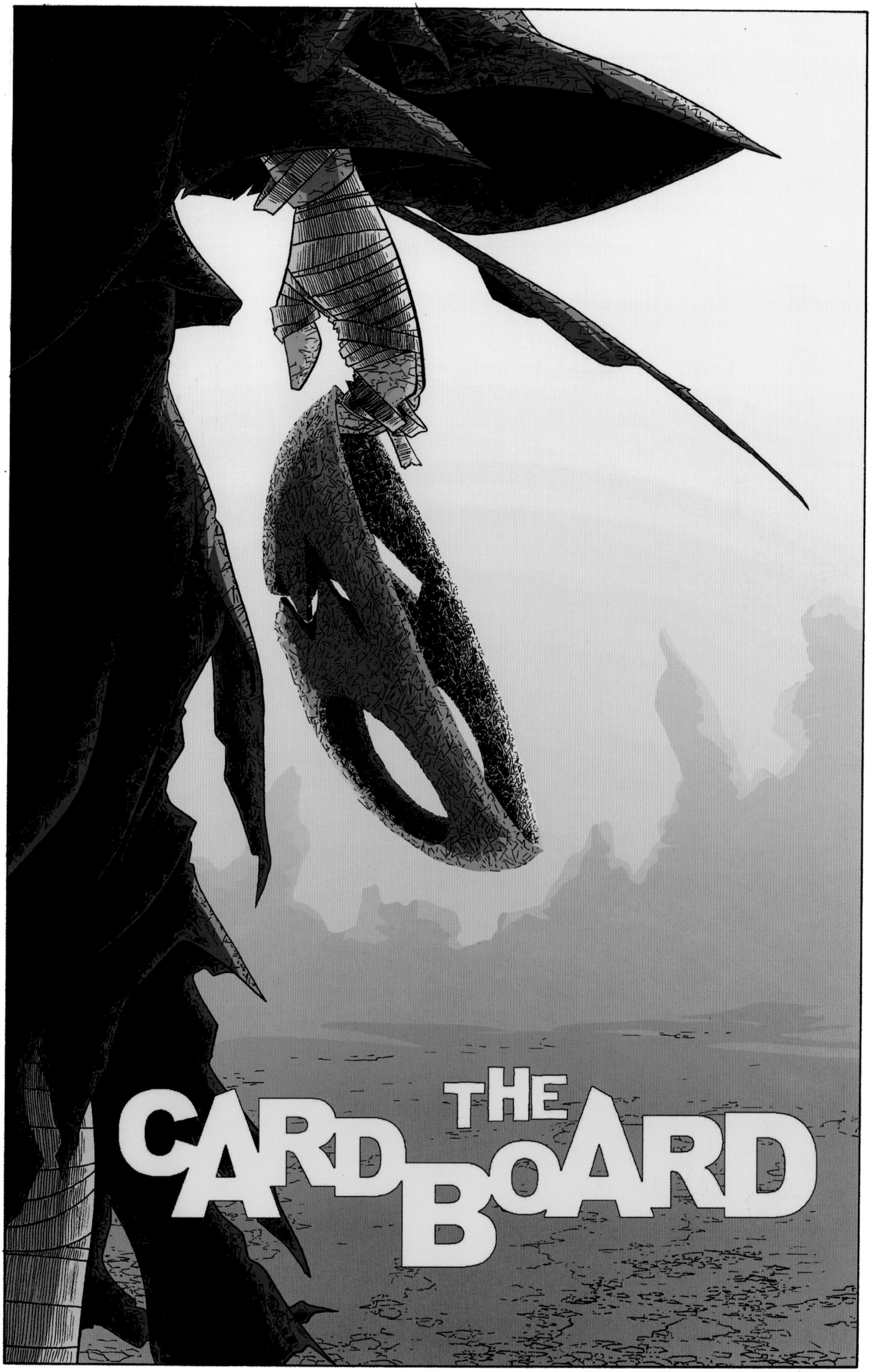
THE
CARDBOARD

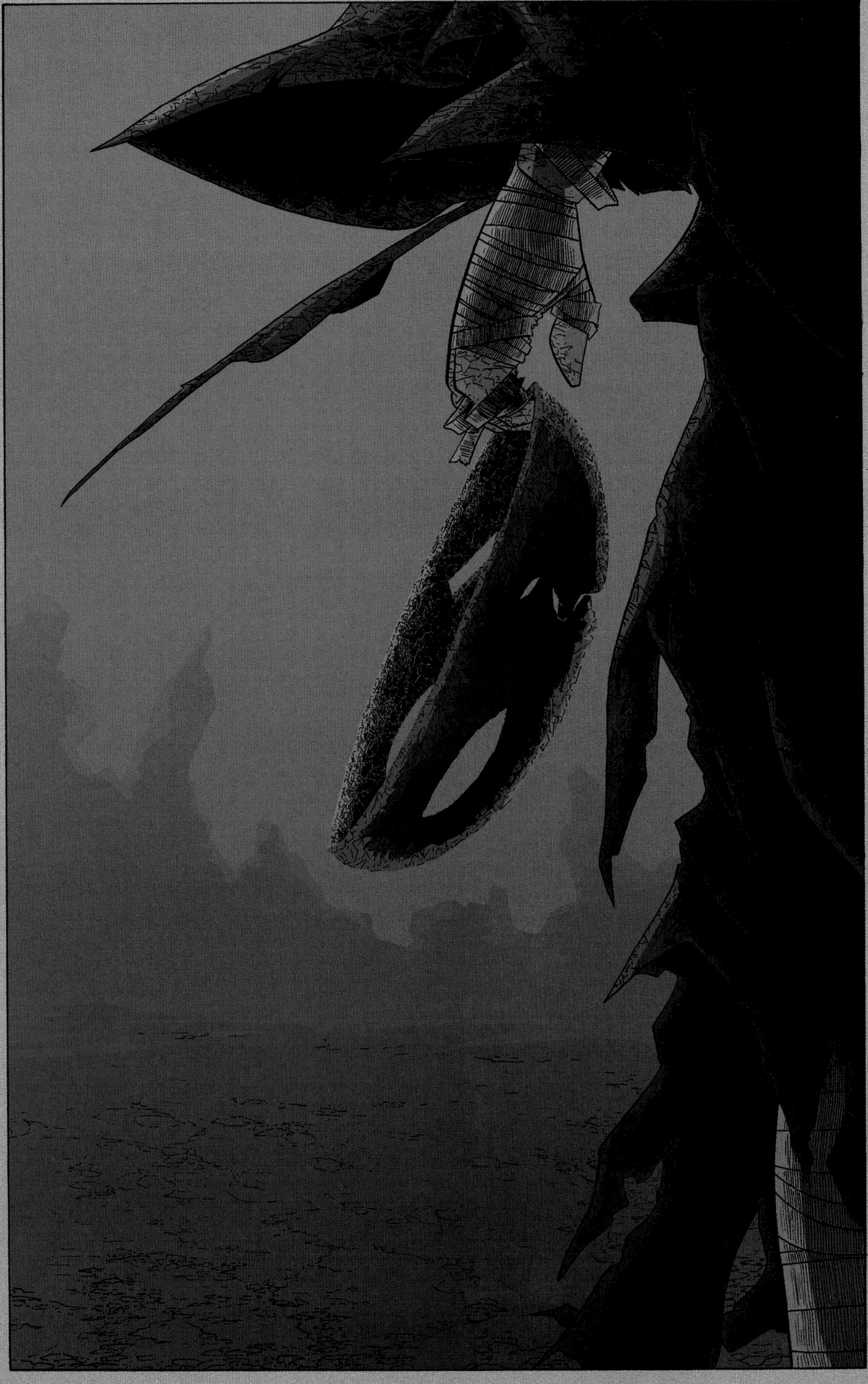

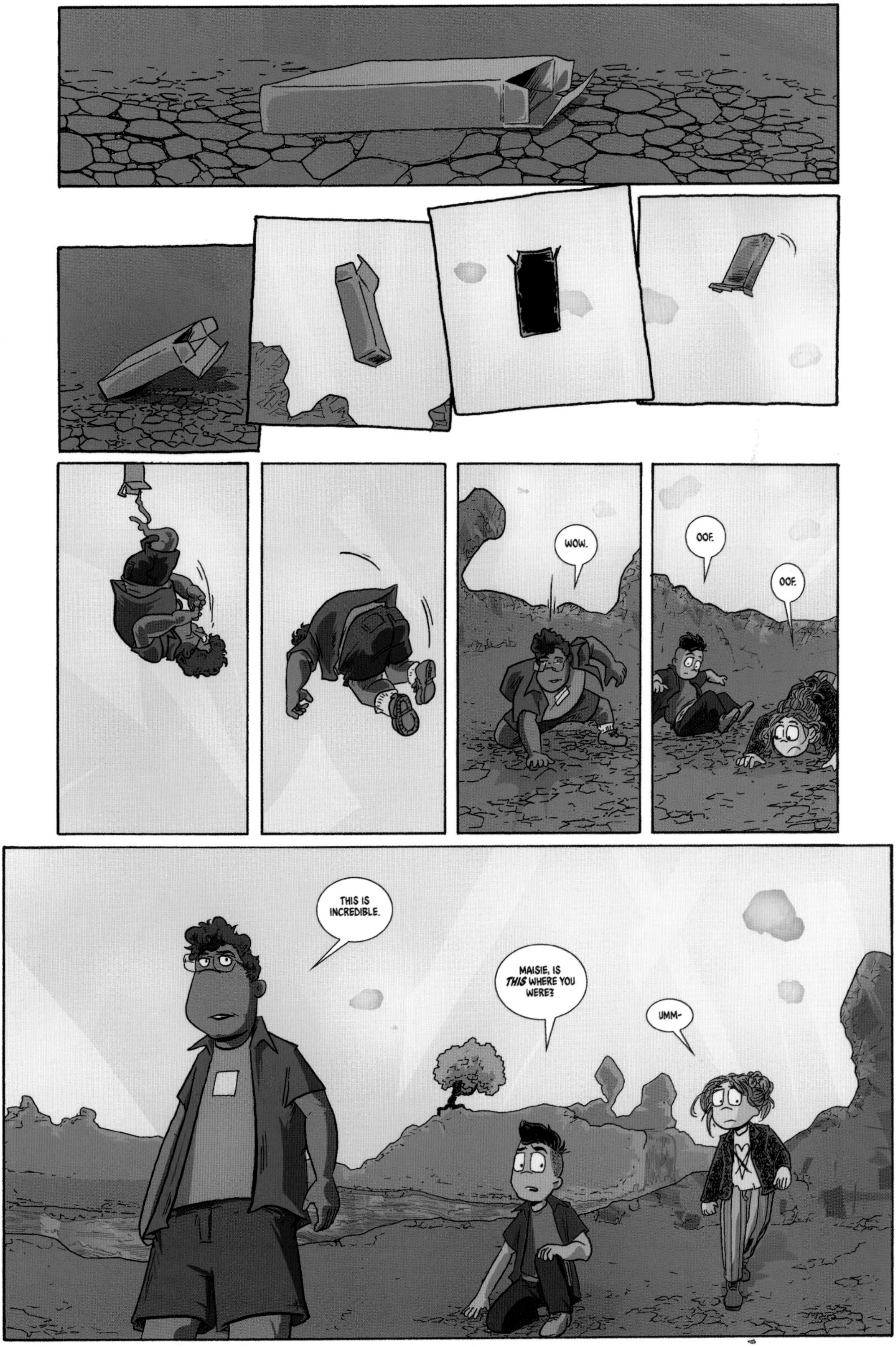
WOW.
OOF.
OOF.
THIS IS INCREDIBLE.
MAISIE, IS THIS WHERE YOU WERE?
UMM-

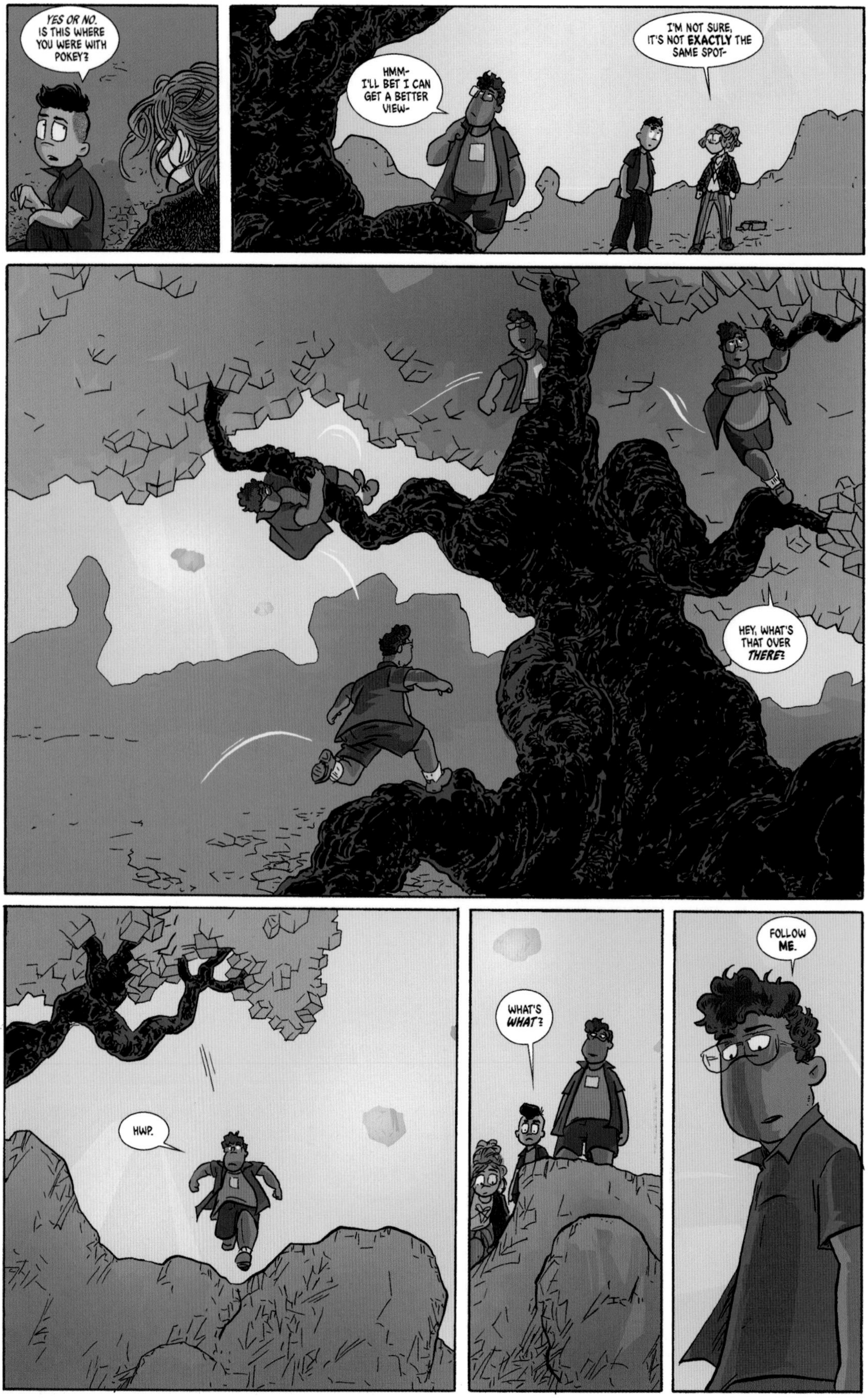
YES OR NO. IS THIS WHERE YOU WERE WITH POKEY?
I'M NOT SURE, IT'S NOT EXACTLY THE SAME SPOT-
HMM- I'LL BET I CAN GET A BETTER VIEW-
HEY, WHAT'S THAT OVER THERE?
HWP.
WHAT'S WHAT?
FOLLOW ME.

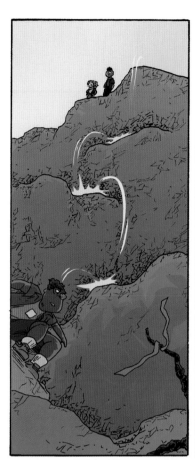

HMM.

YUP, THIS IS ONE OF THE STRANDS OF **PAPER** FROM POKEY'S HAT.

THIS IS **DEFINITELY** WHERE YOU GUYS WERE.

I THINK— I **THINK** THIS IS THE BOX WE CAME HERE THROUGH.

INTERESTING—

I GUESS IF A BOX GETS **WRECKED** IN OUR WORLD THEN IT CAN'T **HOLD** ITSELF TOGETHER HERE.

IT'S LIKE IT'S TURNING **BACK** INTO PULP!

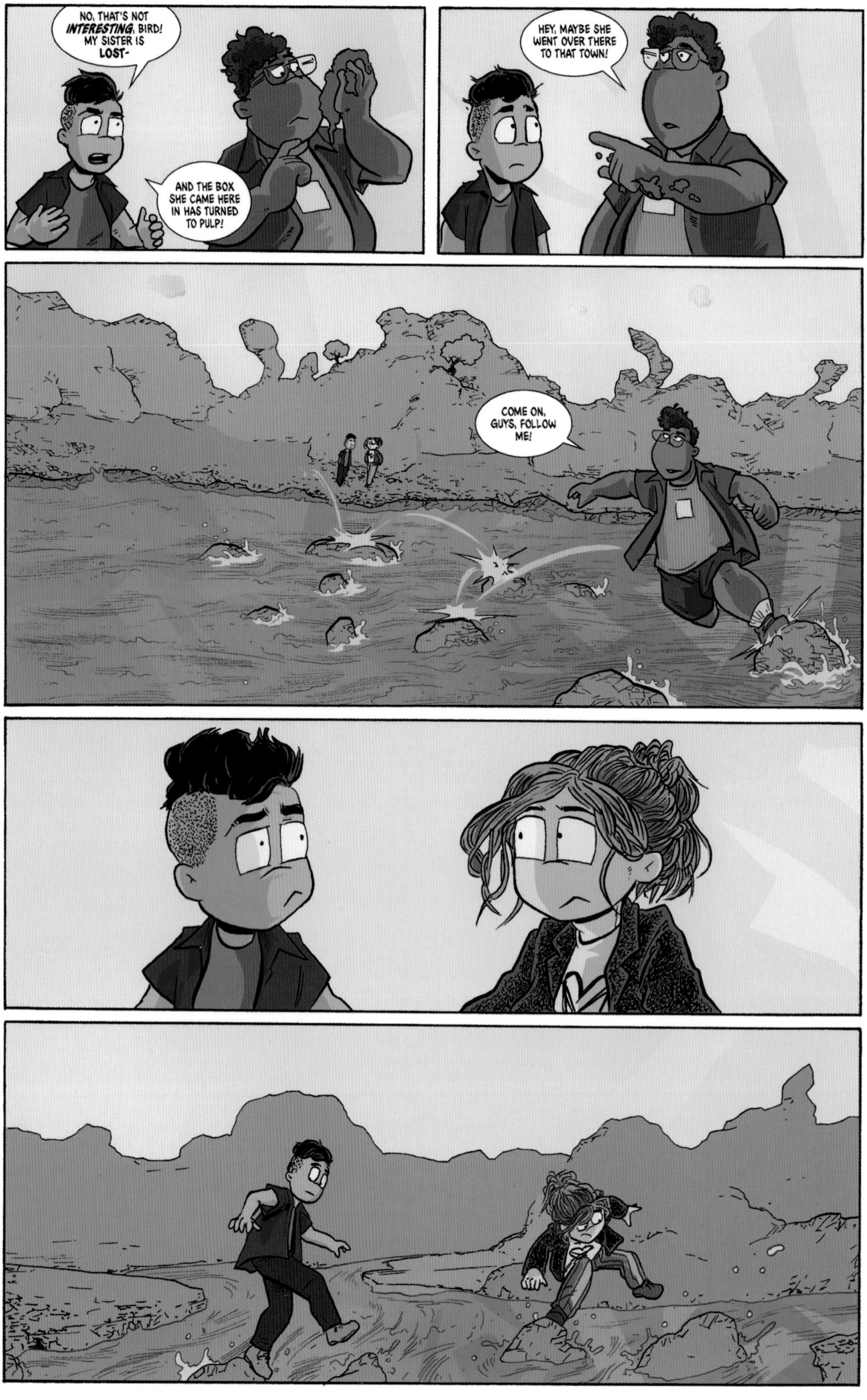
NO, THAT'S NOT *INTERESTING*, BIRD! MY SISTER IS **LOST**-
AND THE BOX SHE CAME HERE IN HAS TURNED TO PULP!
HEY, MAYBE SHE WENT OVER THERE TO THAT TOWN!
COME ON, GUYS, FOLLOW ME!

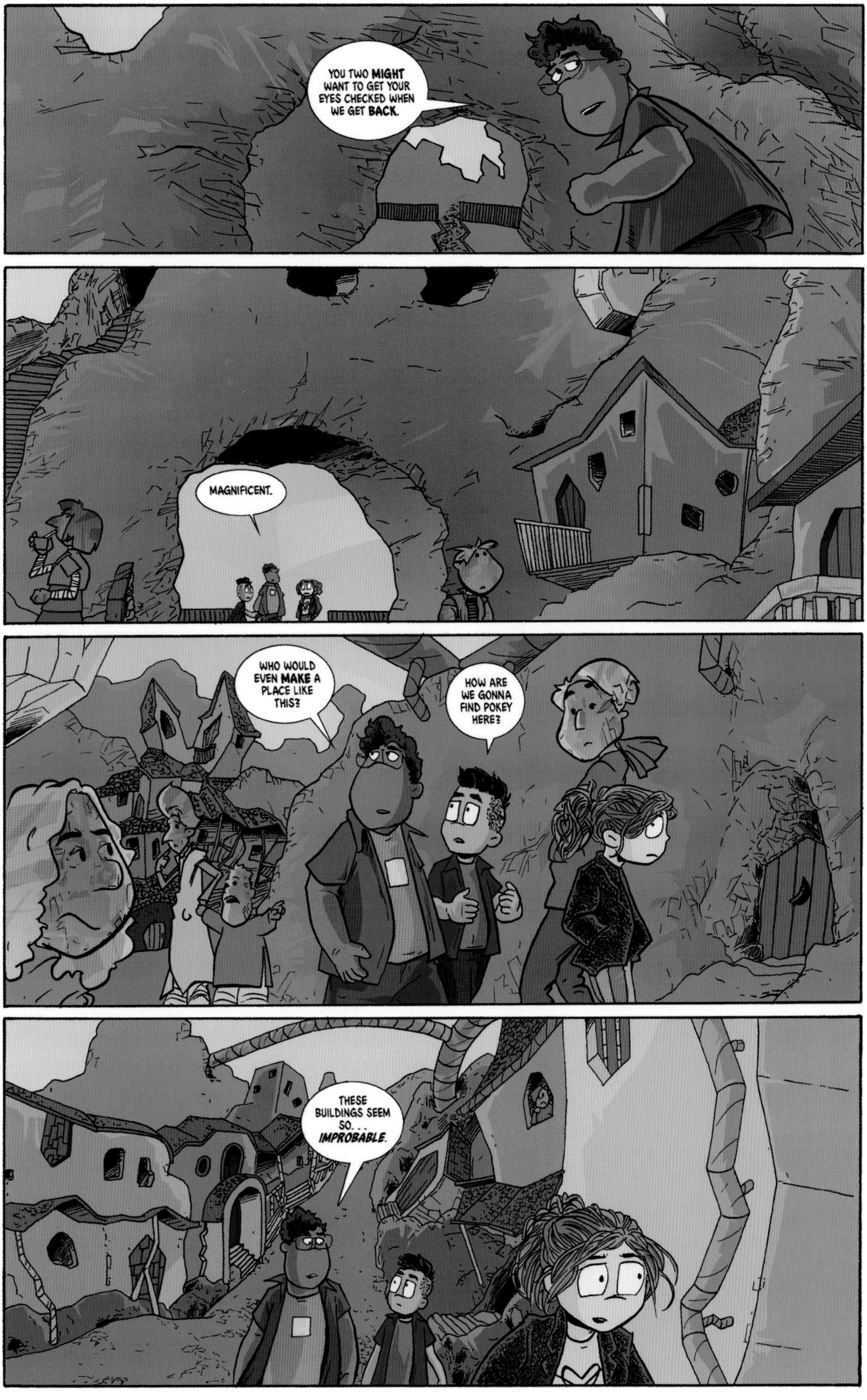
YOU TWO MIGHT WANT TO GET YOUR EYES CHECKED WHEN WE GET BACK.
MAGNIFICENT.
WHO WOULD EVEN MAKE A PLACE LIKE THIS?
HOW ARE WE GONNA FIND POKEY HERE?
THESE BUILDINGS SEEM SO. . . IMPROBABLE.

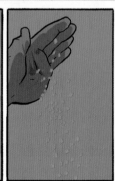

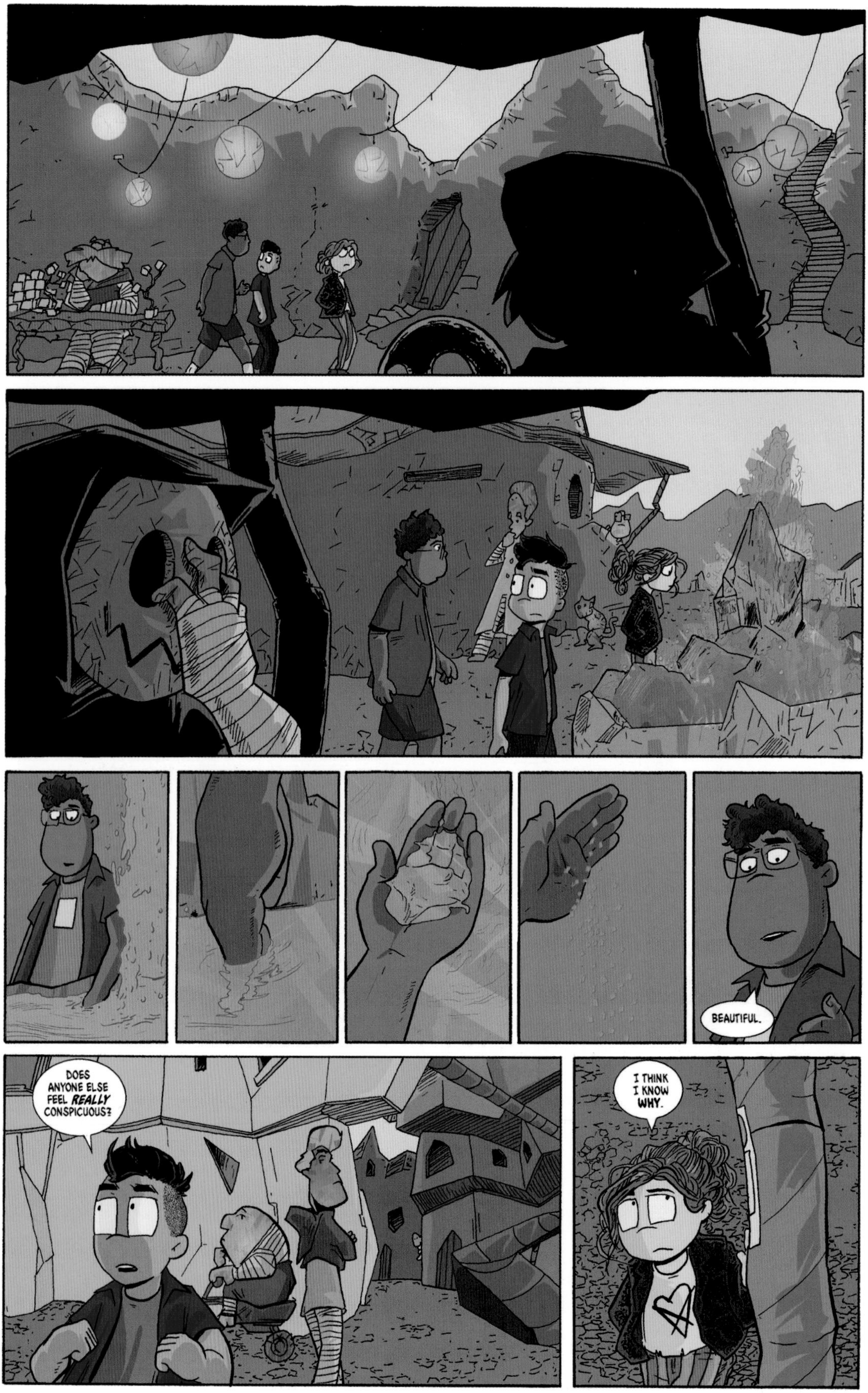
BEAUTIFUL.
DOES ANYONE ELSE FEEL REALLY CONSPICUOUS?
I THINK I KNOW WHY.

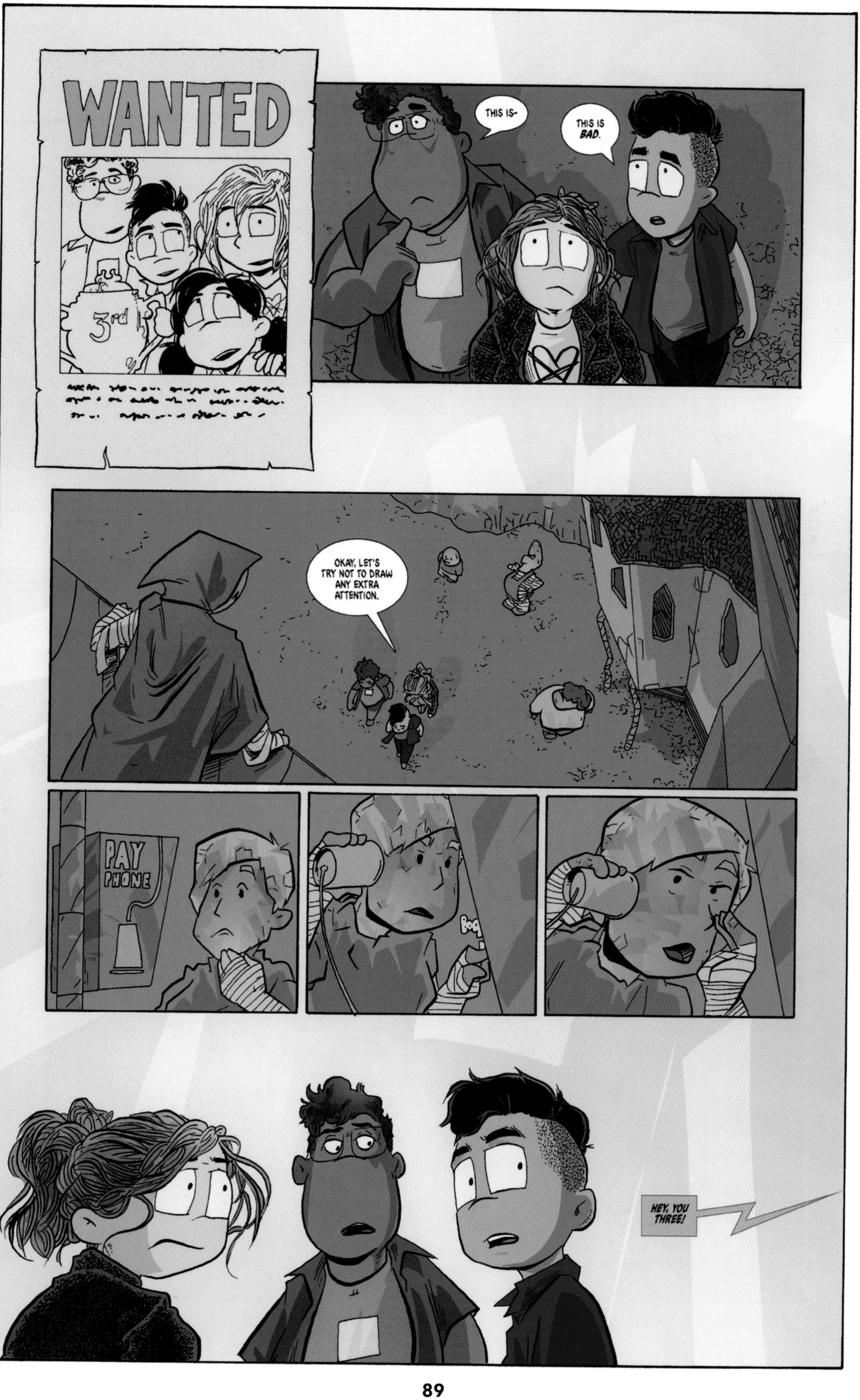
WANTED
3rd
THIS IS-
THIS IS BAD.
OKAY, LET'S TRY NOT TO DRAW ANY EXTRA ATTENTION.
PAY PHONE
HEY, YOU THREE!

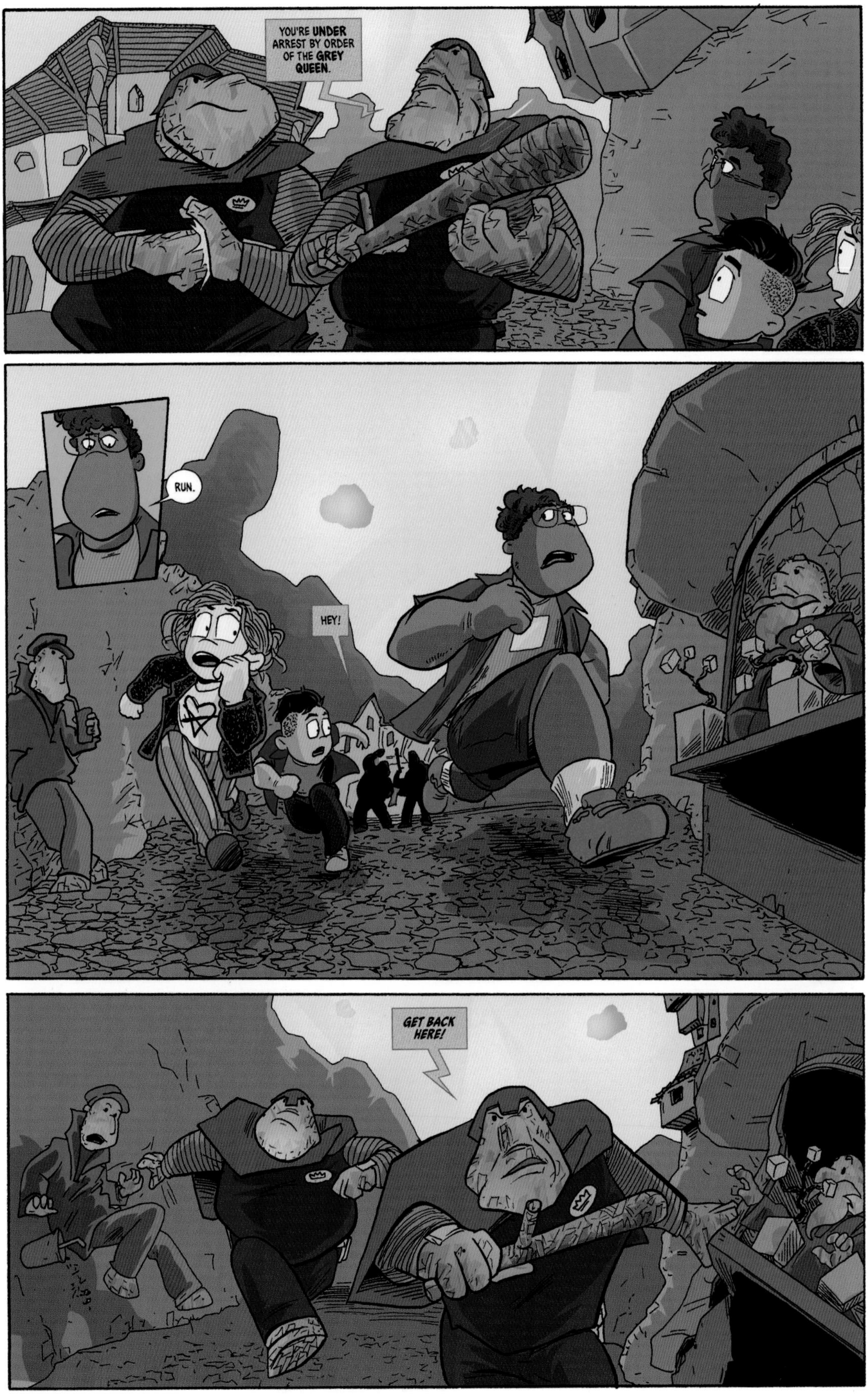

YOU'RE UNDER ARREST BY ORDER OF THE GREY QUEEN.
RUN.
HEY!
GET BACK HERE!

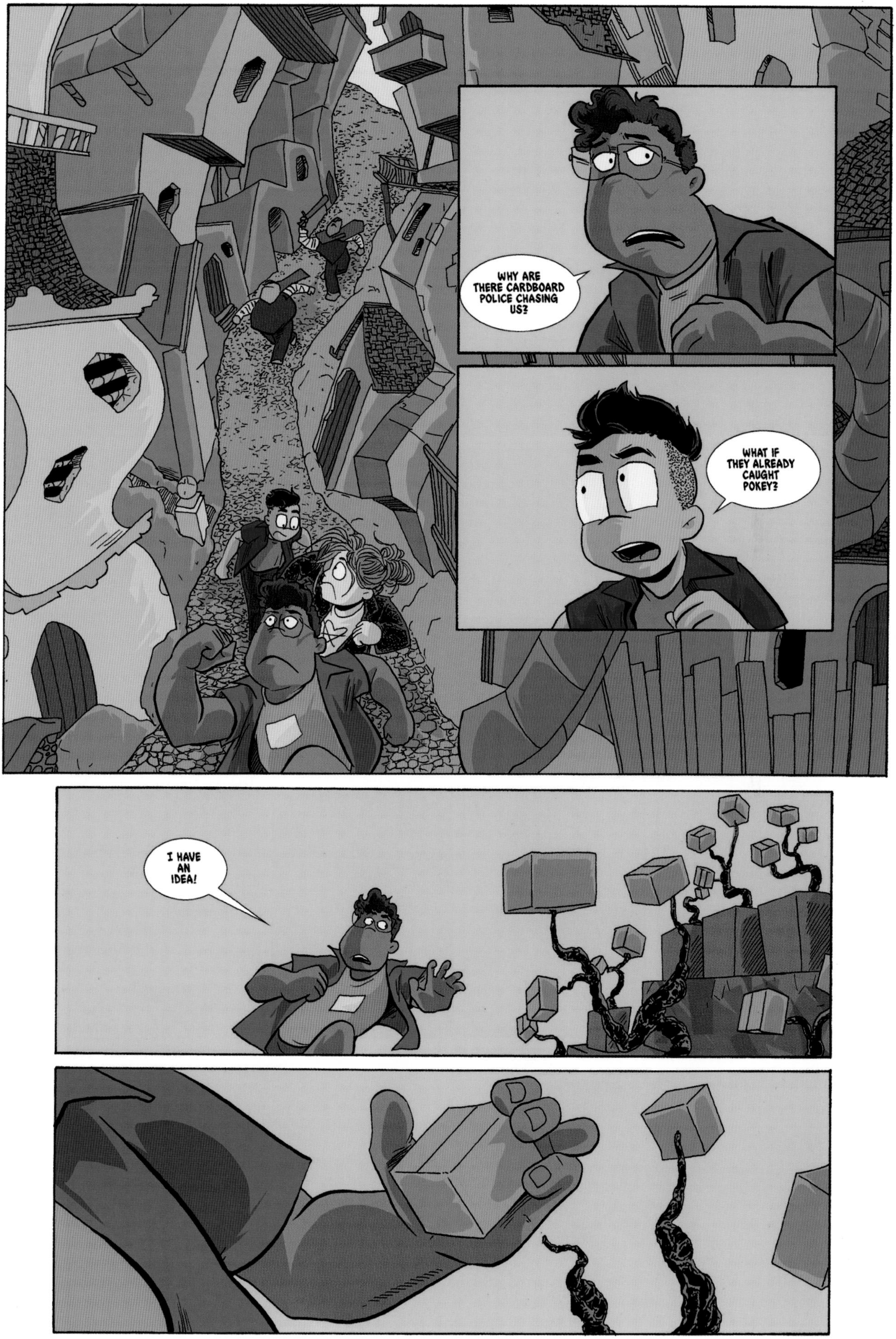
WHY ARE THERE CARDBOARD POLICE CHASING US?
WHAT IF THEY ALREADY CAUGHT POKEY?
I HAVE AN IDEA!

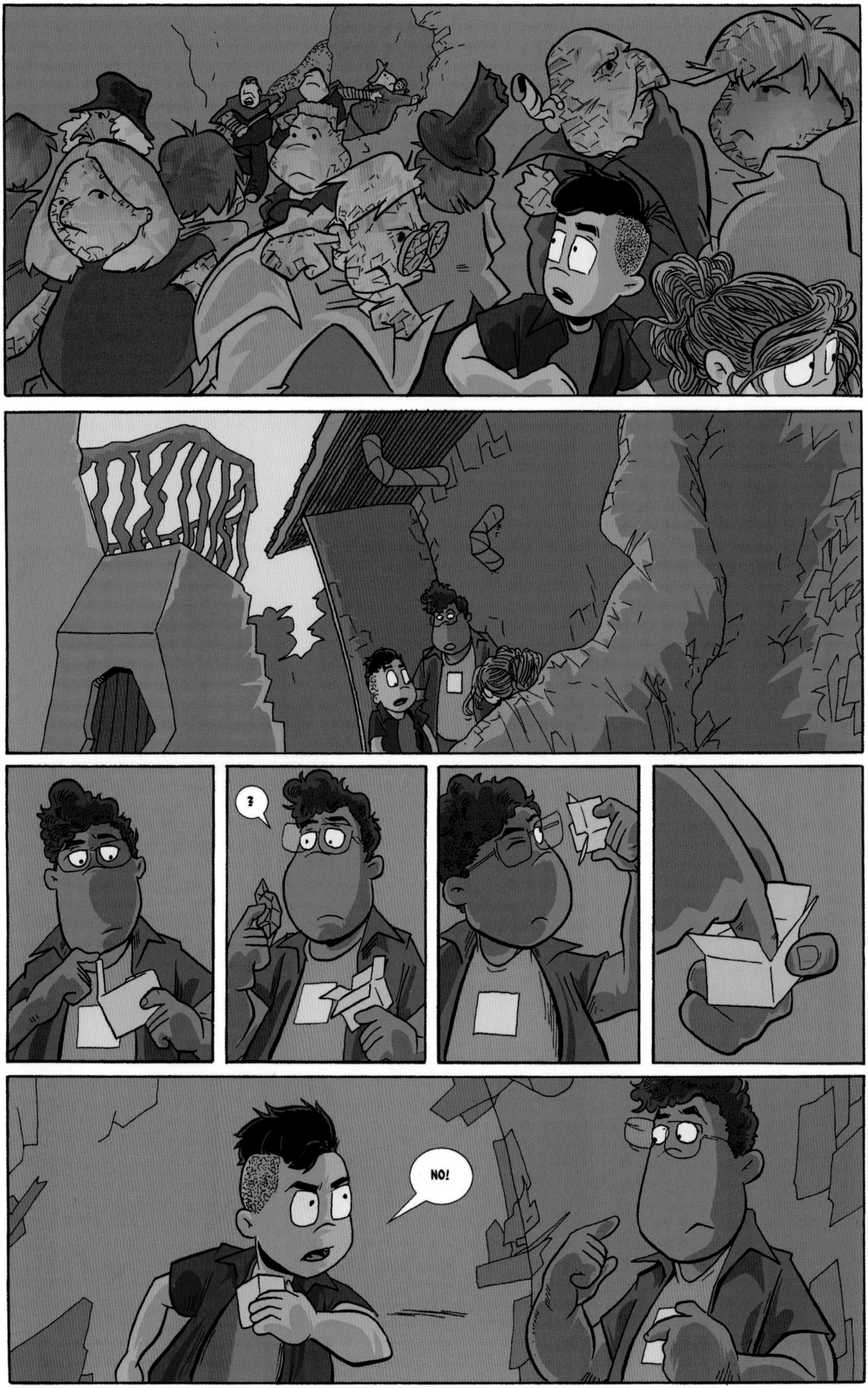
?
NO!

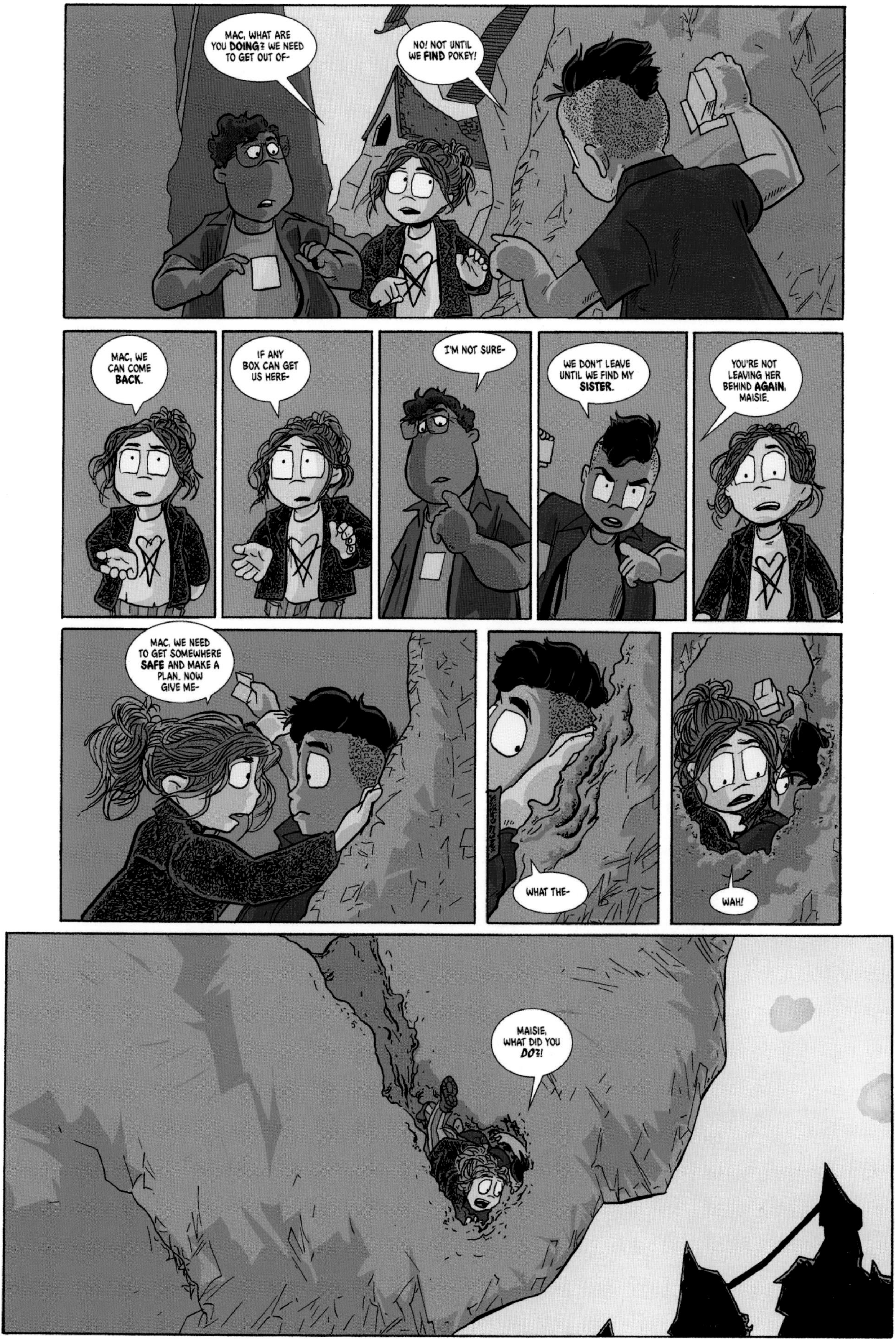
MAC, WHAT ARE YOU DOING? WE NEED TO GET OUT OF-
NO! NOT UNTIL WE FIND POKEY!
MAC, WE CAN COME BACK.
IF ANY BOX CAN GET US HERE-
I'M NOT SURE-
WE DON'T LEAVE UNTIL WE FIND MY SISTER.
YOU'RE NOT LEAVING HER BEHIND AGAIN, MAISIE.
MAC, WE NEED TO GET SOMEWHERE SAFE AND MAKE A PLAN. NOW GIVE ME-
WHAT THE-
WAH!
MAISIE, WHAT DID YOU DO?!

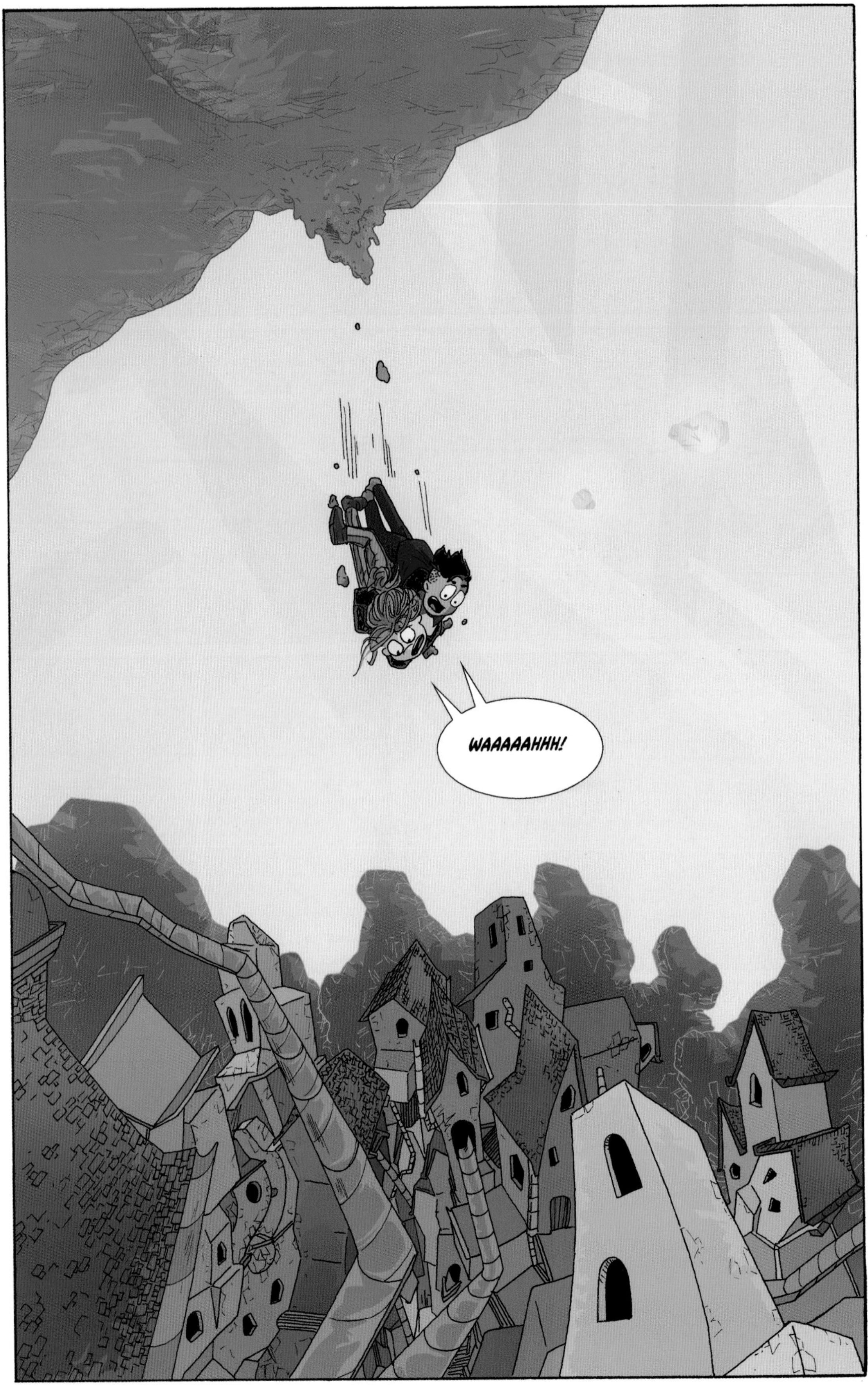
WAAAAAHHH!

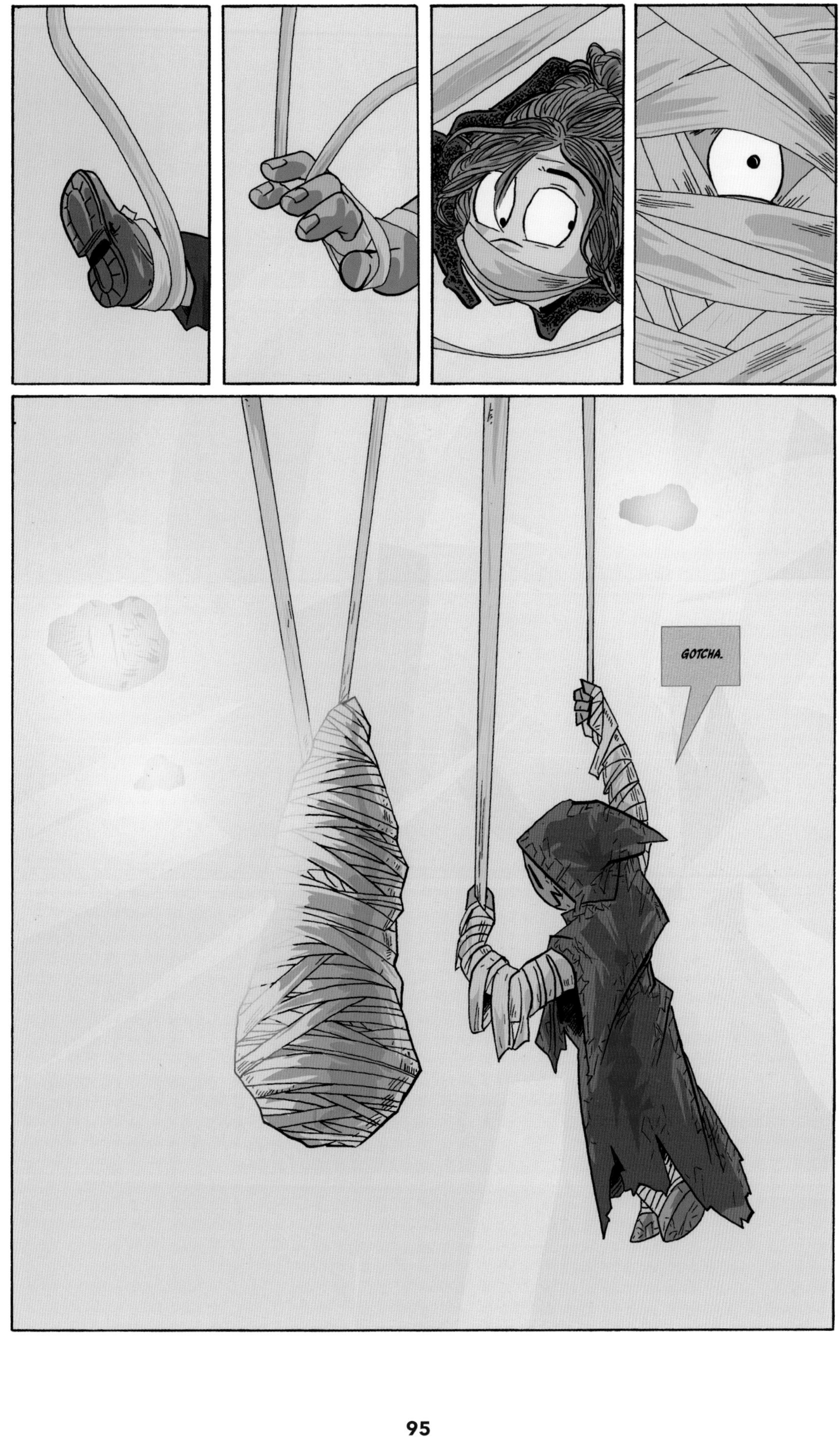
GOTCHA.

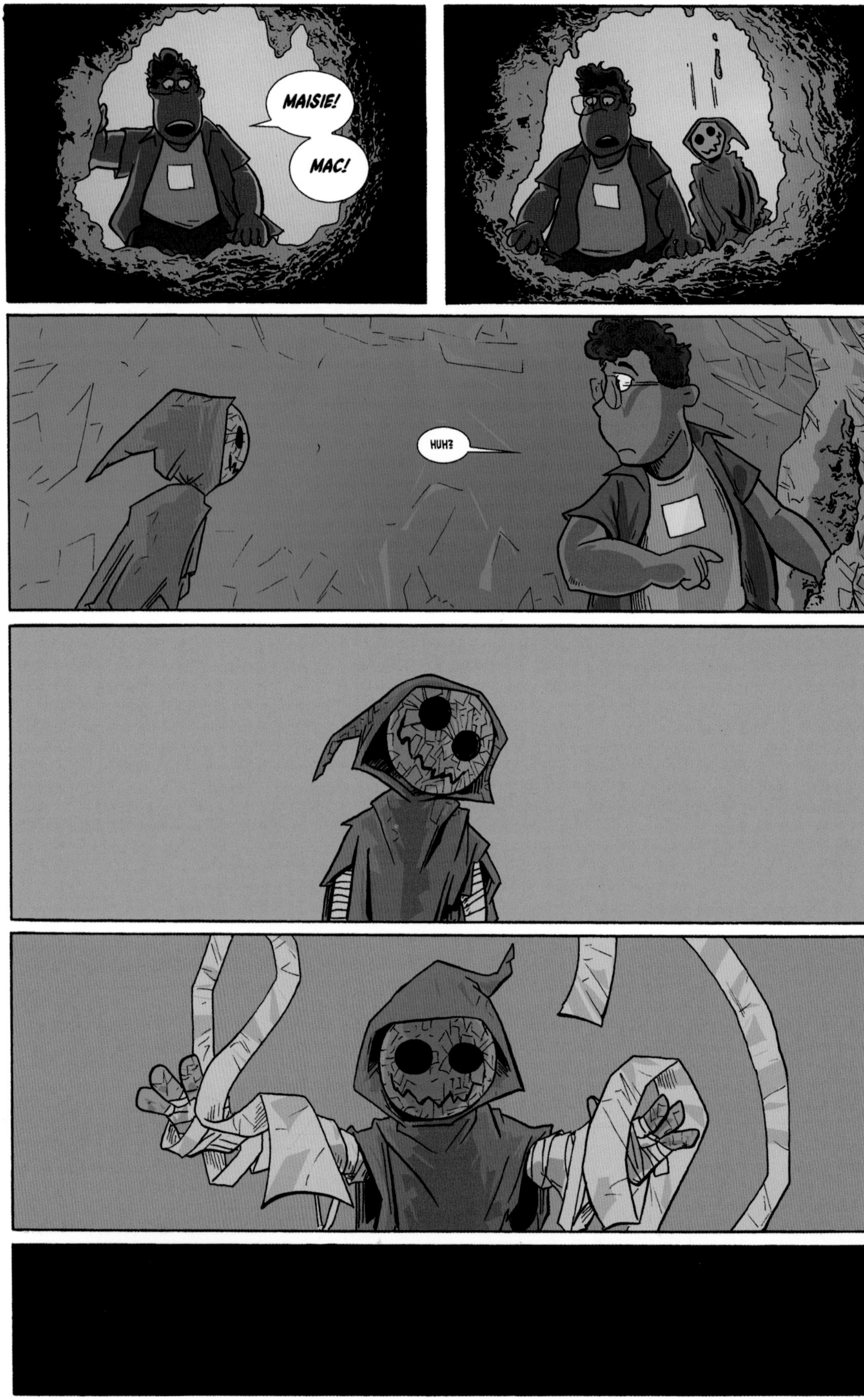
MAISIE!
MAC!
HUH?

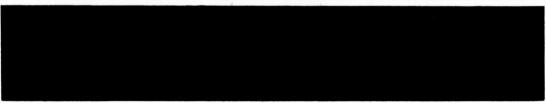

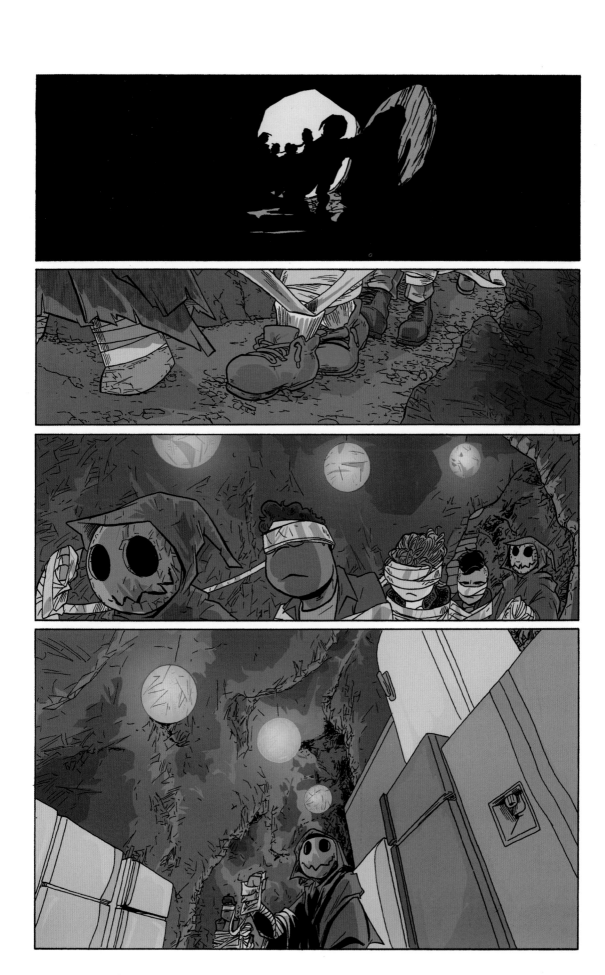

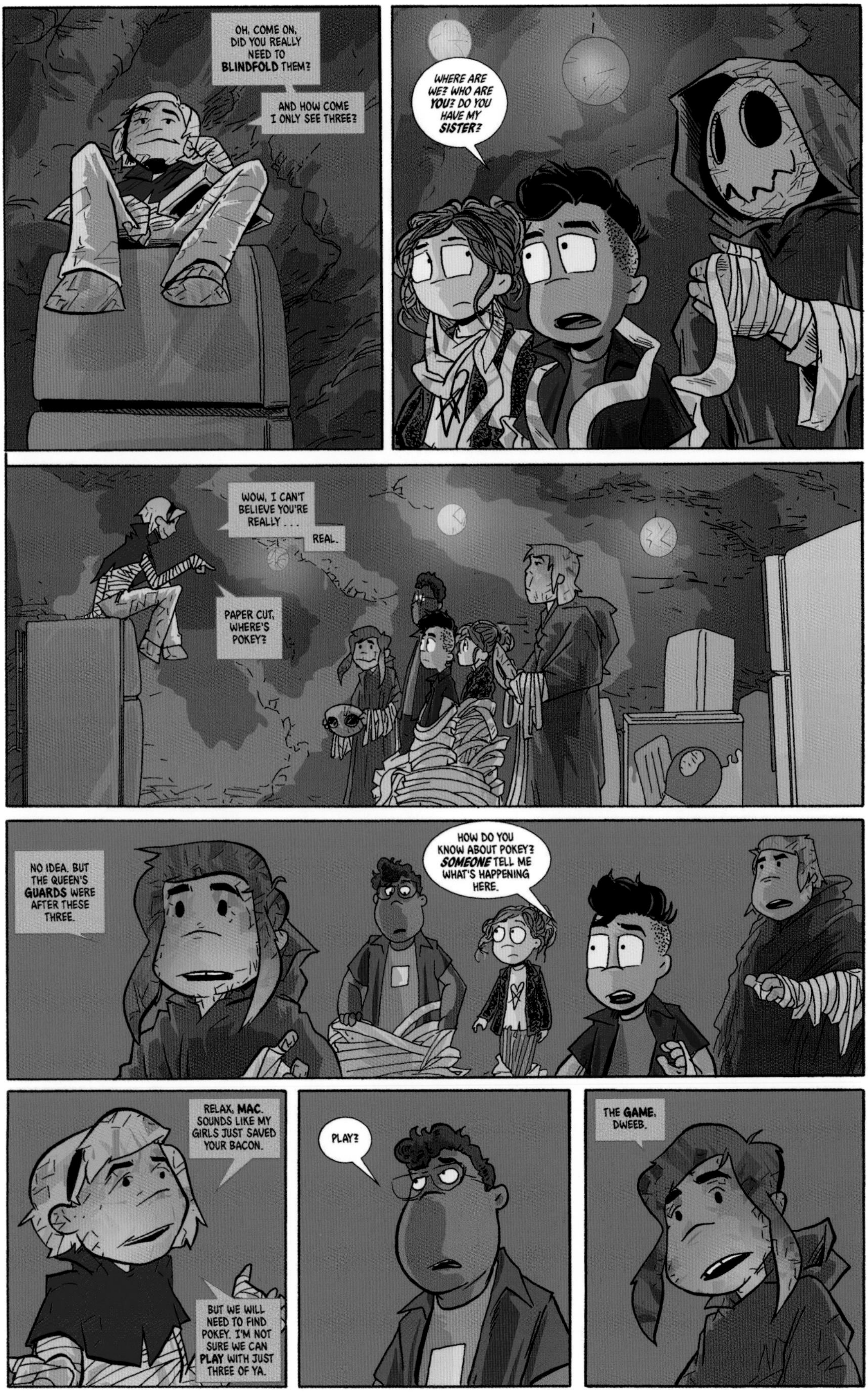

OH, COME ON. DID YOU REALLY NEED TO BLINDFOLD THEM?
AND HOW COME I ONLY SEE THREE?
WHERE ARE WE? WHO ARE YOU? DO YOU HAVE MY SISTER?
WOW, I CAN'T BELIEVE YOU'RE REALLY . . .
REAL.
PAPER CUT, WHERE'S POKEY?
NO IDEA. BUT THE QUEEN'S GUARDS WERE AFTER THESE THREE.
HOW DO YOU KNOW ABOUT POKEY? SOMEONE TELL ME WHAT'S HAPPENING HERE.
RELAX, MAC. SOUNDS LIKE MY GIRLS JUST SAVED YOUR BACON.
BUT WE WILL NEED TO FIND POKEY. I'M NOT SURE WE CAN PLAY WITH JUST THREE OF YA.
PLAY?
THE GAME, DWEEB.

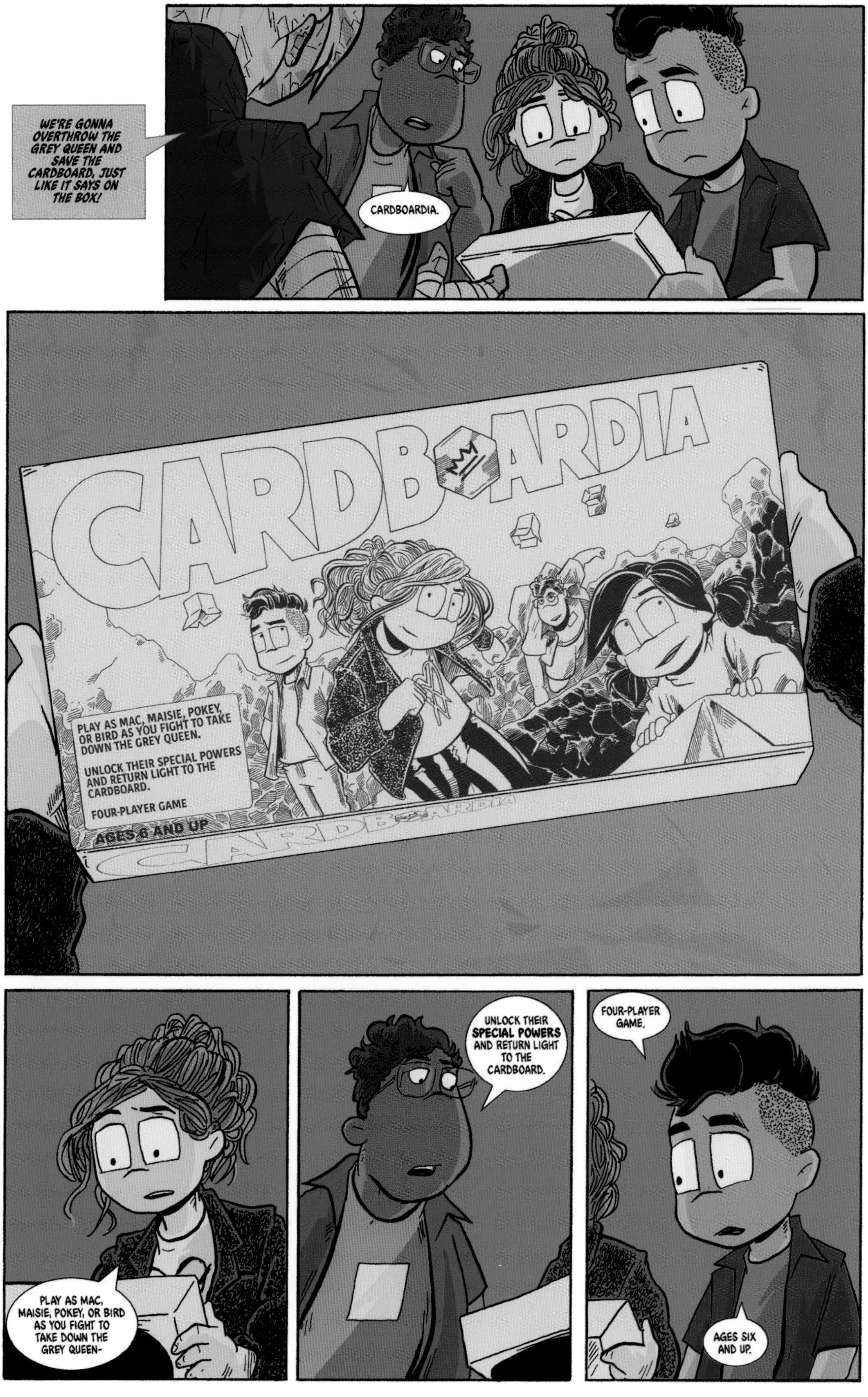
WE'RE GONNA OVERTHROW THE GREY QUEEN AND SAVE THE CARDBOARD, JUST LIKE IT SAYS ON THE BOX!
CARDBOARDIA.
CARDBOARDIA
PLAY AS MAC, MAISIE, POKEY, OR BIRD AS YOU FIGHT TO TAKE DOWN THE GREY QUEEN.
UNLOCK THEIR SPECIAL POWERS AND RETURN LIGHT TO THE CARDBOARD.
FOUR-PLAYER GAME
AGES 6 AND UP
CARDBOARDIA
PLAY AS MAC, MAISIE, POKEY, OR BIRD AS YOU FIGHT TO TAKE DOWN THE GREY QUEEN-
UNLOCK THEIR SPECIAL POWERS AND RETURN LIGHT TO THE CARDBOARD.
FOUR-PLAYER GAME.
AGES SIX AND UP.

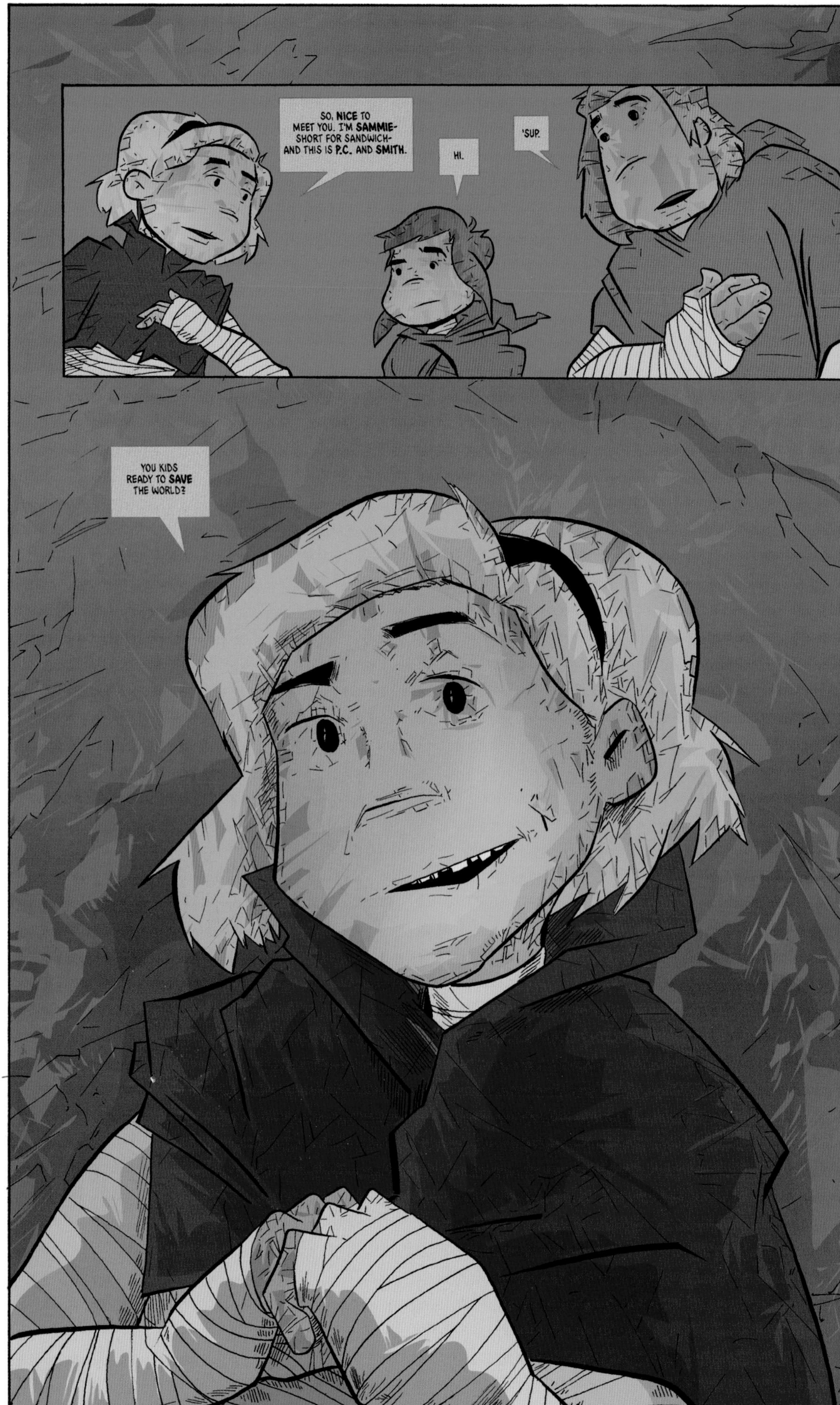
SO, NICE TO MEET YOU. I'M SAMMIE- SHORT FOR SANDWICH- AND THIS IS P.C. AND SMITH.
HI.
'SUP.
YOU KIDS READY TO SAVE THE WORLD?

TO BE CONTINUED.

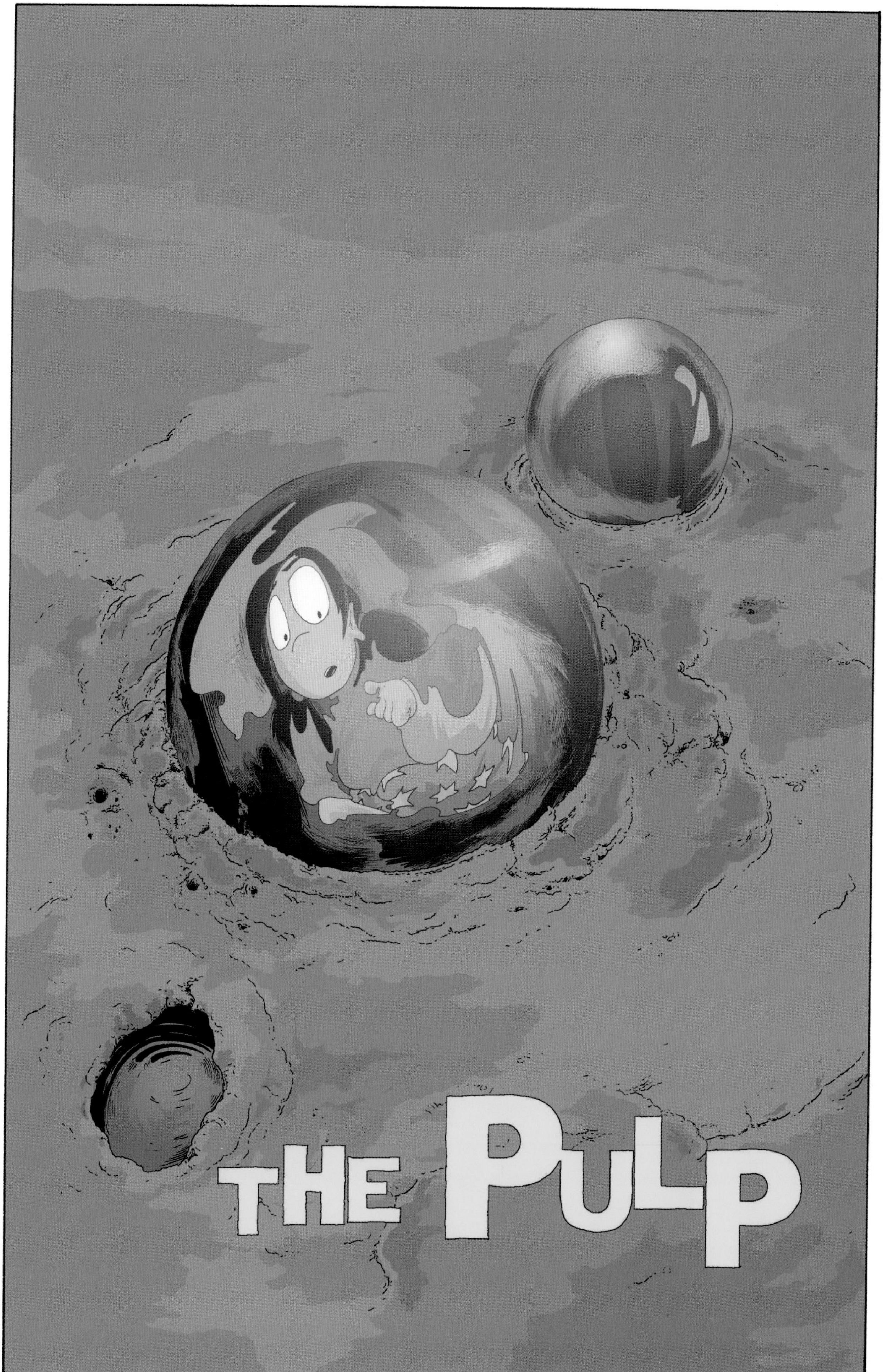
THE PULP

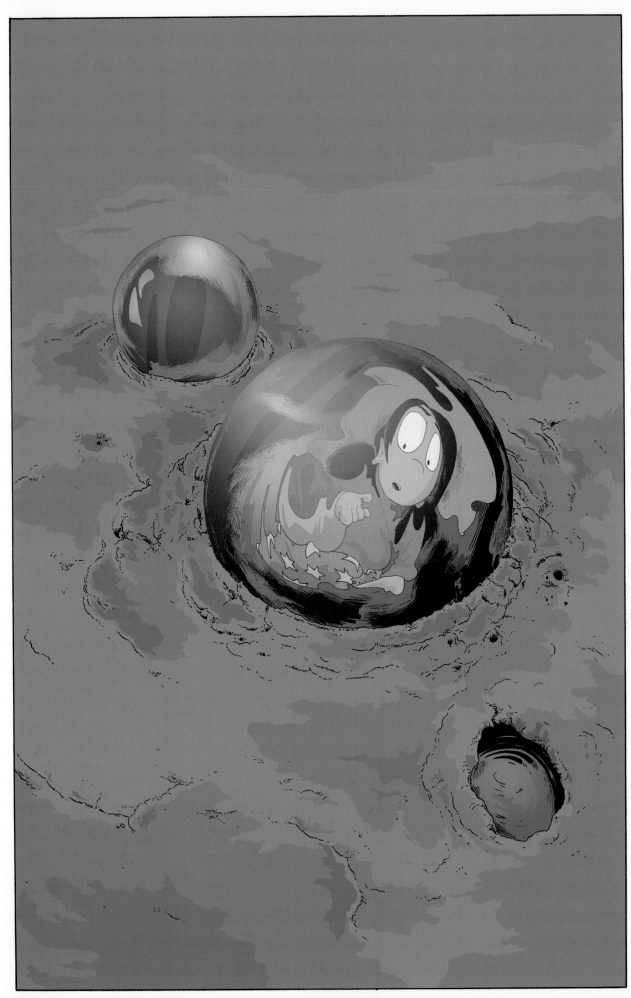

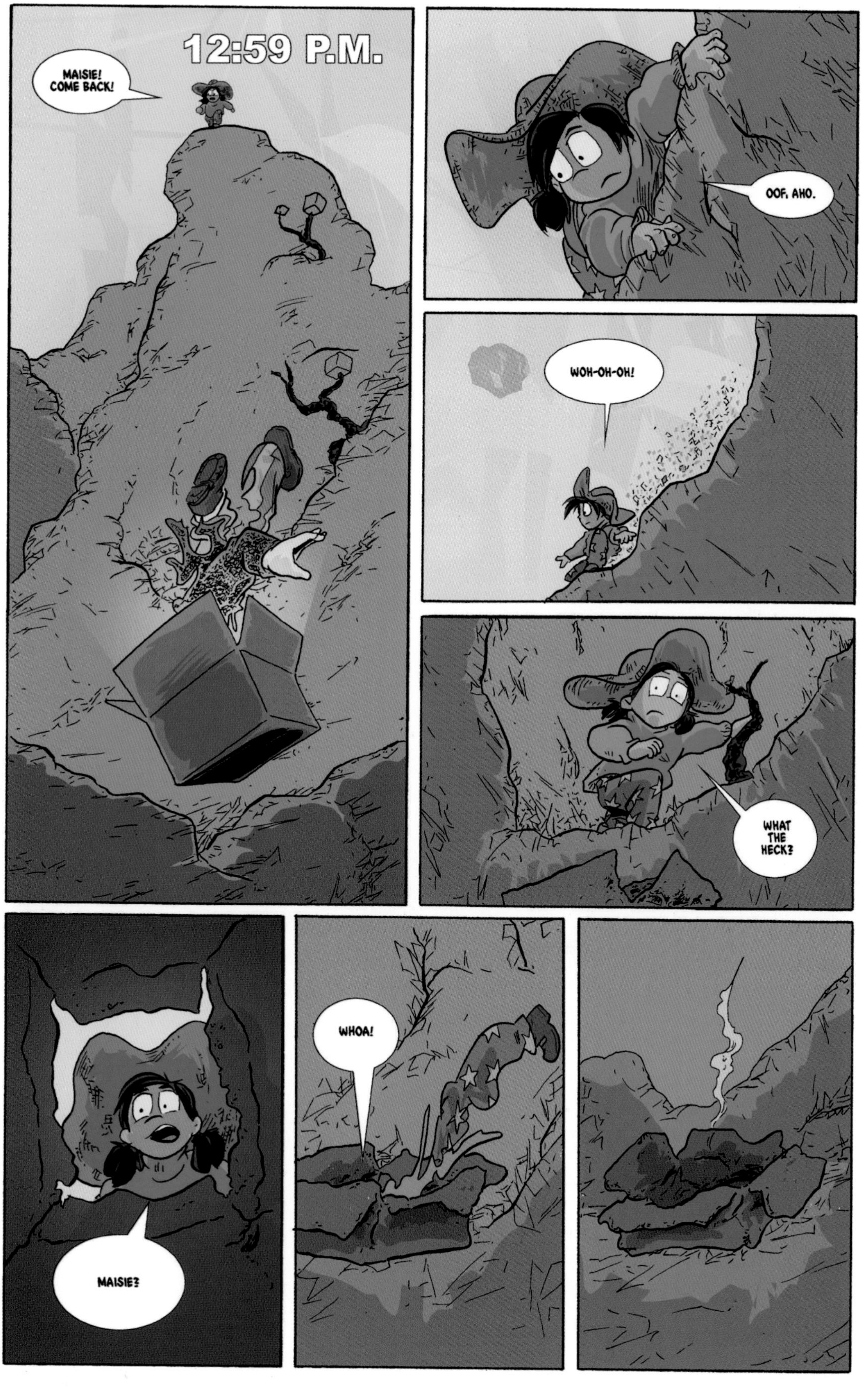
12:59 P.M.
MAISIE! COME BACK!
OOF, AHO.
WOH-OH-OH!
WHAT THE HECK?
MAISIE?
WHOA!

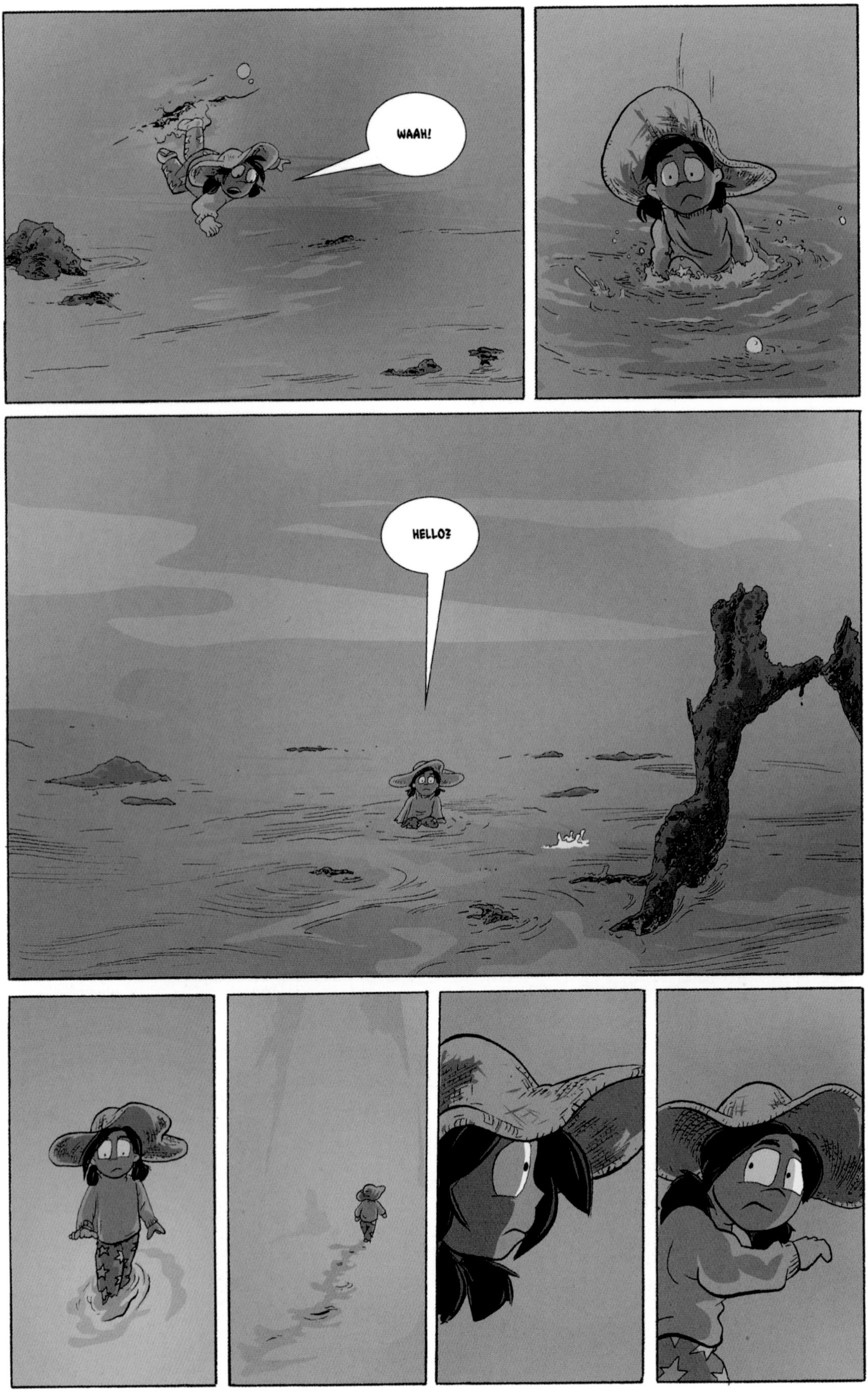
WAAH!
HELLO?

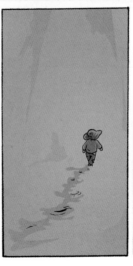

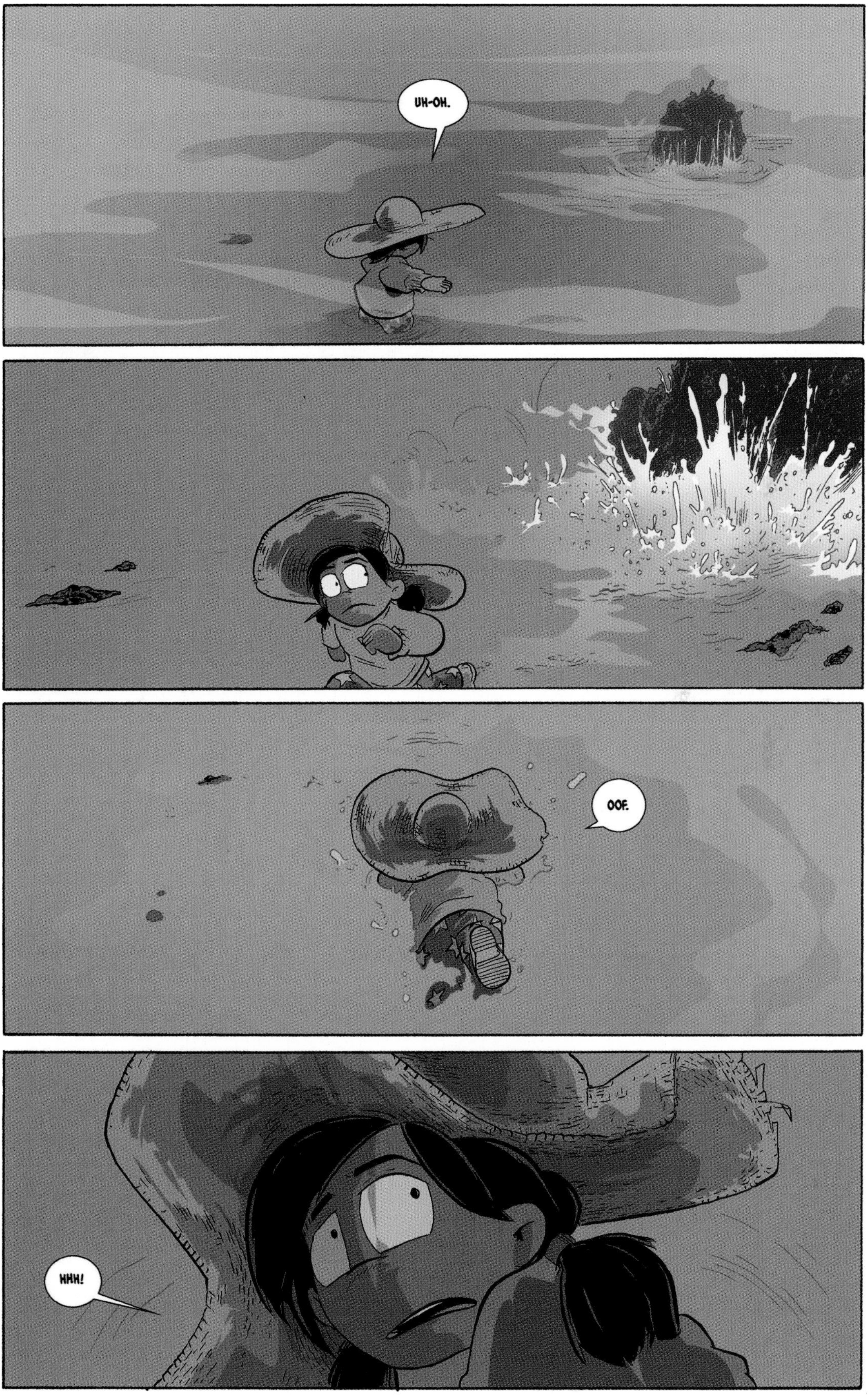
UH-OH.
OOF.
HHH!

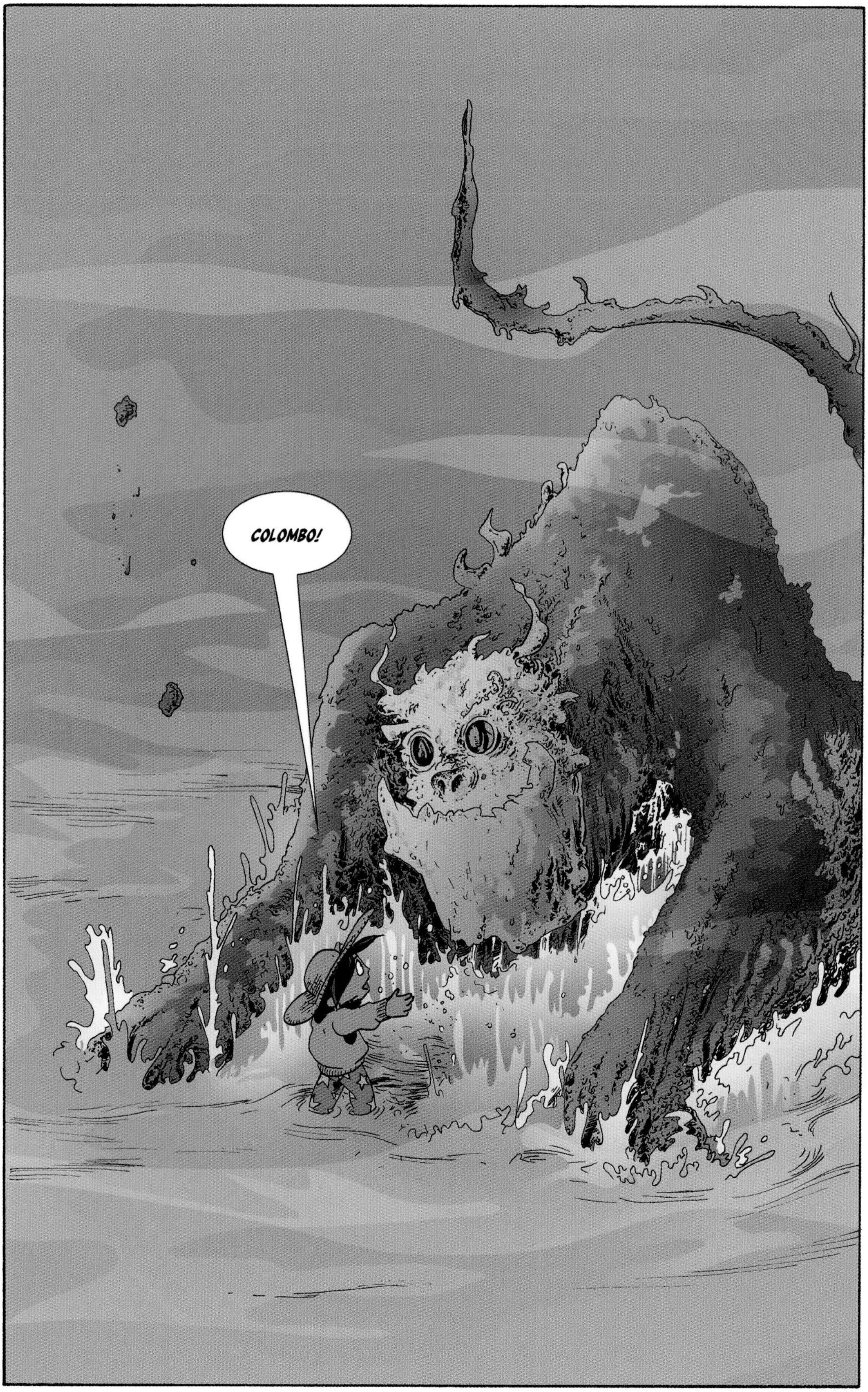
COLOMBO!

TO BE CONTINUED.

OLD CHATHAM BOX FACTORY:
GRAND TOUR WALL OF FAME

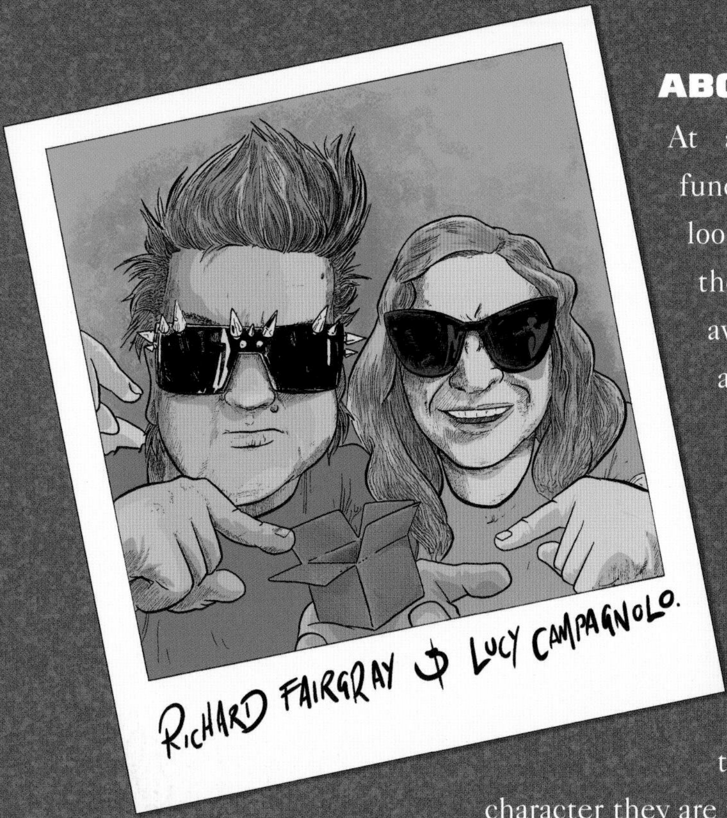
RICHARD FAIRGRAY & LUCY CAMPAGNOLO.

ABOUT THE AUTHORS

At any party, soiree, festival, funeral, or fancy dress ball, if you look in the kitchen, away from the excitement and the noise, away from the party whistles and wailing crowds, that's where you'll find Lucy and Richard. They'll be deep in a conversation about the state of the world, the inconsistencies in McDonald's from one country to the next or the adventures of some new character they are forming in the space between their brains. They'll let you join in, but you'll probably get lost at the third deep dive into the psychology of Crash Bandicoot.

It isn't that they can't engage with the party going on outside (they both have great party tricks: Lucy can lick her elbow, and Richard once ate eight pounds of melted gummi bears in one day), it's just that they are in the middle of something. They're making up something new and that is more exciting to them than anything else. Also, if you haven't completed the secret Skull Level on top of the Nitro Crates in Crash 2 then how do you even have time to party?

What first bonded this unlikely pair was their shared determination to find adventure. If someone walks into the room with a treasure map or a quest, or even just a recommendation of a totally dope local slide, Richard and Lucy will leave that kitchen without a second thought. The math is simple, if something seems like it will be a better story in the movies of their lives then Richard and Lucy will do it.

Lucy is a writer looking for the stories of people who she hasn't seen stories about before. Richard likes ghosts and distortions of the world around him.

ACKNOWLEDGMENTS

RICHARD knows this book wouldn't have been possible without the support of many people. Primarily Lucy, who was the first person he told the idea to and who immediately saw the potential in the world on the other side of the box. Cardboardia has been broken down and rebuilt a thousand times in the five years since the word first popped into Richard's head and Lucy became the engineer who saw which pieces did or did not fit.

Jim, Kenealy, Charlie, RE, Ray, Alex, Paul, Other Paul, Joe, and Rebekah have all been there to listen as I've tried to hold it all together and as I've drawn some of the hardest scenery of my life (so far). Their excitement has kept me going.

Barbra and Bryant and the Fanbase Press community have been a rock during the incredibly trying times when this book was made. They became the high point of many weeks and were a constant reminder that there is kindness out there.

LUCY would like to thank stacks of people, she's like that. But mainly it's Richard. Thank you for opening this world with me and constructing a place where we can make our own magic and mess. Thank you for believing in me when I so often didn't know how.

Thank you to Kate and Kate for sharing your wisdoms in between fighting other fires. Thank you to Rouzie for the motivation and inspiration.

Mum AND Dad, Rachael, Sarah, Jack, Caprece, Zia, Caspar, Milan, and the Pokey Little Puppy—you're my world.

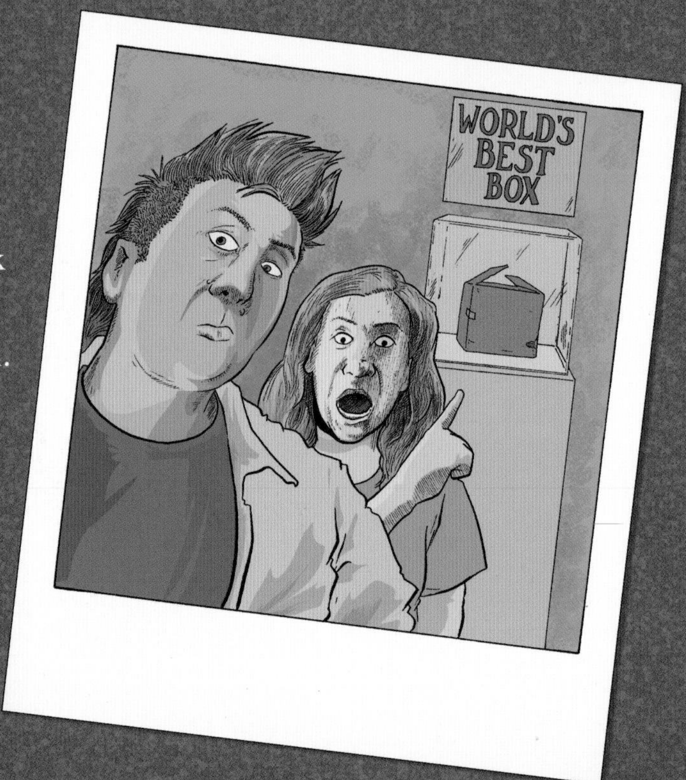
WORLD'S BEST BOX